MEET ME IN MALMÖ

Torquil MacLeod

M^cNIDDER & GRACE CRIME

To Susan – and my special family.

Published by McNidder & Grace
16A Bridge Street
Carmarthen
SA31 3JS
www.mcnidderandgrace.co.uk

Original paperback first published in 2015
Reprinted in 2016
Originally published in 2010
©Torquil MacLeod and Torquil MacLeod Books Ltd
www.torquilmacleodbooks.com

A catalogue record for this work is available from the British Library.

ISBN: 9780857161130

Designed by Obsidian Design

Printed and bound in the United Kingdom by
Short Run Press Ltd, Exeter, UK.

ABOUT THE AUTHOR

Torquil MacLeod is an advertising copywriter and author. Born in Edinburgh, he now lives in Cumbria with his wife, Susan. He came up with the idea for his Malmö Mysteries after visiting the elder of his two sons in southern Sweden in 2000. He still visits Malmö regularly to see his Swedish grandson.

Meet me in Malmö is the first in the series of the best-selling crime mysteries featuring Inspector Anita Sundström. *Murder in Malmö* and *Missing in Malmö* are the second and third titles. *Midnight in Malmö* is the fourth book in the series.

ACKNOWLEDGEMENTS

I would like to thank my wife Susan for putting up with my 'scribblings' and for all the checking she's done. To my son Fraser for the useful photographs and his local knowledge of Malmö – and to my other son Calum for his enthusiastic backing. I would like to thank our friend Karin Geistrand for answering my questions on Sweden and Swedish policing. Any subsequent inaccuracies are entirely my fault. Thank you to Ian Craig for his encouragement and, finally, to the talented Nick Pugh of The Roundhouse for his excellent cover design.

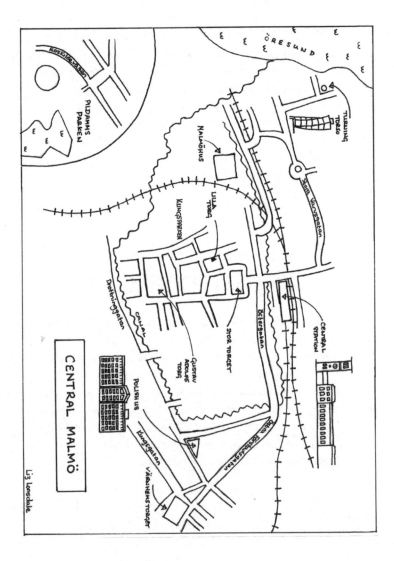

CENTRAL MALMÖ

Liz Lonsdale

PROLOGUE

It was the sound of the sickening thud that he would never be able to erase from his memory. And Alison vomiting straight afterwards.

The evening had started out so well. John Wilson had thought that this was his lucky night. Ever since Freshers' Week he'd been trying to get close to the gorgeous Alison French and then, quite by chance, he had run into her at a crowded end-of-term party in the Bailey. The willowy blonde with the easy laugh had, at long last, turned her winning smile on him. The fact that she had been full of the alcoholic spirit of pre-Christmas probably helped. But there had been no sign of the rugby-playing boyfriend, so the field was clear.

He had been astonished to find himself standing with his arm round Alison's shoulder in front of the brooding expanse of Durham's medieval cathedral. In the darkness of the early December evening, the illuminated western towers and the even larger central one appeared to commune with the night sky.

Alison had shivered and John had clenched her closer. She'd responded and raised her head to his. They kissed, just as they had done when they had staggered out of the party fifteen minutes earlier after he had gallantly offered to see her back to her college across the river. He hoped that this spark of affection hadn't been ignited solely by the drink. She had certainly downed a lot of fancy-looking concoctions and she'd swayed slightly as he'd manoeuvred her along the Bailey and up towards the cathedral.

John knew the lights would be going out soon, so he had begun to move Alison away from the main door of the cathedral. As he did so he glimpsed the lion-like beast that was the famous sanctuary knocker. He suddenly got an overwhelming sense of history. Perhaps it was the alcohol, but he could almost feel the presence of all the souls who'd sought safety in the cathedral over the centuries. He drew the obvious parallel – he felt he'd found refuge with Alison and life could only get better.

They had made their way unsteadily across the grass and round a couple of old tombstones until they were close to the cathedral wall, the central tower looming above. There were some muted sounds of a party going on somewhere nearby, but Palace Green, opposite the cathedral, was quiet. John glanced round and saw that all was deserted. This was his moment. He took Alison's face in his hands and stared into those twinkling, if slightly inebriated, eyes.

'I've waited so long for this moment.'

She blinked before smiling back. 'Do you want to come back to my room tonight? Claudia won't be there. She's round at Andy's.' John could hardly contain his excitement. Alison grabbed his hand, 'Come on!'

But they only managed to take a couple of steps nearer the promised delights of Alison's room. A piercing scream startled them and broke the evening's calm serenity. They hardly had time to look up when the body of a woman hurtled past their heads and landed in front of them; half-bouncing off the grass before slumping back down like a rag doll, its limbs all distorted. Alison was yelling in fright. The lights on the cathedral snapped off.

Twenty-five years later…

CHAPTER 1

She was sitting in front of the mirror. The reflection staring back was beautiful. In her early forties, she could pass for someone far younger. The natural blonde hair was shoulder length, framing a face with high cheekbones that gave it a sculpted look. Yet the deep blue eyes ensured that the overall effect was not that of marble, but full of life. The mouth was wide – a slash of exotic red across cool Scandinavian features. The black dress plunged invitingly, but it was the necklace that caught her attention. The amber glinted in the discreet mirror light. She played with it thoughtfully. A half-smile crossed her lips. Then a noise disturbed her, and her expression changed. She looked round. The sound of someone in the next room perhaps? Her hand went to her throat and her face creased into puzzlement. Yes, there was definitely a person moving around in the next room.

'Rune?' she called out cautiously. There was no reply.

She stood up slowly. This was a woman who was ready to go out to somewhere smart. The dress was short enough to show that she still possessed head-turning legs but long enough to hint that not all was on show – well, not yet. With a certain amount of trepidation, she crossed the bedroom to the door, which was slightly ajar. The room was decorated and furnished in understated Scandinavian elegance. No clutter, no extravagant adornments, nothing that wasn't of some use. She stopped and gingerly opened the bedroom door.

'Ru... oh, it's you.' She sounded disappointed, but the nervousness was gone. The object of her disappointment was just out of sight, behind the now open door. 'What are you doing here?'

She jerked back instinctively as male hands made a grab for her throat. She gurgled helplessly as the fingers pressed around her neck. For a few seconds she tried hopelessly to break the vice-like grip, but she hadn't the strength. The powerful hands were pushing her down onto her knees, her skirt riding up as she went. The unequal struggle ended with her slipping slowly to the floor, all the elegance draining away as fast as her life. The unseen assailant released his grip – then the door closed and the body was left in a still heap.

Ewan Strachan shifted in his seat. He could never sit still, however riveting a film was, but this one didn't come into that category. Was it really that easy to strangle someone? He was sure it wasn't, but that was the magic of the movies. And Christina had it coming to her because she had been starting to annoy him. Even he would have been tempted to do her in, but, he presumed, he wouldn't find out whodunit until the final reel. Yes, she was very beautiful, but some of the lines she had come out with were cringe-making. Of course, that could be down to the translation. You were never sure with subtitles.

Ewan cast his eye round the small but packed cinema. Most of the audience was concentrating fully on the action – or lack of action – until the moment when Christina had copped it. But these were fans of Swedish cinema – and particularly of the director, who was sitting in the front row watching his wife, Malin Lovgren, die dramatically on screen. He was surrounded by disciples. In the question and answer session that followed the screening, there would be no dissenting voices. Not even

Ewan's. He wouldn't get an interview with Mick Roslyn by being critical beforehand.

Sitting five rows in front of Ewan, he still had that familiar long, dark, swept-back hair and the neatly barbered stubble. Not a grey hair in sight, despite his forty-five years. He has certainly aged far better than I have, thought Ewan, who had now lost interest in *Gässen* or *The Geese*. Ewan still hadn't worked out how geese fitted into the story, though maybe they were some obscure Swedish metaphor for... strangulation? Long necks, easy to wring. Or pecking? The Christina character had henpecked her poor husband, who was perfectly justified in murdering her. She hadn't been very nice to her lover either. Then again it might be to do with flight. He would have to come up with something to put in his review. He had to justify his train fare from Newcastle to Edinburgh for the Northern Stars Film Festival. But if he could grab Roslyn for a quick interview afterwards, then even his pain-in-the-arse editor might get off his back for a while. It was a matter of getting Roslyn alone for five minutes. It might help if Mick remembered him.

The chance of visiting a prestigious film festival had seemed fanciful only two weeks before. 'You've got to get off your arse and do something interesting,' Brian Fletcher had said as he tried to remove some wax from his ear with his finger. Ewan couldn't look. What would he do with it if he got the wax out? The operation was unsuccessful and Brian sat down behind his desk in his cramped office. All the offices assigned to the *Novocastrian News* – or *Novo News* as it had become because management felt the name was snappier – were small. It was a small operation run by a big local Newcastle-based newspaper group. They had created the bi-monthly *Novo News* magazine as a vehicle for attracting extra advertising revenue. It was also a good place to hide away their journalists who could no longer do the business – or who had never really been able to in the first place. Ewan often wondered for which group he qualified.

He hoped it was as a hack who could no longer hack it. At least that meant he hadn't always been useless. Brian, on the other hand, always had. But that didn't stop him thinking that he was a born editor, and that any day soon his genius would be recognised and a really good job offer would come along.

'Your arts reviews lack punch. Sometimes I wonder if you actually go and see the things you're meant to be reviewing. And when was the last time you got a decent interview?' Ewan could have answered, if he had been arsed, by pointing out that the group's morning and evening papers got first dabs on anybody in the arts world who was of the remotest interest – leading theatricals, controversial artists, top dancers, even the occasional film star. He was left with all the obscure wood carvers, pretentious potters and loopy candlemakers who seemed to emerge every summer in the touristy bits of the North East. It hadn't always been like this, even though Ewan's own career hadn't been much more glorious than Brian's.

'The boys upstairs have been moaning. They think *Novo* should be more dynamic. And Arts and Social is an important ingredient in our mix. Don't let me down again. Get something fascinating enough to fucking print, or I'll have to find someone else who can!'

After leaving Durham University with high hopes of a stunning journalistic career, Ewan hadn't returned to his native Edinburgh. Too parochial, he had pronounced grandly. He did what he saw as his apprenticeship at a couple of very local newspapers, both of which turned into freesheets and were more interested in advertising revenue than news-gathering. Yet when he did have the chance to move south, he opted for Newcastle. On the evening paper, he did general reporting, before a move to the more prestigious regional morning. He wanted to specialise in crime; nitty-gritty stories. There was certainly enough villainy around Tyneside and its environs to justify a crime correspondent. But the editor, under pressure from the Managing Director, vetoed the idea. It would send out the wrong signals about the region. So he was attached to the sports desk instead. Funnily enough, he quite enjoyed it for a while. As a huge proportion of the Geordie population was far more interested in sport than in anything else, it proved quite lively at first. But then he got bored, got sloppy and got shoved onto *Novo News*. Now he rejoiced in the title of Arts & Social Correspondent. He found it difficult to muster the required enthusiasm as he wasn't very interested in the arts and he wasn't very social. But it was a living of sorts.

'I hear what you're saying, Brian. I'll dig up something that will please upstairs.' Ewan stood up and put his hand on the door handle. 'And you.'

Had he managed to keep the sarcasm out of his voice? he wondered. Brian gave him a sceptical look before nodding. Yes, he had.

Ewan went out into the main open-plan office. It was only open-plan in as much as there were five desks squashed into the one room. He sat down at his computer and stared at it blankly. Opposite, Mary grinned at him. Her hair was a funny off-orange at the moment and she never looked right without a cigarette hanging out of the side of her mouth. In this no-smoking building it meant frequent trips to the back door where she and Ewan used to put the world to rights – well, *Novo News* to rights.

'Another bollocking?' she asked. Her lined face was creased up in amusement. Fortunately for her, retirement was only a year away.

'Not dynamic enough, apparently.' Then he burst out laughing. 'Come on, time for a fag break.'

They made their way along a series of drab corridors. How have I ended up here? Ewan thought for the thousandth time. How come my great dreams have turned into a feckless career? Why have I never escaped the north-east of England? Many people had asked him that. He had made various excuses, most of which weren't believed. Yet, if he was honest with himself – and that had rarely happened in his forty-five years – he knew he could never give them the real answer.

Ewan walked through the large wooden doors and up the wide stone steps of the Newcastle Literary & Philosophical Society. Ahead of him was a large white statue of James Losh, recorder and eminent businessman of Newcastle in the 1800s, though he actually hailed from Cumberland. High on the imposing walls, classical grand relief figures showed that appropriate homage had been paid to the mathematical and philosophical influences that had been taken from ancient Greece. There were portraits, too. Robert Stephenson was there as one of the many important scientific-industrial figures who had been members. Lord Armstrong (warships), Sir Joseph Swan (the electric light) and Sir Charles Parsons (turbine engines) were all to be found on the wooden honours board proudly proclaiming past presidents. When he reached the first floor, swing doors opened into a huge L-shaped room. Tightly packed books rose up from the floor to a gallery with a brass handrail all the way round; then from the gallery floor almost to the ceiling of this huge space. Beyond the reception desk, there were leather armchairs, a round table near the coffee hatch and then, round the corner, long tables and assorted chairs in between further stand-alone wooden bookcases. It was Dickensian. It was unhurried. It was charmingly decrepit. It was Ewan's sanctuary.

In the Lit & Phil he could escape Brian, the *Novo News* and the other aspects of his life that he wanted to forget about. Here, over a paid-for coffee and one free biscuit, he could read the national newspapers, delve into obscure ancient books or plan the novel he knew he'd never write. No mobile phones were allowed. No phones of any kind could be heard. However, quiet talking was tolerated, so conversations could be struck up with some of the more eccentric members, which often proved entertaining and enlightening. One newspaper he always made a beeline for was *The Scotsman*. Why the library stocked it he had no idea, but it was good to catch up with happenings in Edinburgh. Though only an hour and a half away by train, he rarely returned home. Both his parents were now dead and his brother, a successful lawyer, just annoyed him. Most of his old schoolfriends had either moved on or he had lost touch with them. However, the odd one cropped up in the pages of *The Scotsman*. Archie Drymen was the last – he had been arrested for downloading child porn. Ewan hadn't seen that one coming. When they had been in the rugby team together, Archie had always had a 'thing' about other boys' mums. Shows you could never tell.

With *The Scotsman* tucked under his arm, Ewan waited at the coffee hatch. On the other side was Frida, the coffee lady. Though Norwegian, she had lived in England long enough to intersperse her lilting accent with more guttural Geordie phrases. She enjoyed his self-deprecating humour in which he managed to make every episode in his life sound like an amusing disaster.

'Time for coffee?' Frida asked.

'Yes. And I think I'll treat myself to a Bakewell tart, too, please.'

Frida eyed him closely. 'That sounds like you've had a bad day.'

Ewan gave a grimace to confirm her observation. Frida continued to talk as she poured the coffee from the pot. 'You need a break. Go away and forget about your magazine.'

'Still trying to get me to Norway?'

'Norway is good. The air is clean.' She pushed the cup and saucer towards him, 'The mountains are fantastic. Might even find a wife,' she added with a mischievous smile.

'But you had to come over here to find a husband.'

'My second one. My first was Norwegian.'

Ewan settled down to read *The Scotsman* at one of the long tables. As he munched his way through his cake, he caught up on the comings and goings of Hearts, his boyhood football team. By the time he had finished his coffee, he was onto the newspaper's arts section. Over the years it had proved useful for pinching ideas to use in his *Novo News* column. He had been known to use reviews from *The Scotsman*, virtually word for word, of films he didn't fancy, so he didn't have to see the movies himself. He was about to turn the page over when a small article hidden away at the bottom caught his eye. To be more precise, a name in the first paragraph. He stared at it long and hard. It couldn't be – yet it obviously was. He pushed away his cup and glanced up at the gallery above. A librarian was sorting some books. When Ewan looked back at the newspaper, the name was still there. It was another minute or so before he actually read the piece. The article was little more than a straightforward announcement of the events schedule for the Northern Stars Film Festival, which was starting in a week's time. Yet it unsettled him. Then it gave him an idea.

The wind whipped up a discarded crisp packet and tossed it around under the flickering light from the lamps strung across the street. It was cold, and the flurry of snow could soon turn into something heavier. The winter hadn't been as bad as last year, but there was still plenty of time. The crisp packet landed briefly before corkscrewing away into the dark. The man turned his attention to the window on the fourth floor of the building on the other side of the street. He could see the light was still on, though the curtains were drawn. And he knew that she was behind those curtains. What would she be doing at this moment? Watching TV? Having a late meal? Maybe she was painting? He knew she did that. Quite good. He had seen some of her watercolours at that little arty-farty gallery off Lilla Torg in the centre of town.

He adjusted his baseball cap and pulled his coat collar up against the bitter winter chill. He stamped his feet, but it didn't seem to warm them up. He felt in his pocket for his pack of cigarettes. With gloved hands he found it difficult to extract one. He accomplished the manoeuvre and even managed to light it after the second attempt. He took a puff and exhaled slowly, the smoke curling its way through the sodium light into the snow.

CHAPTER 2

Brian Fletcher hadn't been enthusiastic when Ewan first mentioned his idea. He naturally assumed that Ewan wanted to skive off to Edinburgh for the day on company expenses. Didn't the Tyneside Cinema show enough obscure foreign films without his having to swan off to Scotland?

'Look, Brian, this is different.' After seeing the article in *The Scotsman*, Ewan had spent the next hour on the internet finding out as much as he could. And yes, it had been *that* Mick Roslyn. And yes, he was what the article had claimed – "the modern Bergman", even if he wasn't Swedish. 'Mick Roslyn is huge in Sweden. Like…' and Ewan tried to think of a film director whom Brian might have heard of. 'Like a… Spielberg.'

'Now if he was a Hollywood director…' Brian began as he half-suppressed a burp, confirmation that he had just had a very large pub lunch.

'No, the point is that it's a big local success story. "Geordie-made-good-in-foreign-land" approach.'

'Ah, you didn't say he was a Geordie.' Brian's interest was now piqued.

Ewan had already mentioned that Roslyn was from the Heaton area of the city, but Brian hadn't been paying attention at that stage of the conversation. 'Yes, he's a Geordie who has conquered Swedish cinema. And he happens to be married to one of their top actresses. Malin Lovgren.'

Now Brian really started to look interested. 'Blonde?'

'Of course.' And very attractive, too, judging by the photos he had managed to find on the web. Typical of Mick, thought Ewan.

'And you say this Roslyn bloke is going to be at the Northern Thingamajig?'

'Yes. He's introducing his latest film, and there's a question and answer session with him afterwards.'

'And will his wife be there?' Brian was already imagining putting a glamorous photo of a sexy Swedish film star on the front page of his magazine. That would impress upstairs.

'I don't think so. There's nothing in the article about Malin Lovgren being in Edinburgh, though she stars in the movie.' Brian looked disappointed, but he could still legitimately use her photo if she was involved.

'But we'd want more than a review of his film.'

'Of course. I could do a big piece on him. The works. Local background. How he ended up in Sweden and how he became a celebrity over there and part of a glamorous couple.'

'Sort of Posh and Becks.'

'More Madonna and Guy Ritchie.'

Even Brian had heard of Madonna. His face lit up. He could see the possibilities. And he could scoop the editors of the group's two big local newspapers. He loathed them as much as they despised him. Then doubt crossed over his ample features. 'What makes you think you'll get an interview with him? He might not be keen on being associated with such a sma...' – he managed to correct himself – 'a publication of our size.'

'I think he'll speak to me. We were at university together.'

Of course, doubts set in the moment he boarded the train to Edinburgh. When he arrived at Waverley Station, he nearly jumped on the first train back. Mick might not want to see him. He was a big deal now. That was obvious from the way he adroitly handled the question and answer session after the film had finished. It helped that most of the questions were sycophantic, but he retained that enormous charm he had exercised at Durham. There was no doubting his charisma. Still handsome, still remarkably lean, and still with that arrogant swish of thick black hair, he commanded a room. Always had. The winning smile, the polite way he answered questions, the flashes of humour – but he was good at concealing his ego when it mattered from his public.

As Mick held his audience spellbound, Ewan was amused to note that he had lost all traces of his Geordie accent. He had been proud of it once upon a time. In fact, it had been a badge of honour in a university that was awash with 'public school ponces', as he called them. He made great play of being a Geordie. He even gave the impression of being a working-class hero, even though his family were reasonably well off. That's why the Michael who had turned up at Freshers' Week had become Mick three weeks later. His chosen persona went down well with posh girls from down south – their bit of northern rough. He had always been surrounded by attractive women.

Sadly, in this case, there was no Malin Lovgren, but he did have a stylish PR woman sitting with him, alongside a young actress who had appeared in a small role in the film as the murdering husband's bit on the side. Ewan didn't catch her full name in the credits: Tilda something – but she was not your archetypal Swedish blonde; quite dark in fact. But undeniably attractive. And appreciably taller than the older Lovgren. Mick didn't introduce her during his talk, so she wasn't there for the publicity. Maybe she was the producer's girlfriend; the producer being an earnest young man with very trendy red-rimmed spectacles who had taken the stage with Mick, but wasn't asked any questions and whose only contribution to the discussion was to say that Mick Roslyn was a brilliant visionary. It was an observation with which Mick seemed entirely in agreement.

After a gushing thank you from the festival organiser, the audience started to filter out of the cinema. The organiser was ushering the VIP party out through a side door. The producer attached himself to the young actress. A gentle hand in the small of her back as he guided her out hinted that they were in a relationship. Ewan moved towards the retreating group. Mick was talking to the PR woman when Ewan tried to attract their attention.

'Mick. Can I have a word?'

The PR woman turned and with an icy smile said,' Sorry, Mr Roslyn isn't doing any extra interviews at the moment.'

Ewan ignored her. 'Mick. It's me.' Mick Roslyn turned round and looked at Ewan blankly. 'Ewan. Ewan Strachan from uni. Durham.'

The PR woman tried to spirit Mick away, but Mick hesitated. He stared hard at the man in front of him. Slowly it began to dawn on him that he recognised the person who was shifting awkwardly from one foot to another. Though standing at six foot like himself, the Ewan Strachan he remembered was much thinner, had a lot more reddish hair (certainly not greying and fraying around the temples) and a boyish face. That was gone, though there was still the same twinkle in the deep blue eyes.

'My God,' Mick said slowly. 'Ewan bloody Strachan. I don't believe it.'

'Sorry, Mr Roslyn, we must get on. *The Scotsman* want their interview, then we have to get you to the airport,' said the PR woman insistently.

Mick held up his hand. 'Isobelle, just give me a minute.'

His smile part-placated Isobelle, who wasn't happy that her timetable was being disrupted, but she didn't want to upset her client. 'Only a minute.'

Mick held out his hand for Ewan to shake. 'What are you doing here?'

'Trying to get an interview with the great Swedish-based film director.'

'Journalist?' His surprise was obvious. 'Thought you'd end up as a teacher.'

'I wouldn't have known what to do with all the holidays.'

'So what rag are you working for? A Scottish one, I presume.'

'No. In Newcastle actually.'

Mick gave him a quizzical look. 'So you've never escaped. And your newspaper?'

'Magazine. You wouldn't have heard of it. After your time.'

'Course I would. My folks still live there.'

'*Novo News.*'

He pursed his lips. 'No, I haven't heard of it.'

'Mr Roslyn, they're waiting for you,' said a still-hovering Isobelle.

'Sorry, Ewan. Looks like I must dash. But we must catch up.' He paused for a moment as a thought struck him. 'Tell you what; get your rag to send you across to Sweden. I'll give you the works. The whole Mick Roslyn story. And, off the record, my new hush-hush project,' he said with a conspiratorial wink. He reached into the inside pocket of his jacket and fished out a card. 'Ring this number. It's our production company. Ask for Agnes. She'll sort out a convenient time. Fly across. Meet me in Malmö.'

He knew she was alone. Where the man had gone, he wasn't sure, but there had been no sign of him yesterday or the day before. He would have to make his move when he wasn't there. Not tonight. But he was going to have to do something soon. As far as he was concerned, it had gone on too long like this. A group of youngsters sidled past him, noisily making their way homeward – or maybe they were going to call in for a carry-out at that place he sometimes frequented round the corner. They were enjoying their own company too much to notice him. A couple of drunks, mumbling incoherently to themselves, huddled under the shelter of the small terracotta-coloured Skånetrafiken bus station on the opposite side of the road. The youngsters disappeared in the direction of the falafel shop. As he turned back, he noticed a police car moving slowly towards him, coming from the city centre. He slipped into the shadows.

The police car turned left at the lights and was well out of sight as he took up his former position. He noticed that the light on the fourth floor was no longer on. 'Shit,' he whispered to himself.

CHAPTER 3

Ewan hated aeroplanes. They were frighteningly claustrophobic. When the plane door slammed shut, he always got that panicky urge to rush up the narrow aisle and try and force his way off. And the Cimber Air flight from Newcastle to Copenhagen's Kastrup airport was particularly enclosed as it was a small aeroplane. But it was still a better way to spend a Monday morning than in the office. That he was on the flight in the first place amazed him. Brian hadn't been very happy when he returned without his interview. 'All that expense to go to Edinburgh to see some bloody Norwegian film...'

'Swedish.'

'As if there's a bloody difference!'

It had taken a couple of days to persuade Brian that this was quite a story – and would be a real feather in his cap. Roslyn might have only made Swedish-based films, but he had quite an international reputation, as Ewan had discovered on further internet research after his return from Edinburgh. One of his films had even been nominated for a BAFTA – Film Not in the English Language – a few years before. Though that had completely passed Ewan by at the time, the information brought a smile to Brian's chubby cheeks. What was more, Ewan promised (but doubted it would happen) he would try and get an interview with Malin Lovgren as well. He had produced a photocopy of a near-naked shot of Lovgren from one of Mick

Roslyn's earlier films as confirmation that she was worth it. The fact that Brian stopped eating his sausage roll in mid-bite was a good sign. His 'Can I hang onto that?' rubber-stamped the decision. A return flight abroad and two nights at a hotel – booked by Brian's sulky secretary Val – was almost unheard of in the annals of *Novo News's* expenses.

'Watch the spending. And I want receipts for everything, mind,' were Brian's parting words.

The weather was dull when the plane took off. Would there be snow at the other end? Ewan wondered. Pity he couldn't have done this in the summer but buggers like him couldn't be choosers. He had to admit that he was surprised that he wasn't going to Stockholm. It was the obvious place for celebrity Swedes. And the star-studded duo did have a flat in the Swedish capital to make sure they were at the hub of all things artistic. However, further reading had revealed that Malin Lovgren was from Malmö and that she was happier living in her home town. Hence Mick's invitation. Of course, when Mick had said 'Meet me in Malmö' he had pronounced the umlaut so it sounded like 'Malma'. So Swedish, so Mick. In the three weeks it had taken to set up the meeting with Mick, Ewan had delved deep into his chosen subject. He had lost touch with Mick's movements after university.

According to his web autobiography, Mick Roslyn had gone into advertising in London. From copywriting jobs in a couple of the top agencies, he had moved on to directing commercials. It was while filming one of these in Sweden that he had fallen in love with the country – and with an up-and-coming actress called Malin Lovgren. He decided to stay, and from Swedish commercials he moved onto movies. The rest was history. It all sounded so easy. Whether Malin had made Mick, or Mick had made Malin, it was difficult to tell from the sketchy details. One thing seemed certain – their fates and subsequent success were inextricably linked.

Ewan had seen as many of Mick's movies as he could get his hands on. He had also canvassed Frida's opinion. She had heard of Roslyn and Lovgren though, being Norwegian, she was scathing about the Swedes. And the Danes. And the Finns. 'Not my kind of thing,' was her verdict. She could never understand how Roslyn could film his own wife naked – and sometimes making love to other men – in front of all those viewers. 'That should stay in the bedroom is what I have to say on the subject.'

Ewan mulled over this less-than-in-depth critique of Mick Roslyn's body of work as the plane began to bank over flat fields and squat hamlets. Then there was a great expanse of sea with land further to the left, which he took to be Sweden. Why did the plane have to lean so alarmingly? During his rather nervous flight he had buried himself in the flight magazine, which carried a feature on the Scandinavians who had made it in Hollywood. Of course, there was no Mick Roslyn or Malin Lovgren. They seemed content to make their names in the domestic market. Were they happy to be little fish? Surely they must have thought about dipping their toes in the bigger waters across the pond. Or was it fear of failure? Mick never liked to fail. Rejection wasn't his thing either, unless he had changed in the last twenty-odd years and there had certainly been no evidence of that in Edinburgh. Maybe Malin really was a home bird who didn't want to spread her wings. Mick had never been short of ambition, so was she holding him back? It would be interesting to find out, but first he had to cope with the landing.

At the top of the aeroplane steps he stood for a moment and took in deep gulps of air. He didn't feel comfortable in the old, black woollen coat he had come in. He had bought it for his father's funeral years ago. It was too formal. It wasn't him, but it was the only warm outer garment he possessed, and he had assumed that Sweden would be bloody freezing at this time of year. Though it was chilly, it wasn't as cold as the Newcastle he had left an hour and a half ago. However, he was grateful for the shelter of the warm bus which ferried them to the terminal. Kastrup was Ewan's first experience of Scandinavia. It met his preconceived ideas of Scandinavian cleanliness, efficiency (the bags emerged very quickly) and sleek modern design. He made his way straight through to the airport railway station, which was underneath the terminal and reached by a horizontal escalator. As the Malmö train was arriving, lights in the platform floor lit up to show where it would stop. This fascinated Ewan.

The train was fairly crowded, so he was happy enough to stand. Within a few minutes of setting off, the train emerged from a tunnel under the sea into the daylight and onto the elegantly curving Öresund Bridge, which linked Denmark and Sweden by both rail and road. Over seven kilometres of modern engineering had bonded two disparate cities in two separate countries into one metropolitan area. Through the girders of the railway section, which ran under the elevated road, Ewan could see Malmö's latest landmark and Scandinavia's highest building, the huge fifty-four storey Turning Torso. This massive, slender, white skyscraper, twisting 90 degrees from top to bottom, seemed far too big for its surroundings – an awkward, gangling Gulliver in a Lilliputian landscape. In any other modern city it would be lost among a mass of gigantic towers but here, on flat terrain either side of the seaway, its only rival was the bridge itself. On the Swedish side, the train arced its way in a semicircle through the outskirts of Malmö.

The concrete buildings became more interesting and less boxlike as the train came nearer Malmö Central. As the line approached the station, a canal appeared on the left-hand side, and tall, elegant apartments in a variety of colours overlooked the water. The austere station platforms gave way to a lively and pleasant tiled terminal with shops, food outlets and a tourist information area. A cosy tunnel of a building. Here Ewan picked up a *Welcome to Malmö* map. He decided to find his hotel first before he planned his movements and discovered where Mick Roslyn's flat was situated; the venue for the following morning's interview.

The Hotel Comfort was less than five minutes' walk from the station. Situated in the old docks area behind the station, Ewan's heart sank when he saw the solid red façade of the four-storey building. It had all the appeal of a Travelodge, but inside it was better than the exterior suggested. The large atrium, tiled floor and comfortable mock-tartan-clad chairs were more promising. The woman on reception was very friendly and spoke immaculate English. She informed him that the hotel had a no-smoking policy for which he quietly cursed sulky Val. She would have done it on purpose. The receptionist also told him that the establishment was allergy adjusted. He hadn't a clue what that meant. His room was small, functional and noisy – they were in the process of building the City Tunnel project, an underground railway connecting Malmö Central directly to the Öresund Bridge.

It was still light enough to go for a wander to gain his bearings. Map in hand and his new *Rough Guide to Sweden* under his arm, Ewan made for the centre of the city. He crossed over the canal by the elegant station exterior, with its Italianate clock tower, and headed into Stortorget, Malmö's oldest square. Impressive buildings surrounded the square in the middle of which sat a statue of King Karl X Gustav on his horse, flanked on three sides by trees. One of the buildings, the surprisingly flamboyant town hall, built in 1546 in the Dutch Renaissance style (according to the book), took up one sizeable chunk. Behind it towered the spire of Sankt Petri Kyrka, one of the city's main churches and oldest building. In a gap in the corner of Stortorget was the entrance to its smaller companion square, Lilla Torg. Here among the cobbles and old, colourful 16th-century buildings were the bars and restaurants which the young and trendy of Malmö made a beeline for at the end of the day. Being neither young nor trendy, Ewan settled for a drink in a bar called the Moosehead to watch the Swedish world go by. He wasn't sure whether the beer was expensive as he hadn't got his head round the exchange rate yet.

It was true that the streets of Sweden were paved with golden-haired beauties. And many other different hues, too. It really wasn't fair that a country with such a small population should have such a high percentage of attractive people. Ewan started to count the ugly ones just to make himself feel better. His attention returned to the map. The address that Mick's PA, Agnes, had given was on Östra Förstadsgatan. Based at Mick's production headquarters in Stockholm, she had arranged the eleven o'clock meeting in Malmö, and for a photographer to come at 11.30. Apparently, Mick was coming down from Stockholm first thing as he had some engagement that night, but promised to be there on time. Malin would be in residence, and he might get the chance to have a word with her. The hint Agnes gave was that it could depend on what sort of mood Miss Lovgren was in at the time. She wasn't as keen on meeting journalists as Mick. According to the map, Östra Förstadsgatan could only be about twenty minutes' walk from his hotel. Agnes had said that it was opposite the *Systembolag*, the state-owned off-licence.

Ewan also cast around for a few sights to visit in the afternoon after his interview. He had promised the deputy editor of the morning paper that he would do a travelogue piece on Malmö for the Saturday *Lifestyle* section. That way he could split the cost of the flight, so Brian didn't have to fork out for the full trip. That had placated the editor who found it impossible to exclude budget constraints from any decision he made. He would visit the Malmöhus castle, which now incorporated a museum. He would also take in one of the many parks, for Malmö was a city of large green spaces.

After finishing his beer, Ewan sauntered back to his hotel.

It was dusk now. The neatly laid-out shops were all aglow, if not very busy; the restaurants looked inviting; the bars were starting to fill while commuters were beginning to gravitate towards Malmö Central. He would go back and have a shower, and then come out again for something to eat and try and savour the city's night-time atmosphere. But he took a wrong turning out of Lilla Torg and found himself walking along a darkened street behind the Rica Hotel Malmö. It was only by chance that he caught a fleeting glimpse of someone whom he thought he vaguely recognised. But then the woman, along with a companion, disappeared into a doorway of a modern apartment building at the end of the street. Ewan shook his head. No, he was mistaken. Definitely.

CHAPTER 4

The chatter in the bar was loud and lively. It was extraordinary to be in Sweden: the bar could have been in any town in Britain. Which probably explained why The Pickwick had a large expatriate clientele. He struck up a conversation with two of the regulars. Alex and David were both British, both lured to the country by Swedish women and both were now separated from their sirens. But they had stayed. Alex now had another woman in tow, David was between girlfriends. Ewan had found the bar by accident and had almost beaten an immediate retreat when he had seen the British decor and ye olde traditional bric-a-brac and wooden-framed pictures that cluttered the walls and window sills. There were photos of the Queen and Prince Philip, and a model of a Spitfire hanging from the ceiling. And then the final British touch – a dartboard, which was in noisy use. The only concession to Swedishness was the tealights on every table. It was the *Bombardier* pump that had persuaded Ewan to give it a go. He was pleased he had stayed because the atmosphere was congenial, the company interesting. As they sat on a low-slung, thick leather sofa opposite the bar, he was also picking up pointers as to what to see during his limited time in Malmö.

Alex seemed to be a perpetual student, having gone back to university as the only way of being able to find a job in Sweden, while David was running his own export business. Both were members of the Malmöhus cricket club. It had never occurred to Ewan that they would play cricket in Sweden. Eventually, Ewan managed to steer the conversation round to the subject of Mick Roslyn. Mick certainly didn't mix with the expat set and they assumed he spent most of his time in Stockholm. Many of his films were set there. 'He's big over here,' said Alex in a strong Glaswegian accent.

'The Swedes reckon Roslyn understands them. The way they think,' put in David, who certainly hadn't lost his estuary twang despite having spent twenty years in Scandinavia.

'The Swedes seem very normal. Like us really.' Ewan's assessment was based on exchanges in the restaurant round the corner where he had an evening meal, the barman in Lilla Torg earlier and the hotel receptionist.

Alex and David exchanged smiles. 'They may seem the same on the surface but they are very different, believe you me,' said David.

'But you reckon Roslyn has got under the cultural skin of the nation?'

'So they say,' Alex nodded. 'But I still don't understand a lot of his films. Sometimes he tries to out-Bergman Bergman.'

'But with more tits,' David smirked.

'Yes, he's not afraid of exposing a lot of flesh.' Ewan was all for a bit of gratuitous nudity, but it helped if it seemed to fit in vaguely with the plot. With Mick's films, much of it seemed to be there for shock value.

'Are you meeting Malin Lovgren? She's a bit tasty,' Alex pronounced, and David nodded agreement.

'Maybe. If I'm lucky.' Ewan's accompanying leery grin won him some laughter and another pint.

His vigil continued. She had gone out earlier in the evening. It was the first time he had glimpsed her for twenty-four hours.

He knew she was at the TV station, but there had been no point in following her there. She had returned at about half nine. Now she was in the same corner room. What was she doing? And where was the man? Why did he leave her so often?

At this time of night, it was bitterly cold, but he didn't feel it. Not tonight. He was well wrapped up and his baseball cap kept his head warm. Excitement was starting to mount. Adrenaline, he supposed. This was the night. He had decided to make his move. He took one last drag of his cigarette then flicked it away. It landed next to the hardly touched kebab he'd regretted buying twenty minutes before. He didn't know what the outcome would be, but he had to stop all the tension that was building up inexorably inside him. He would explode if he didn't do something positive. The only thing that troubled him was that the man might have returned while he had been buying his kebab. But the chances of that were slim. He'd only taken ten minutes.

He glanced around to make sure no one would see him. A couple of taxis passed and a local green bus came into the station opposite and waited under the neon-lit Skånetrafiken sign. Once the bus had pulled out, there were only the two drunks left. They seemed too caught up in a world of their own to notice him. He glanced at the turning clock face on its tall pedestal at the end of the bus station – 12.03. Then he saw a couple coming out of the Broderstugan bar just down the road. They wandered hand-in-hand towards the apartment block entrance. He cursed and slipped out of sight into the shop doorway. They stopped to kiss, before the cold drove them off. No one else. This was it. He kept in the shadows for as long as possible until he crossed over the road to the main door of the apartments. He knew the combination, so he would have no trouble getting in.

CHAPTER 5

Ewan woke early. He eased himself out of bed and went over to the window. Parting the curtains revealed another dull, grey day. Before he could gather his thoughts, the workmen on the underground began in earnest. He felt a bit queasy. It was nothing to do with anything he had eaten or drunk the night before but more a nervous tension as to how the morning would play out. He needed a cigarette. Like a naughty teenager, he sat in the en-suite bathroom to have a smoke as though no one was going to be able to smell it in there. After flushing the offending cigarette stub down the toilet, he showered and shaved. Even after his best efforts, the bathroom mirror didn't offer much encouragement. The boyish looks, which had given him a certain cheeky charm, had disappeared into his more swollen middle age. Only the eyes showed there was still some life left in the carcass. He put on his black shirt in an effort to disguise the weight he was becoming increasingly conscious of but lacked the willpower to do anything about.

He decided to skip breakfast. Cheese and cold meats weren't his idea of starting the day the proper way. Computer bag slung over his shoulder, he walked past the station out of which were emerging the day's first commuters, wearing the blank, zombie-like expressions fellow office workers anywhere in the world would recognise. He still felt sick, so he was quite happy to walk the tension off. About fifteen minutes later, he reached Triangeln, a large modern glass and white-pillared temple to shopping, pinned into place by a skyscraping Hilton Hotel.

Though it was too early for shoppers, he was able to buy himself a coffee on the first floor. The café court was situated in the middle of the complex on a podium that floated between the shopping floors, which swooped up on either side. Ewan sat down on a chair with a ridiculously high back, turned on his laptop, and took a gulp of coffee as he waited for the computer to spring into life. He spluttered, and the coffee nearly came back up. After it had stripped his stomach lining, it would threaten to shred his intestines once it got that far. None of the guidebooks had warned him about the dangers of Swedish coffee.

Ewan tapped idly at the keys in an attempt to get started on his travelogue article, but he didn't feel inspired. To take away the taste of the coffee, he bought himself an ice cream. Full fat. What would Mick be like? Ewan's thoughts drifted back to Durham. Through the prism of time he couldn't even recognise himself, physically at least. That was another person. Yet the man he had become was shaped in Durham. Distorted, more like. But the Mick of all those years ago was sharply defined in his mind. Mick was someone a timid first-year student like himself happily latched onto. As his friend, you could take shelter within Mick's aura of confidence. Mick was always at the centre of things, which meant that Ewan was always there too. The tolerated guest, even if he hadn't been invited. Often Mick hadn't been invited either, but he still turned up to be welcomed with open arms.

And yet Ewan couldn't help feeling slightly uneasy at Mick's magnanimous summons to Malmö. He hadn't expected it. And he knew the nagging at the back of his mind was a natural consequence of past experiences. There had always been a reason behind everything that Mick did: a subtext that couldn't be read at the time. The ulterior motives would only be comprehended later. Maybe success had negated the need to be duplicitous. A great career, ravishing wife and enviable lifestyle. And yet?

Ewan made sure he turned up on time. He was surprised that the apartments weren't more prestigious, on the outside at least. He had seen plenty of elegant blocks on the way from the hotel. The *Systembolag* opposite had some seedy-looking customers at that time in the morning. Värnhem didn't strike Ewan as the city's most salubrious area.

The apartment stood at the end of the busy Östra Förstadsgatan where it opened out into yet another square, Värnhemstorget, which had a small interchange bus station. The block curved pleasingly round into the next street, which was the beginning of the wide-avenued Kungsgatan. Number 35B must have been a very smart building when it was on the edge of Malmö, but time hadn't been kind to it. Light beige in colour, the rendered concrete was surprisingly appealing. Mick and Malin lived on the fourth floor. A wire mesh grille covered the entrance with what looked like a cage door in the middle of it, barring his way to the formal wooden and glass-panelled front door. He looked at the list of occupants on the wall and pressed the buzzer for the flat marked *M Lovgren*. There was no answer. He tried again. No response. It would be typical of Mick to drag him all the way over to Sweden and then not turn up. Maybe his flight was delayed.

The wind whipped up. Ewan shivered. A third press of the buzzer was as fruitless as the first two. Then he saw a woman in her twenties coming out of the main entrance and approaching the grille. The cage door opened. Ewan smiled at her, but got no response. However, he managed to step inside before the door clanged shut. Once through the front door, he was at the bottom of the block's stairwell. The staircase was wide and had once been elegant. Now it needed a lick of paint. The lift, to

Ewan's right, beckoned. He was tempted to save the climb, but his fear of enclosed spaces got the better of him – and this lift was particularly narrow.

Ewan was panting heavily by the time he reached the top floor. The Roslyn apartment was straight in front of him. As he regained his breath, he looked at his watch: 11.08. He didn't like being late himself – he hated it even more in others. And it appeared that if Mick was going to turn up, he would be fashionably late. He pressed the doorbell. He could hear it ringing inside. If someone didn't come to the door soon, he was going to lose his nerve. A second attempt didn't stir any occupants. Mick should be here, must be here. Ewan tried the door handle. It opened. Now he was left with a dilemma. Should he go in or wait outside? Do nothing and he could be standing here for ever. No interview and he would have to face the wrath of Brian, brandishing his P45. He half-opened the door and knocked on it loudly. Silence. 'Mick?' he called out. Then he tried 'Miss Lovgren?'

Ewan stepped into a narrow lobby. Some coats hung from a line of hooks. To his left, there was a toilet. Ahead of him, the door was open. Through it was a reception room with only a small table and two chairs of the very minimalist Scandinavian style. A large, unused fireplace took up one corner. The high ceiling was impressive. These apartments had been built for the wealthy citizens of Malmö, possibly in the 1920s, Ewan concluded. The wooden floor was beautifully polished – there wasn't a carpet or rug in sight. Ewan began to panic. He didn't want to be caught here. He thought of turning tail but found himself rooted to the spot. Ahead of him was a door leading into a further hall with what looked like a bathroom beyond. To his right, elegant wooden double doors were slightly ajar, through which shone a finger of artificial light.

Three slowly taken paces got Ewan to the door. Opposite must be two very large picture windows if the still-drawn curtains were anything to go by. The light came from two ultra-modern, squat table lamps flanking a buff leather sofa. It looked expensive. This wasn't IKEA territory. Where the hell was Mick? It was at that moment that he saw the slumped figure on the floor next to the sofa. In that strange light, he wasn't even sure it was a figure at first until he made out the thick blonde strands of hair that covered her face. She was wearing a long, black skirt, which had ridden up her legs. Her jumper was a deep blue. Ewan just stared. Was this a drunken repose? He took a step nearer. He couldn't hear her breathing. As he peered closer, he noticed how stiff the body appeared.

Ewan began to tremble. This wasn't right. This wasn't meant to happen. He must phone for help. But he had better make sure. Carefully, he got down on his haunches so that he was hovering just over the corpse. With a quivering hand he gently brushed back her hair. Then, without knowing why he did it, he slipped a hand under her rigid body and cradled her. He found he was stroking her hair. Malin Lovgren was a truly gorgeous woman. She was beautiful in life, now beautiful in death, despite the blueish-purple hue of her face, which gave her a ghostly look. His hand was still on her hair when he heard someone cry out, 'What the fuck are you...?'

Then there was a flash of blinding light.

CHAPTER 6

She looked hurriedly around. Where the hell had she put her bag? It had the car keys in it. She was going to be late again. She knew she shouldn't have gone for that run in Pildammsparken. But it had cleared her head, which she needed now that she had two days off work. She couldn't see the bag in the kitchen. Where was it? The leisurely shower had taken longer than she had planned, too. And the pampering afterwards. That happened once in a blue moon. Even she admitted she didn't look that bad when she wasn't hassled, which she was most of the time these days. At such moments she could even imagine she appeared far younger than the forty-two she now was and usually felt.

She glanced at her watch – just past 12. She would never make Simrishamn by lunch. Should she ring Sandra now and tell her she would be a bit late? The overnight stay with her old friend would do her good. She needed to get out of Malmö. The place was suffocating her. Back home in Simrishamn, she would blow the cobwebs away. Clear the brain. And a few drinks tonight with Sandra would be a laugh. Maybe some of the other girls would come round. And tomorrow morning, a walk along the lovely beach at Lilla Vik would dispel the inevitable hangover.

She moved into her bedroom. The bag wasn't there either. The room was in a mess – so was the rest of the apartment, but

33

she wasn't going to waste her precious two days off tidying up and cleaning. She would do that one night later in the week. Well, maybe. Though she knew she couldn't possibly have left the bag in Lasse's room, she went in anyway. Of course it wasn't there. Then a pang of guilt. Her son's room was tidy, everything neatly in its place – even his posters of a goal-scoring Zlatan Ibrahimovic and a sexily-clad Izabella Scorupco were perfectly aligned on the wall above his bed. How could Lasse be so organised? Just like his father. But Lasse was a student for God's sake! Students were meant to be the messy ones, not their mums. She quickly shut the door. She missed Lasse, but he would be home for a few days in a fortnight's time. They would do a few things together. That's if there wasn't anything too pressing at work. The cinema? Take in a concert? Usually, they went to support Malmö FF at their stadium on the other side of the park, but the Swedish season didn't kick off until April. The Sky Blues hadn't done much in recent years, but Lasse was doggedly loyal. Yes, he was a loyal kid. Now that *was* different from his father.

The bag was in the bathroom, under the towel she had flung on the floor. Typical of it to hide there! She did a quick check of everything she needed. No, the keys weren't in her bag. She cursed. Then she spotted them on the side of the basin with her mobile phone. Yes, she had been organised after all. She had simply put them there while she had applied some eye-shadow. One last look in the mirror. At least she had her new spectacles on, which had gone missing on several occasions. Lasse had called them trendy. Anita had called them expensive.

A minute later, she was out of the apartment and across the road to where her car was waiting patiently on the park side of Roskildevägen. The ranks of trees guarding the edge of Pildammsparken were bare. She longed for the summer, but that seemed a long way off. They hadn't had their share of snow yet this winter. She was about to open the car door when her mobile rang. Would she answer it or pretend she hadn't heard it? It might be Sandra. Or Lasse. She took it out. When she saw the number, she sighed heavily. It was from work.

'Anita Sundström.'

'Anita, Paula here.'

'Hi, Paula. Hope it's nothing important as I'm just off to Simrishamn. It's my day off,' she added with exaggerated emphasis.

'Sorry, Anita; not any more. There's been a murder at Östra Förstadsgatan. Moberg wants you over there right now.'

Anita's eyebrows shot heavenwards. 'Some wino's got into a scrap outside the *Systembolag*?'

'No. This is a big one. It's Malin Lovgren.'

'But I just saw her on TV last night.'

'Well, she'll be on again tonight.'

As Anita edged her way through the door of the fourth-floor apartment, there were people everywhere. She recognised most of them. She had already had to push her way through a crowd on the street outside. They had been attracted by the sudden police activity. She was curious that Malin Lovgren should live here – *had* lived here. There were plenty of smarter places round town she could have taken with the money she must have made. If she'd had Lovgren's money, Anita would have chosen somewhere along Limhamnsvägen overlooking the sea. By the looks of it, most of the polishus were here – the police headquarters was only five minutes' walk away. And there was Chief Inspector Erik Moberg directing operations. A bear of a man, Moberg was hard to miss in a crowd. The general consensus at the polishus was that he was far too fat for his own good. He would have a heart attack soon if he didn't cut down on his huge intake of food and drink. And the sooner the better, Anita thought unkindly. The badly dyed, nicotine coloured hair didn't help his aesthetic appeal either. He was a good cop in a bad body.

Moberg turned and saw Anita. 'Ah, Inspector Sundström. You've kindly decided to turn up.' Anita bit her tongue. When he wasn't trying to belittle her, he was undressing her with his eyes. 'Nice of you to dress up.'

'I hear it's Malin Lovgren.'

'Yes, we've got ourselves a proper celebrity this time.' Anita knew Moberg would be loving this situation. This would get him on TV and in the national newspapers.

'How?'

'Strangled. Doctor's been and gone. Body's in there,' he said, nodding in the direction of the open double doors. As she turned to go into the room, Moberg warned, 'This is an important one, Anita. We need to pull out all the stops. The whole of Sweden will be watching us. We need a quick result.'

Inside the living room, a police photographer was busy taking his ghoulish snapshots. Anita wondered what his family album was like. Eva Thulin, in a plastic bodysuit, was standing back examining the spot where the body lay. The experienced forensic technician was a friendly face. She smiled grimly at Anita. 'I saw her on the TV last night.'

'Same here.'

'Wearing the same clothes.' The photographer had finished and left the room. 'Lovely woman,' Thulin said as she bent down for a closer look.

'When did it happen?'

'Early days, but I would guess between eleven and one this morning.'

'The Chief Inspector said she was strangled.'

'The colour of the face and the swollen tongue certainly indicate strangulation. And neatly done.'

Moberg came in. 'Two lovely ladies together. It's my lucky day.'

'Did her husband find her?'

'No,' said Moberg. 'It was a journalist. From England. That's why I need you here. My English is crap. Yours is good, as we all know.' Again the sarcasm. 'Her husband is here, too. And a photographer. We need to talk to all three now and piece together what's happened here.'

'Where are they?'

'I've got Mick Roslyn and the photographer in one of the bedrooms. I've only had a brief word. Got more sense out of the snapper – Mjallby, I think he called himself. Roslyn is very upset.'

'Only natural, I would think.'

'I never know with these arty types. Never seem real.'

'And the guy who found her?'

'Through there.' Moberg gestured towards another set of double doors at the end of the room. 'He's shaken up, too. But don't go easy on him. Never trust a fucking journalist. Certainly not him. Don't like the look of him. And you'd better take young Olander in with you. Don't want him complaining about police harassment in a foreign newspaper. One-on-one can be dangerous. Bastards like him can twist the truth unless you have a witness.'

'I'll go and find Mats. But first I'll have a good look around.'

Moberg didn't bother hiding his impatience. 'I'll do the looking, you do the talking.' As usual, Anita tried her best to ignore him. She found Mats Olander in the kitchen on the opposite side of the internal hall.

'I thought it was your day off,' Olander said brightly.

'So did I!'

It was a beautiful kitchen. Every modern gadget you could think of, every appliance a top brand, every surface spotlessly clean. They must have a cleaner, Anita thought tetchily. It was more a creation of a style magazine than somewhere that was actually lived in. They probably ate out on their trips to Malmö and never actually cooked at home.

'Anything of interest in here?' Anita asked, knowing that Olander had an observant eye.

'Yes. Those two mugs on the side.'

They were black and white striped with a badge on the front.

'Football?'

'Newcastle United. Newcastle's where Mick Roslyn comes from.'

'Yeah, my Lasse likes them. Alan Shearer, right?'

'Used to play for them.'

'And this kettle looks half full.'

A kettle was an unusual sight in a Swedish household. Olander must have read her mind. 'Again, must be Roslyn. It's actually British made, or bought there. There's an adapter.'

'Have you a spare pair of gloves? As you can see, I didn't come ready for such a situation.'

Olander fished out a pair of plastic gloves and Anita slipped them on. She inspected the mugs. Next to them was a box of teabags. Lipton's English Breakfast Tea. Roslyn might live in Sweden, but it seemed he liked reminders of home. 'And no one has been in here since last night?'

'Not sure. The photographer phoned us because Roslyn was too upset. Poured Roslyn a whisky. There's a drinks cabinet in the living room.'

'So she was about to make someone a cup of tea. What stopped her? What made her go back through there?'

'Do you want forensics to go over all this?'

'The whole apartment. But we'd better let the Chief Inspector give that instruction.'

'What instruction?' Moberg had lumbered in.

'I was saying to Mats that you would be ensuring that the whole apartment is gone over by forensics. Particularly in here.' Anita nodded towards the two mugs.

'Ah, a welcomed guest as opposed to an unwanted intruder.'

Thulin appeared at the door. 'Lovgren wasn't killed in the living room. Marks on the floor. The body was moved or dragged through there.'

'What are you waiting for?' Moberg shouted at Olander, 'Get forensics to take this fucking place apart.'

Ewan wondered what was happening. He could hear lots of activity next door, but no one was coming to see him. He hadn't spoken to anyone other than the huge policeman with the angry attitude. The uniformed policeman left in the room with him hadn't said a word and didn't seem likely to break his Trappist silence. Ewan still felt sick. Not so much from what he had seen and was caught up in, but from the punch that Mick had thrown at him. That was before the photographer pulled him off. First appearances hadn't looked good, so Mick's reaction had been understandable. This was all so weird. He had stepped into a Swedish surreal world; like one of Mick's bloody films.

Ewan had spent time gazing out of the window watching the growing crowd. He had noticed the woman with the glasses come in. Was she police? Quite attractive. When he was interviewed, as he realised he must be, he hoped it was her and not that man mountain who liked to shout. One thing Ewan had noticed when watching all these Swedish films of late was that when the actors raised their voices, there was no change in inflection, no subtle shifts of emphasis. It was as though someone had just turned up the sound to 'yell level'. It sounded bizarre.

At least the room was interesting because this was Malin Lovgren's studio. A number of watercolours were propped up against the walls, mainly seascapes. They were fresh and vibrant. Did they reflect her character? She certainly had some ability. He had been to too many gallery openings not to be able to spot the difference between the talented and the talentless. Two paintings were on easels. One was nearly finished. It was of a coastal scene. A fishing village with gaily painted cottages, a few boats and a low harbour wall. The other had hardly been started, but there was the vague outline of a church. Would her paintings be worth more now that she was dead?

The door opened. It was the woman. And a young officer. She nodded to the uniformed policeman, who left the room. She was a vision of blue under her beige jacket. A blue jersey, rather tight-fitting, striped blue-and-white pants and an elegantly sweeping scarf wound casually round her neck, the two ends draped down over her breasts. Did she always turn up to murder scenes dressed like that? Ewan wondered. Her hair was short and blonde with a centre parting that was no longer exact, as the wind outside had tousled the effect she had tried to create. The wisps of flopping hair made her more natural, more earthy. Her eyebrows were so blond that they were scarcely visible, which drew one's gaze hypnotically towards her clear grey-green eyes. The glasses acted as a perfect showcase for them. To Ewan, they formed a rather sexy combination.

'Inspector Sundström,' she said, introducing herself. 'Police Assistant Olander,' gesturing to her colleague who looked too young to be a policeman. Her eyes scanned the paintings before she spoke again.

'And you are Mr Ewan Strachan?' She hardly had an accent, but she couldn't quite get her tongue round his name, so it came out as *Straak-en*.

'Strachan. Ewan Strachan.'

'It was you who found the body of Miss Lovgren?'

'Yes.'

'Did you move her?'

'Er... no. I came in and found her lying there. Slumped on the floor. I think I was holding her when Mick came in. To see if she was OK. See if she was dead.' Ewan realised he was starting to ramble, so he stopped.

'That's when Mr Roslyn came in?'

'That's right. He went mad. Punched me on the side of the head.' Ewan's hand automatically went to the tender spot. 'Before that, there was this flash. It was the photographer. Instinctive reaction I suppose. Fortunately, he was quick-witted enough to get Mick off me.'

She moved over to the large, curving window and took a peek at the throng below. 'Then what?'

'Mick was beside himself. But it was obvious that I hadn't killed her. Even he could see that she was stiff. Must have been dead for a while.'

'Are you used to seeing dead bodies?'

'Only my mother's.' He stared down at his feet, as though embarrassed. 'I held her, too.'

She turned back and faced Ewan. 'So what were you doing here?'

Ewan was amazed at how accurate her English was after the error-strewn efforts of the shouting policeman. 'I came to interview Mick.'

'You say, Mick. You know him?'

'We were at university together. In England.'

Ewan went on to explain the arrangements that had been made for him to come over for the interview, where and when to meet, and how he had come into the apartment on finding the door unlocked.

'Just as a matter of interest, why Malmö and not Stockholm? That's where they spent most of their time.'

'I have no idea. The girl I dealt with to arrange the trip is based at his production company in Stockholm. And it seems odd because Mick was up in Stockholm yesterday and wasn't coming down until this morning. Maybe it just fitted in with his schedule.'

She tugged thoughtfully at one of the ends of her scarf.

'We will need to speak to you again, Mr Strachan.'

'But I've got a flight back to Newcastle tomorrow.'

She smiled, though it contained no warmth. 'That is not possible. Where are you staying?'

'At the Hotel Comfort.'

'Please leave your details with Olander here. We will speak later.'

'But why? I haven't done anything. I just found... I need to –'

'Later,' she said brusquely and turned away. Then she paused at the door and swivelled round. 'For the record, where were you last night between about eleven and one?'

'In bed. Asleep. Where the hell did you expect me to be?'

Her eyes narrowed and the stare was uncompromising, but she didn't say anything. Ewan wondered how he was going to explain this mess to Brian.

Anita came out of the studio and closed the door behind her. Malin Lovgren's slender frame was being eased into a body bag. The operation was being supervised by Thulin. The bag was about to be zipped up when Anita said, 'Wait a second. Eva, did you notice whether she was wearing a pendant?'

'No, she wasn't, though there were signs that there had been something about her neck. But I really need to have a closer look because naturally there are a lot of abrasions in that area.'

'Last night, on the telly, she was wearing a pendant. I noticed it because I've got one that's similar.'

Thulin laughed. 'They're paying you too much.'

'No. It's not expensive. It's just that it's made by a girl I know in Simrishamn. Lotta Lind. She specialises in these colourful glass starfish designs. That's why I noticed it last night. It was blue.'

'She probably took it off when she got home.'

'Possibly, but she still had all the same clothes on. We can soon check.'

As Anita left the room, there was the loud rasping metallic sound of the zip finally closing on the world of Malin Lovgren.

*

He hovered at the back of the crowd. Who was it they wondered? Speculation was rife; theories were already being bandied about. It was a businessman, someone suggested. A prostitute, assured another. No, it was one of the alkies who spend their life in the Systembolag *opposite. Committed suicide by mistake. It was a knifing, the policeman over there had said to the woman in the fur hat standing behind those two students. Malmö was turning into New York. It was dreadful. It was bound to have been committed by an asylum seeker. Couldn't trust them. A drugs deal gone wrong.*

But he knew the truth. He knew who it was.

He had seen the female cop with the glasses standing up at the window. Was she good at her job? Would she ask the right questions? Would she come after him?

CHAPTER 7

Ewan drew long and hard on his cigarette. When he exhaled, it was difficult to tell whether it was smoke or cold vapour. Despite the deep winter chill, he was sitting on a bench between an old-fashioned green lamppost and a modern green waste bin on Kungsgatan. The wide avenue of leafless trees channelled the eye towards St Pauli Kyrka, a four-sided red brick church with a confection of curves, straight lines, and rounded windows, all topped off with an iced cake of mini-spires and a central clock tower shaped like an inverted ice-cream cone. Maybe, after he had finished his cigarette, he would take sanctuary inside and gather his thoughts.

The last hour had already played havoc with his clear initial impressions and begun to blur them. One minute he was going to interview an old university acquaintance, the next he was found clutching the dead body of the wife of the interviewee. He hadn't had time to panic, as Mick had burst in and thumped him. Thank God for the photographer, or he would have been pulped. And why had Mick not been there in the first place? The police hadn't been very friendly. Surely he couldn't be a suspect? He supposed they would find his prints on the body as he had held her, but she had been dead a long time, so they couldn't place him at the scene. But you never know with police under pressure. They would want a

44

quick conviction in a high-profile case. He hadn't got an alibi so was an easy target. They might ask awkward questions. Maybe not the big, fat, aggressive one, but that Sundström woman looked sharp. She didn't appear the sort who would take prisoners.

He had been glad to be able to escape the increasingly claustrophobic flat after giving his details to the young police sergeant – home address, mobile number, hotel room number. He had managed to slip out of the block as the crowd were pushing forward to try and ghoulishly catch a glimpse of the body as it was wheeled out. He hadn't seen Mick, which was a relief. What do you say to a man who has just had his glamorous wife murdered? The interview was out of the window. Brian would go ballistic. This would probably cost him his job, which was hanging by a thread anyway. And Brian would be happy to snap it and get rid of him. Well, fuck him! He'd find another job. Still, he would wait until he returned to the hotel before calling Newcastle with the bad news. First, a couple of drinks.

He took a last drag on his cigarette and dropped it to the ground. As he was crunching it out with his heel, he became aware of someone standing next to the bench. Ewan turned his head – it was Mick. Despite the cold, he was only wearing a fashionably expensive leather jacket. Their eyes met. Mick's gaze made Ewan feel uncomfortable. Mick appeared totally calm now.

'Now you really have a story.'

Ewan stood up. This was an awkward situation. All that he managed was a mumbled, 'It's dreadful.'

Ewan found himself walking slowly towards the church with Mick at his side. In this time of difficulty, the church seemed to be pulling them towards it.

'I didn't mean...'

'I know,' said Ewan. He found it easier to walk slowly alongside Mick as he didn't have to look at him.

'When I saw you there... for a minute I...' Mick's voice trailed off.

'It's OK.'

They had now reached the far side of the church. A flight of steps led up to a studded wooden door, framed by three arches.

'She looked beautiful.' Ewan felt it was his turn to instigate a conversation. 'Malin, I mean.'

Mick's eyes followed the lines of the church up to its main tower. He was still looking heavenwards when the reply came. 'She was the most beautiful person I have ever known.' His head suddenly dropped as though he had received a blow. 'And I have spoilt it all.'

'Don't be daft.'

'I have.' When he turned to Ewan there were tears in his eyes. Ewan didn't know where to put himself. He was bad at dealing with raw emotions. He found it hard enough to take when women cried. In men, it was just embarrassing. He had only cried once before in manhood and it wasn't even when his mother had died. And afterwards he had sworn he would never cry over another human being again. Yet here was the most self-possessed man he had ever met letting tears spill slowly down his cheeks.

The appalling spell was broken by the sudden burst of a mobile phone. The tune was familiar, but it wasn't Ewan's. Mick looked startled before realising that it was his. It was still playing away as he took it out of his jacket pocket. Then Ewan remembered where he had heard the tune before. It was the theme from Mick's last film, *The Geese*. Mick stared at the mobile's panel. He held it out in the palm of his hand towards Ewan. 'Please. I can't.'

Ewan took the phone. 'Yes?'

'*Hej, Mick, hur är det?*' The voice stopped. 'Mick?'

'This is Mick's phone, but I'm Ewan Strachan.'

'Ah, the interview. Sorry to interrupt you.' The voice had

switched to English. 'I'm Bengt. Bengt Valquist. I produce Mick's movies.' He was the man who had been so attentive to the actress in Edinburgh, Ewan remembered. 'Can you tell Mick to call me when you are finished, please?' His English was very precise as though thinking through the words before he said them.

Ewan could see that Mick was in no state to call anybody.

'You won't have heard.'

'Heard?'

'Malin Lovgren.'

There was a pause at the other end. 'What about Malin?'

'She's dead.' There was no other way he could put it. The long silence at the other end made Ewan think that Valquist had hung up. 'Hello?'

'Yes. I heard.'

'Last night. She was... killed.'

'*Herregud*,' came a hoarse exclamation from the other end. '*Var är...*,' he quickly corrected himself, 'Where is Mick now?'

'With me. We're by some church near his flat.'

'I must come. I must see him. Tell him, please.' And he was gone. Ewan lowered the phone from his ear and offered it back to Mick, who took it with some reluctance.

'It was Bengt. He's coming over.'

Mick nodded but didn't move. His tears were dried up now. 'And you? The police?'

'I'm meant to be flying back tomorrow, but they say I've got to stay. I don't know for how long.' This wasn't the time to go into the problems this would cause him or how it might stuff his career.

'I'll go back. Wait for Bengt.'

'Right.'

Mick cut a pathetic figure. All the cocksure demeanour was gone. It was as though someone had sucked all the vitality out of him. Without that he was nothing. He had visibly aged.

His face was as gaunt as that of his wife lying in that impersonal body bag. Ewan watched him wander back in the direction of Värnhems torget and the busy road. What Ewan needed was a stiff drink.

The room was full of expectant faces. Commissioner Dahlbeck had just addressed the assembled detectives on the importance of the case. How the whole of Sweden would be looking at their every move. They had to combine speed with thoroughness. The public still hadn't forgotten the assassination of Olof Palme and all the questions that that had raised. Fortunately, catching the murderer of Foreign Minister Anna Lindh had been more straightforward, but this one being such a high-profile case, they couldn't afford any slip-ups. It was a cover-your-arses speech that was doing nothing to push forward the investigation. Anita grew impatient and her attention wandered to the window.

Below them was the wide canal that encircled the old part of the town like a moat. In the summer, pedal boats made the round trip. It took about an hour, but if you were a few minutes over your time you were charged for a second hour. She had been taken round on one of her disastrous internet dates by a pedalo gigolo. She couldn't remember his name, but having dawdled past Kungsparken, he had suddenly realised that the hour was nearly up. She thought he was going to have a heart attack as his increasingly desperate pedalling got the boat back with a minute to spare. His triumphant but sweaty face hadn't created the right romantic impression.

In fact, the whole internet dating process depressed her. It had been Sandra's idea after the divorce. It emerged that there were three types of date. The first was frightened off as soon as they found out that she was a cop. The second thought that as an inspector she would want to be the dominant partner and that went against good old Swedish male chauvinism. The third type wanted her to don a police uniform and handcuff them to the bed. She had had her fill of Swedish men. She had requested the site to remove her dating 'nickname' and photo.

'I'll hand over to Detective Chief Inspector Moberg.' Anita's concentration returned.

'Thank you, Commissioner.' Moberg's strained smile was the signal for the commissioner to beat a retreat so that the real policing could start.

'Keep me posted hourly,' was the commissioner's parting shot. He was followed out of the room by the elegant Sonja Blom, the new public prosecutor. She was said to have a brain that was as sharp as her clothes. Anita didn't know her, but she had made up her mind that she didn't like her. The couple of times Anita had come across the public prosecutor, she had felt scruffy and inadequate by comparison.

Once he was out of the room, Moberg looked round at the assembled group. 'Now that you know how important this is...' He waited for a low murmur of laughter. 'Right. The victim is Malin Lovgren.' He looked at the large whiteboard that had been set up against the wall, and tapped the photo of the actress – a publicity shot that had been downloaded from her internet site. 'She had been strangled and was found in the living room. But, according to Thulin, she wasn't killed there. We don't yet know where in the apartment she was actually murdered. We're awaiting details from forensics. She was found at her apartment this morning at about 11.30 by an English journalist called Ewan Strachan.' He wrote down Strachan's name in blue felt pen. 'You know what I think about journalists, so I'd like to assume that he did it!' Further amusement. 'However, the murder was committed last night, somewhere between eleven and one in the morning. We'll get a more exact time later, but it puts our journalist in the clear. Is that right, Anita?'

'I think it's probably a case of the wrong place at the wrong time. He came over to interview Lovgren's husband, Mick Roslyn.' As she continued, Moberg wrote up Roslyn's name on the board. 'Roslyn set up the time and the place. Strachan says he arrived on time but hung around for Roslyn to turn up. Getting impatient, he tried the door, which he found unlocked. He went in, and on entering the living room, he found Lovgren on the floor. For some reason, he cradled her – he doesn't know why – and it was in this position that Roslyn turned up and found him. He was with a photographer who had been booked to take shots for the article. Roslyn, seeing Strachan on the floor with his apparently unconscious wife, lost it and attacked him. The photographer, Jonas Mjallby, pulled Roslyn off Strachan.'

'Do we need to pursue the journalist any further?'

'I would like to talk to him again. There are one or two things that may or may not be significant. The two men were at university together, so there may be a history there. The other thing is that Roslyn set up the trip and dictated its timing. He was meant to be in Stockholm last night and came down early this morning. Strachan thought it was strange that they were meeting in Malmö and not Stockholm, where Roslyn and Lovgren spent most of their time. His production company is up there. So is their main residence.'

'OK, let's check that Roslyn was in Stockholm last night.'

'And why was he late?' put in Anita. 'If he had been on time, he would have discovered the body himself.'

'Maybe he was meant to.' This was Henrik Nordlund. A man of few words, and those he did use were usually well chosen.

'A possibility,' mused Moberg. 'If that was the case, then it was premeditated. Whatever, we need to talk to Roslyn as soon as possible. He was too upset to be coherent earlier.'

'He's volunteered to come in later,' said Anita.

'Good. You talk to him. If he's upset, he'll probably find it easier to talk in English... and we all know how good the lovely Anita's English is.' The men smirked. Anita's two female colleagues in the room scowled. 'But be gentle with him.

He's just lost his wife. More importantly, he'll have powerful friends in Stockholm, so don't upset him – yet.'

'Now, Malin herself. I want her movements traced for last night. We know she was on the telly, but what time did she go to the studio and what time did she return to the apartment? Did she do anything in between? Meet anyone? The one thing we know is that there was no forced entry. In fact, she may have known her murderer because she was about to make two cups of tea. So who would turn up that late? She wasn't dressed for bed, so she might have been expecting someone.'

'A man friend?' Karl Westermark would suggest that, thought Anita. He was the station Romeo and the resident creep. He had even grabbed her arse at the last Christmas party. He wouldn't do that again in a hurry. 'Husband away, coast clear. He wasn't expected until the next morning.'

'You look into that. She might have been having an affair. She might have other admirers. See if she has ever had any stalkers or guys pestering her. Attractive women in the public eye often do. Check with our colleagues in Stockholm if they have anything along those lines. Basically, we need to build up a complete picture of this woman. What was she like? Was she a down-to-earth girl or a brainless prima donna? Was she saint or slut? She certainly didn't mind getting her kit off for the cameras.'

'That doesn't make her a slut.' Anita's interjection brought an awkward silence.

Moberg stared at the board for a few moments and puffed out his bloated cheeks as if he were searching for inspiration. Anita took advantage of the break to take out her snus tin and pop a miniature bag of tobacco next to her gum. She was quite pleased with herself that she had been off cigarettes for six months.

'We also need to check the internet. They have some strange sites out there. There may be some lunatic fans around.'

Moberg hardly knew how to work his computer; not even to access porn. 'And I want any CCTV in that area looked at. There will surely be some footage available at the bus station.'

Moberg scratched his huge stomach. 'Henrik, I want you to go down with as many people as you need and blitz the area. Talk to the neighbours in the block. Did they hear anything? Did they see anyone or notice anything suspicious? In fact, talk to everyone down there. Drunks included. Maybe someone saw him go in.'

'Are we sure it's a man?' interrupted Klara Wallen. Anita had once been on holiday with her, but it hadn't worked out. They discovered that what they only really had in common was a taste for red wine, which was what had united them in the first place on a few girls' nights out and department booze-buying runs to Germany. They still spoke but were never as friendly again.

'I think strangulation rules that out,' Moberg said dismissively. 'A woman would have to have been a professional shot-putter to have done that.'

'Why don't we just keep an open mind until we hear back from the pathologist?' Anita suggested.

'All right,' Moberg conceded grumpily. Wallen flashed Anita a grateful glance. 'I'm doing a press conference in half an hour and I'll do an appeal for witnesses. That might bring someone out of the woodwork.' Moberg licked his thick lips in an unappealing way. 'So, let's find ourselves a killer.'

A buzz of excitement broke out in the room. A big case often got the communal adrenaline flowing. This one had glamour attached.

'One last thing,' called out Anita above the sudden din. Moberg wasn't happy. He didn't like to think he might have missed something. 'When Malin Lovgren appeared on the TV last night, she was wearing the same clothes she died in. She was also wearing a glass pendant. In the shape of a starfish.

Colour blue. She wasn't wearing it when we found the body. So far, there is no sign of it. It's not among her jewellery. It hasn't turned up at the apartment yet. It may have come off in the struggle. If so, where is it? Find that starfish, and we'll probably find our murderer.'

CHAPTER 8

Ewan stared at the phone for at least a minute. He nearly picked it up but decided he needed to visit the bathroom again. It was the third time since he had returned to the hotel room. He had had two beers, which were guaranteed to set his bladder off, but he knew he was just putting off the inevitable. Then there was the whisky. That hadn't helped him either. He wasn't sure what had shocked him the most – the events since his arrival in Sweden or the price of the Scotch. As he stood over the toilet bowl trying to coax out some pee, he glanced at his watch. It showed 4.10 pm. That would make it ten past three back in Newcastle. Brian would probably have staggered in from a large lunch, lubricated with a couple of pints of *Black Sheep*. That was the best time to catch him.

It was Mary who answered. A friendly voice. Just at this moment, he didn't want to have to battle through the unhelpful Val to get to Brian.

'Hello, jet-setter! How are all those gorgeous Swedish girlies?'

'Gorgeous. You'd like the men, too.'

'Bring one back for me and then I can boot out that dull old hubby of mine. How was the interview?'

'There wasn't one.'

There was a sharp intake of breath at the other end.

'Ooohhh, dear.'

'Extenuating circumstances.'

'They'd better be good, or Brian is going to twist your balls off.'

'They are very good, but I had better tell him first. Is he in?'

'Yes. I'll put you through. Good luck.'

Ewan waited for a moment as Mary put him through. An upbeat- sounding Brian came on the phone.

'Was it great? I've already got some smashing photos off the internet of that Malin babe.'

'Well, you can still use them.'

Brian's tone changed. 'What happened?'

'She did. I didn't get the interview.'

'You fucking what!' exploded Brian at the other end. 'I send you all the way to fucking Scandinavia and you have the bottle to tell me you didn't get the fucking interview.'

'I couldn't.'

'You told me you fucking could!'

'I couldn't get the interview because Malin Lovgren is dead.' There was silence at the other end of the line. 'She has just been murdered.'

Brian came back to life. 'Murdered?'

'Yes. Last night. Erm… I found the body this morning.'

There was a bark of laughter. 'You're making this up.'

'Brian, it's the truth. I turned up this morning to interview Roslyn and there's Malin Lovgren lying on the floor, dead as a doornail. I've been interviewed by the police. That's where the problem lies – or one of them.'

'They don't think you've done it?'

'I bloody hope not. No, they've said I've got to stay on. I don't know for how long. But I'll be back as quick as I can. I'll do that travel piece, though.'

'Did this character Roslyn do it? It's usually the husband in these things.'

'Doubt it.'

'Who do the police think it is?'

'Haven't a clue.'

There was a pause. Ewan could hear Brian's breathing, which was just loud enough to cover the sound of the cogs turning in Brian's head.

'Don't worry, it's OK.'

Ewan was genuinely surprised. 'Are you sure?' he asked guardedly.

'No. I want you to follow up this story. The murder of a glamorous film star is always good news.'

'No one in Newcastle will have heard of her.'

'Not the point. Not the point. Famous Geordie director's beautiful actress wife is murdered.'

'No one has heard of him either.'

'No matter. We'll big him up... say he's the Swedish Hitchcock or something. And you are at the heart of it. You found the body. This is fantastic! You can get an interview with your mate, but now the angle is the grieving director. All that shit.'

'Brian, I just want to get out of here as fast as I can. I don't want to get mixed up in all this beyond giving the police a statement or whatever they want from me. Then I want to piss off home.'

'Forget that, sunshine. We can really make something out of this.' It was "we" now. 'This will put those tosspot editors' noses out of joint and will impress upstairs.' Ewan didn't have to see Brian to know that he was already envisaging himself taking up the reins of one the group's flagship publications.

'I'll see what I can do,' he said doubtfully.

'Look, you're always moaning on that you wanted to be a crime reporter. Well, here's a crime, so fucking report it! But I want everything to come through me. All the inside info. One or two of the nationals might report it, but I want you to delve deep. Dig up the dirt.' The excitement was rising in his voice. 'Glamour, beautiful couple, films, Sweden, sex – if you can find some of that it would be helpful.'

Ewan couldn't believe he was having to listen to all this. Brian was talking like some hot-shot newspaperman in the movies, not a half-baked editor of a crappy little provincial magazine.

'Brian, the *Novo* isn't that sort of publication.'

'Leave that to me. Might have to push it through one of the other papers, but it's our scoop.' After the newly energised Brian had rung off and disappeared into his fantasy world, Ewan was left to reflect on what lay ahead. It made him nervous.

Bengt Valquist always wore a worried expression. Mick had always assumed it came with the territory. A film's producer had a lot on his plate. He was in charge of every practical detail from raising the finance to trying to ensure a film's shoot passed with as little hassle as possible. He had to think on his feet. React to each new disaster, each unreasonable demand. Organising the location caterers one minute, soothing a temperamental star's ego the next. He was good at these things, which was why Mick had taken the bright, enthusiastic, young graduate from Lund University, keen to make his name in the movie business, under his wing. Valquist had quickly proved himself and worked his way up in Roslyn's production company, R&L Films. He had produced Roslyn's last three films and was as much a part of the team as Mick and Malin. He was good at spotting talent, too. It was he who had unearthed Tilda Tegner at some small theatre group in Stockholm. They were an item now. Valquist's face was riddled with concern as he watched Mick pace round the bedroom of his apartment.

'Come and stay with me in Lund.' He spoke in Swedish.

Mick stopped and gazed out of the window. He had returned to the apartment to await Valquist's arrival, but he knew he couldn't remain as this was now an official murder scene.

'Tonight, if that's OK.'

'Of course.'

Mick absent-mindedly ran his fingers through his hair.

'Why? What had Malin done to anyone?'

'I don't know. Nothing, I'm sure.'

Valquist got out his mobile phone. Mick turned round and saw him.

'Tilda. I've been trying to get hold of her. Hasn't been answering. Probably shopping. You know what she's like.'

Mick didn't answer. He was battling to keep his emotions in check.

'The police? Any ideas?'

Mick shook his head. Valquist took off his spectacles and twiddled them nervously in his hands.

'As I was driving over here, all sorts of thoughts kept turning over in my mind. And there was one that I couldn't get rid of. The project.'

'What do you mean?' Valquist had caught Mick's attention.

'You know. We've been treading on dangerous ground.'

'No. No, there can't be a connection.'

'We're getting in pretty deep. There are people out there who might want to make sure that it never comes out.'

'After all this time?'

'It may have happened over twenty years ago, but the guy who pulled the trigger may still be out there.' Valquist put his spectacles back on and blinked. 'Getting to Malin is a good way of...'

'Shutting me up?'

Anita had taken a moment to call Sandra on her mobile to tell her that she wouldn't be able to come over the next day either as all leave was cancelled. Sandra had seen Moberg on the TV calling for witnesses. Despite saying how dreadful it all was, Anita could tell that Sandra sounded almost excited. Anita was always amazed at the public's morbid delight in murder – they never had to see the bodies.

After she'd finished, Olander informed her that Rolsyn had arrived with a bloke called Valquist. Anita said she'd be down in a minute, but popped into the ladies' toilet to compose herself. As she washed her hands, she had a good look in the mirror. She didn't like these situations; not that they had happened too often. But talking to the husband, wife, son or daughter of someone who had just died wasn't easy. They were trying to come to terms with their loss, and yet questions had to be asked. It seemed like an unwanted intrusion into their grief, making them put their mourning on hold. And sometimes things emerged which only made the situation more awkward. This interview – or chat, really, as it wasn't an interrogation – might throw up some very personal questions for Roslyn to answer. She was going to have to go into Malin Lovgren's background, ferret around to see if there were any skeletons that could give them a lead. Admirers, rivals, enemies.

Anita dried her hands. She realised that she didn't know much about Roslyn. She wasn't a great one for watching films. She got bored too easily. It drove Lasse mad whenever he persuaded her to try out a new film that he thought she might like. Within minutes she would make her mind up whether she was going to enjoy or hate it. Often she didn't get much beyond the credits. She had seen Roslyn's picture in the papers often enough without taking a particular interest. As Anita made for the door, Klara Wallen came in.

'Thanks, Anita. For before.'

Anita smiled. 'Moberg speaks before he thinks.'

'He's a big fat bastard; I hate him…' Klara said in a rush and promptly burst into tears. Anita didn't have time for this, but she took a sobbing Klara in her arms and gave her a reassuring hug.

'It's OK. I'm sure he didn't mean it.' But Anita knew that he did.

The sobs started to recede and Anita was able to let Klara go. She fished out a paper tissue. 'Come on, Klara, get yourself cleaned up.'

Klara took the tissue and wiped her eyes. 'Did you see him on the TV? He's so full of himself.'

'Yes, but he usually knows what he's doing. He gets results, whatever it costs the rest of us.'

Klara sniffled into the tissue. 'How do you put up with that slob?'

'Just try to ignore him.'

If only Anita found it as easy to take her own advice as to give it.

CHAPTER 9

Mick Roslyn seemed calm, but Anita had no idea what awful thoughts were ricocheting around in his mind. He was handsome in a flashy sort of way that would have impressed and attracted her a few years ago. Experience had taught her that those who spent so long cultivating their looks had little time for cultivating meaningful relationships, except with themselves. She had explained in English that she understood that this conversation might be difficult, but they couldn't afford to put it off as they had to act as quickly as possible to catch the killer. This was part of the information-gathering process, and he was vital to that. He might be able to point them in the right direction. As she spoke, Mick Roslyn stared at his manicured hands, which were placed palm down on the table, as they sat in the middle of a soulless interrogation room. Sitting opposite him next to Anita was Olander, who appeared to be in awe of the director. He was an avid movie buff and was well acquainted with Roslyn's work.

'What I need to ask you first is to confirm your movements prior to going to the apartment at Östra Förstadsgatan.'

He started to drum his fingers. 'I spent last night in Stockholm. I had a meeting; then I wanted to go through some follow-up research material for my next project.' Anita could see out of the corner of her eye that Olander was champing at the bit to ask what it was, but he had the sense not to interrupt.

'I didn't go to bed late because I had to be up for a very early start. I got the flight down to Sturup, then came into town by taxi.'

'You were meant to meet Mr Strachan at eleven, but you didn't reach the apartment until half past. Why were you late?'

'Plane was delayed.' He shrugged.

'So you arrived at half past.'

For the first time he looked up and stared at Anita. 'The photographer was just arriving downstairs, so I let him in. We entered the flat together and when we went into the lounge, there was Strachan bending over my wife, who was on the floor.' A tremor came into his voice and his splayed hands curled into fists. 'I just flipped.'

Anita gave him a second to compose himself.

'Your wife. Had she been worried lately? Anything unsettling her? Had anybody being pestering her? You know, ardent fans?'

Mick Roslyn paused, as though weighing up the question in his mind.

'She had a stalker. It'll be in police records somewhere.'

'In Malmö?'

'No, in Stockholm. Couple of years ago. We had to take it to court. He was called Jörgen Crabo.'

'And has he been a nuisance since?'

'I saw him in the crowd at a premiere of *Gässen* last year in Stockholm. Fortunately, Malin didn't spot him. Or she certainly didn't let on if she had. But after what we had been through, you are always on the lookout. Apart from that, he's kept to the court order as far as I'm aware.'

'We'll check his whereabouts. He didn't threaten her life at any stage?'

'No.'

'Has anybody? Or is there anybody you would have regarded as a threat to her safety?'

Mick took a sip from his coffee, which by now was probably cold, but he didn't make any comment.

'Have you any snus?'

Anita took out her tin and pushed it over the table. He thoughtfully unscrewed the top and slowly reached in for a sachet. 'She had these letters.'

Anita and Olander sat up a little straighter.

'What sort of letters?' Anita asked.

He put the snus in his mouth.

'It was some fan. Said he was in love with Malin.'

'I would have thought she would get many such letters,' put in Olander.

'Of course. But these were different. When she didn't reply, they became more explicit, more threatening. Not that she could reply because he didn't include an address after the first one.'

'So there was an address on the original letter?'

'I believe so, but it didn't get past Agnes at our production office. Her job is to sift out that sort of thing so that Malin isn't... wasn't bothered with all the correspondence. When the other letters came to light, we looked into it. Agnes thought the first one might have come from abroad.'

'Where abroad?'

'India, Pakistan, somewhere out there. But as the others came from Sweden, we thought that Agnes must have been mistaken. Mixed it up with another fan letter.'

'So how did your wife react?'

'At first Malin laughed them off. But then they started to unnerve her.'

'Have you still got them?'

'No. Malin wouldn't have them in the house. She burnt them. She wouldn't even show me the last couple.'

'Were they signed?'

'He only put H.'

63

'Where were they posted from?'

'Here in Malmö. Initially, they were sent to our production company address in Stockholm. But the last few were delivered by hand. Shoved through the letterbox.'

'So he had discovered where she lived.'

'Yes. Made it seem even creepier.'

Anita made a note on the pad in front of her.

'Is this H another Crabo situation?'

Mick shook his head. 'No. Crabo kept turning up wherever Malin went. H is very different. We've never seen him.'

Anita scribbled something else.

'Did your wife spend much time down here? In Malmö?'

'When she could. She comes from here. This is where her family are. Her mother, Britta, still lives in Rostorp, opposite the park. Where Anita Eckberg came from,' he added unnecessarily. 'Malin never did like Stockholm much. And the Crabo situation didn't help.'

'Were you apart a lot?'

'What are you implying?' he said with a hint of anger.

'I'm not implying anything. All I'm trying to establish is whether your wife spent time by herself in Malmö. That would give your H, or anybody else, a chance to find her alone. Someone knew you weren't there. Presumably, that's why they turned up last night.'

The anger disappeared and his eyes began to water, though she could see he was fighting back the tears. 'I should have been there,' he gulped. 'Yes, we were apart quite a lot. She wasn't into the business side of film-making. I had all that. And the Stockholm creative scene – she loathed it.'

Anita continued to make notes as Mick wiped an eye with his index finger as though he had some grit in it.

'Any other people who might be a potential danger?'

Mick looked up, almost startled. Anita thought he was about to say something, but he merely shook his head.

'Any personal relationships that could have tipped over into violence? I hate to ask this but did she have any other…' she couldn't phrase it any other way… 'men?'

'Of course not!' That smouldering anger resurfaced with a vengeance. 'Just because she was an actress, it doesn't mean she fucked around!'

Anita held up her hands in gesture of placation. 'I'm not saying she did, but we have to explore every avenue.'

'We were happily married. End of story.' It turned out to be the end of the interview. Mick Roslyn got up and walked out.

'He what?' Moberg couldn't believe what he was hearing.

'He just got up and walked out. We weren't holding him, so there was nothing I could do,' Anita explained.

'And why?'

Anita shifted uneasily in front of Moberg. She knew she was giving him more ammunition. 'I asked, in as polite a way as possible, if she had anybody on the side.'

'Brilliant! We're going to get fuck all co-operation from him from now on.' She let him rant on until he ran out of steam. Maybe it was time for the transfer she had promised herself. Ystad would be OK – Simrishamn better.

'What I did get out of him were a couple of potential suspects.' This changed Moberg's mood when she told him about Jörgen Crabo and the anonymous H.

Moberg turned to Westermark. 'Give Stockholm a ring.'

'Won't get much out of them at this time of night.'

Moberg's finger started to wag in Westermark's direction. 'I don't care what bloody time it is. Get them off their arses and get someone to track this Crabo down and find out if he was in Stockholm last night and not peeping through windows on our patch.'

A chastened Westermark slunk off to make his call.

'Henrik, any luck with the neighbours?'

'So far, a blank. No one heard or saw anything suspicious. But we have tapes from a couple of CCTV cameras – one from the bus station and the other for the *Systembolag*. Unfortunately, there's nothing covering the entrance to the apartment block, but at least we've got something from either side of the road, so our killer may be on there somewhere.'

'That's something.' Moberg hitched up his trousers, which were constantly under pressure from his overhanging stomach. 'That leaves this H character. Might just be a lovesick loon, but we have to try and identify him.'

'Unless H is the same person as Crabo,' suggested Olander.

'That's a point. Tell Westermark to get Stockholm to send down a photo of Crabo. He may have come down here but kept out of sight.'

Olander went off after Westermark. Moberg watched him leave the room. 'Smart boy, that one. Better watch your arse, Anita.'

'I thought that's what you did.'

Moberg was temporarily taken off guard by Anita's retort. Nordlund smirked. Before Moberg could come back with a sarcastic remark, Anita said, 'If H was dropping off his letters at the apartment, then he may have been hanging around the area for some time. It's probably worth looking at CCTV footage going back a few weeks.'

Nordlund sighed heavily. 'Thanks.'

'No, fru Sundström's right.' He emphasised the 'Mrs', making her sound like a hundred and three. 'I want someone looking through that stuff tonight. This H is the only real suspect we've got so far – so let's find him!'

Ewan was restless. He couldn't get Malin Lovgren out of his head. He kept seeing the blue of her jumper. Not the face, just this blur of blue. He found himself shaking, and he automatically teased out a cigarette from a packet he wasn't really aware he was holding. He was about to light it when he stopped. He'd got away with lighting a cigarette the day before in the bathroom, but decided he wouldn't push his luck. He didn't want the Swedish health police battering down the door the moment his first puff set off some hidden smoke alarm. He left the cigarette unlit in his mouth. At least it felt comforting in there.

He pulled back the curtain and gazed into a cold Scandinavian night, the lights of Malmö spread out in front of him. He hadn't had the heart to go out and socialise with Alex and David as promised. He'd rung David to say he couldn't make it. 'God, what a shitter,' David had sympathised on hearing the reason. But they'd arranged to meet next day for David to show him around.

He had had one drink in the hotel bar but hadn't been able to finish it. And he certainly couldn't eat anything. He knew he wouldn't be able to keep it down. He tugged at the curtains roughly and shut out the Swedish city. It was no good; he couldn't banish thoughts of Malin Lovgren's dead body.

He looked up at the apartment. The fourth floor was in darkness. There would be no one there tonight. Malin Lovgren would never return. What was he going to do now? The bitter wind off the sea was bringing flurries of snow with it. He stamped his feet in an attempt to warm them up but nothing could stop him shivering at the chill and the thought of what had happened up there in that room. What he knew.

He pulled his coat collar tight to the neck and turned away for the last time. His cold vigil was at an end.

Anita stared at the contents of her fridge – two eggs, a half-eaten pack of Danish salami, a nearly squeezed-out tube of caviar, a tub of Turkish yogurt and a small lump of Kloster cheese. Nothing looked that appetising. She had expected to be in Simrishamn so hadn't stocked up. She half-heartedly took out the cheese and dumped it on the small kitchen table. The opened bottle of red wine had already taken centre stage. She was on her second glass. She glanced around for the knäckebröd. She knew she had put it somewhere yesterday. She wasn't actually that hungry, despite not eating since a late, leisurely breakfast. It was well after midnight and she was tired.

They were no closer to any new leads by the time Moberg had called it a night. It would be an early start. She would talk to the journalist again on the way into the polishus. Then Malin Lovgren's mother. She wasn't sure whether Roslyn had been completely honest with her. Just a feeling, nothing more. Strachan might throw more light on the charismatic director. He was certainly that, which meant he was capable of manipulation. Strachan might offer a few clues as to Roslyn's character. Yet all it would amount to was background. It was Malin Lovgren's background that really needed looking into. Anita hoped that her mother would paint a broader picture than the one they got through the usual media coverage and cinematic hype: the real person behind the public persona.

Anita sipped her wine. Was this really the life she wanted for herself? She had had such expectations, both personal and professional. It was sad to reflect that her professional male relationships had been more successful than her personal ones. Except Lasse. He was the one joy to have come out of her increasingly joyless marriage. He dutifully phoned every week. She wasn't sure what she would do if she hadn't got him.

And why had Malin Lovgren not had children? Would a family have interfered with her career? On first acquaintance, Roslyn hadn't struck her as being a family man. Was it even relevant to the enquiry? Yet she couldn't get out of her mind his final outburst: 'We were happily married. End of story.' The protest was too strong. What was he hiding?

CHAPTER 10

The blue body lay crumpled on the floor. The blonde hair kept flapping up and down as though blowing in the wind. But there was no wind because he was inside a windowless room. And standing over him was the big fat detective who kept shouting, 'You've murdered her, you've murdered her!' And he was trying to explain what he was doing there in the first place but the fat man wouldn't listen. He was now cowering in front of the policeman who yanked him up roughly from the floor. As he was held in a vicious grip, he looked down. The dead blonde opened her eyes and slowly raised her arm; a thin finger unrolled in his direction. She was about to speak when...

Ewan sat up bolt upright. He was covered in sweat. He rubbed his eyes, trying to become accustomed to his strange surroundings. Yes, he was in his hotel room, but it didn't make him feel any better. He dragged himself out of his bed and without turning a light on he walked to the window. He drew back the curtain. Snow was falling. All was quiet outside. He gathered his scattered thoughts. He tried to order them, but they still added up to one thing – he had stepped into a nightmare.

Anita saw him sitting by himself in the corner, toying with some cold meat. As she approached, he looked up in surprise as though taken aback to see her in the hotel dining room – and at that time in the morning.

'I am sorry to disturb your breakfast, Mr Strachan.'

His bloodshot eyes surveyed her suspiciously before he forced a smile. 'Saves me eating this stuff. Not my idea of breakfast.' She could see he was nervous. Her presence seemed to be intimidating him.

'You look tired.'

'Couldn't sleep. Given the circumstances... Sorry, please take a seat.'

He even stood up as she slipped into the chair opposite.

'Would you like a coffee?' She nodded. Ewan filled a spare cup from the coffee pot. She watched him carefully. Compared with his friend Roslyn, he wasn't much to look at, though he had a pleasant face when he smiled. He obviously didn't take much care of himself. Too much English beer?

'I'm afraid the coffee is not as strong as you probably like it. I asked for it to be weaker this morning.'

'I thought the British always had tea for breakfast.'

'Coffee wakes me up in the morning. I take tea at night to send me to sleep, if the booze doesn't do the trick.'

Anita tried not to betray the fact that the coffee was far too insipid for her liking. After her first sip, she pushed the cup gently away. Though she had Moberg's natural dislike of journalists, she thought the aggressive approach would be counterproductive. She preferred to wheedle information out of suspects. She left the heavy-handed treatment to Moberg and Westermark.

'Are you OK? It's been difficult for you.'

She could see him visibly relax.

'Yes. It's all been a bit of shock.'

'I understand. We will need you to come down to the polishus... the police headquarters... for you to make an official statement.' Ewan produced another weak smile. 'Then you might be able to go back to England in the next day or two.'

To her surprise, he grinned at her. 'That is no longer a problem. My idiot editor thinks it's a great idea if I cover the murder story for my magazine. I'm an official reporter. I've got a real crime to report. So, if you're not careful, it'll be me who'll be interviewing you.'

The twinkle in his eye was mischievous and oddly appealing.

'Well, the sooner we discount you as a suspect, the sooner you can start reporting.'

'Suspect?'

'Everybody connected with the case is until we decide they are not.'

Ewan made another stab at his cold collation before giving up.

'I was talking to your friend Mr Roslyn last night.'

'Poor guy must be in a state.'

'What is he like?'

'Mick? He's a good guy. Full of himself, of course. Certainly used to be, and I doubt his success has made him any humbler.'

'And you know him from…?'

'University. We were at Durham together in the early eighties.'

Anita couldn't help the smile that formed. 'Durham. I know Durham.'

'You do?'

'I lived there when I was younger. We went there when I was about ten. My father was chief designer at Electrolux. At the factory in Spennymoor. But we lived in the city. I went to school there.'

'That explains your English. It is incredible.'

'I also had a year seconded to the Met in London a few years ago. That helped, too.'

'God, how did you survive that sexist mob? An attractive blonde like…' He spluttered to a halt and stared down at the table. He began fiddling with his fork. She noticed, with amusement, that his face had gone red from embarrassment.

'Mr Roslyn. Did you know him well at university? Or was he just someone you came across occasionally?'

He tore his eyes away from the fork. 'Oh, no. I knew Mick very well. We shared a room in our first year. Did everything together. Inseparable. He was a laugh.'

'As you knew him so well, would you say that he is an honest person?'

Ewan took a sip of coffee before answering. 'I suppose so.'

'You would trust him?'

There was a pause before he answered. 'Yes.' Then he added as an afterthought. 'Except with your girlfriend.'

'Ah, as you say in England, a ladies' man.'

He laughed. 'A ladies' man. He was always that. At Durham, anyhow. I can't tell what he's like now. He must have settled down because he's been with Malin Lovgren quite a number of years, I believe.'

'Thirteen years.'

'There you are. He's changed his ways. In the old days he was never short of female admirers. Funnily enough, I always thought that he'd never settle down and I would.' A momentary sadness flickered across his face.

'No wife?' she asked.

'A couple of near misses.'

'Maybe you didn't meet the right women.'

'Oh, I met the right women, but I think the problem was that I was crap in bed.' Anita screwed up her face, almost as though she hadn't heard him correctly. Then she saw his amusement at her response and she found herself laughing. 'You see, that's exactly the reaction I kept getting.'

Anita remembered why she had felt at home in Britain. She always loved their self-deprecating sense of humour.

She would never have heard such a confession from a Swedish man, even in jest.

She asked a few more questions about Roslyn, but his answers were of little use. He hadn't seen him for over twenty years since they left university, so there was no fresh light he could shed on the Roslyn of recent times – nor on his relationship with Lovgren. She checked her watch and stood up.

'I need you to come to police headquarters. Porslinsgatan. The big modern building by the canal. At about three?'

'I have nothing else to do. Will you be taking my statement?'

'No. My colleague, Mats Olander, will.' He actually looked slightly disappointed at the news. She was about to go when she stopped. 'One last thing. You say you hadn't seen Mr Roslyn until you met him in Edinburgh. When you saw him for the last time before that, did you part as friends?'

'That's a strange question.'

'I still ask it.'

'Yes. Why shouldn't we? We just went in different directions after we left university. He went off to London. I stayed in the North East. Didn't keep in touch. One of those things.'

Outside the hotel, Anita stepped into the thin layer of snow. She was convinced that Ewan Strachan wasn't telling the whole truth – just like Roslyn.

CHAPTER 11

Olander came into the office bearing two cups of coffee. Anita drank it greedily. Black and strong. It made her feel better. Without coffee she didn't think that Sweden would be able to function in the mornings.

'Get anything new out of the journalist?'

'Not much. Except he was a bit too keen to let me know that he and Roslyn were great friends. Just seems strange that such great friends hadn't been in touch since university days until a few weeks ago.'

'Is it relevant?'

She took another long sip of coffee and let it glide down her throat. She sighed. 'Probably not.'

'Neither can be serious suspects. Strachan has no reason to kill Lovgren. He had never even met her. And Roslyn was in Stockholm.'

'You're right. What lies behind their relationship is between them and doesn't affect Lovgren's death. However, I wanted to get some background on Roslyn because there may be something in his relationship with Lovgren that throws up a motive for someone else. Did she have a lover? Did he? Was their marriage as wonderful as we are led to believe? That would change the picture.'

'Could be nothing to do with any of those things. Just some mad fan.'

Further speculation was curtailed by the arrival of Eva Thulin. She had a file under one arm. She flashed a tired smile.

'Working all night, Eva? Coffee?'

'I've had enough to keep me up for the next week.' She dropped the thin file on the desk in front of Anita.

'Pathology report and preliminary findings. Malin Lovgren was strangled. But we can rule out any sexual motive. No sign of sexual assault or activity.'

'That's something. We needn't follow up the usual list of perverts. So, man or woman?'

'Probably a man, but it could have been a woman if they had done something like judo. Whoever killed her used a chokehold. Normally it's a restraint hold in martial arts. The arm goes round the neck... look, I'll show you on Olander.'

Thulin stood behind Olander, who bent down slightly because he was taller than she was. She wrapped her right arm round his neck and locked his neck in the crook of her elbow, both hands clasped just above Olander's left ear for leverage. 'If I've got the strength, or the right technique, I can then apply real pressure. I can cut off the supply of blood to the brain as a result of the compression on the sides of the neck. The airway is blocked at the front of the neck. In martial arts and combat sports, it's a self-defence system. Normally it doesn't go as far as strangulation, but it has in this case. The person who did this knew what they were doing.' Thulin let go of Olander, who felt his neck gingerly. 'Sorry,' she said smiling apologetically.

'Malin Lovgren was small, so, as long as the killer was taller, a man or a woman, with the right knowledge, could have done it?' pondered Anita.

'I think so.'

'So we're looking at...?'

'Could be someone with a military background or maybe a person who was into martial arts. Certainly combat sports.'

'Then she was moved?' asked Olander.

'Definitely. As well as discernible scrape marks on the wooden flooring, there was bruising under her upper arms that is consistent with the body being dragged. I'm pretty sure the murder was committed in the kitchen. Forensics found a single link from a chain under a unit.'

'From the pendant?' Anita asked.

'Could be.' Thulin paused and pursed her lips. 'I went back to the scene of crime first thing this morning to have another look. That's when it really got interesting.'

The avenue of high trees opened out into a massive grassy arena. It was circular in shape with more trees all the way round. It was an awe-inspiring space to find in the middle of a city. It was known locally as *talriken*, the plate. Ewan was soon discovering that Malmö was a city of parks. 'It's gorgeous in the summer,' David enthused. Pildammsparken was the biggest, an easy walk south of the old centre of the city. David explained that the park had been built for the Baltic Expo in 1914, but hadn't been completed until the 1920s. Now they hold a huge bonfire and party here every 30th April. Known as Walpurgis Night, it is the celebration of the arrival of spring.

They took another tree-lined path out of the green arena and came to a large man-made lake. The water's edge was covered with geese and ducks, happily immune to the extreme chill. Some were being fed by a couple of hardy, well-wrapped-up souls. David mentioned that the goose was the symbol of Skåne, Sweden's southernmost province, of which Malmö was the main city. That was probably why Mick's film was called *The Geese*. But Ewan didn't really take in what David was saying, as his mind kept replaying his breakfast chat with Inspector Sundström.

Her appearance at the hotel had disconcerted him. Caught him off guard. Had he been too effusive about his old friendship with Mick? Had she read things into it that weren't there?

He was having difficulty enough coping with the situation without a suspicious policewomen adding to his troubles. He just wanted to get back to the relative safety of North Shields. Yet, if he was to cover this case, Sundström might be a useful contact. She was more approachable than her bully-boy boss. Be pleasant and co-operative and she might slip him some usable information. He also found her a rather good-looking woman. When she had left his breakfast table, he had noticed her arse. That was attractive, too.

They turned away from the lake. David pointed ahead of him. 'One place you've got to see is Malmöhus.'

'What's that?'

'The castle. It also served as a prison. One of the most famous prisoners was one of your lot.'

'My lot?'

'Yeah. A Scotsman.'

The main members of the investigation team were gathered in Moberg's office. Anita, Nordlund and Westermark. There was quiet as they digested the information that Anita had passed on from Thulin.

'Let me get this straight,' Moberg said. He was squeezed in behind his desk in a seat that was too small for him. 'According to Thulin, Malin Lovgren was left sitting on the leather sofa. So how did she end up on the floor? Did the journalist lay her down there?'

Anita was trying to make sense of it herself and chose her words carefully. 'Eva reckons that the dead body was placed on the sofa and that it slid down before it became stiff. The position of the body on the floor wasn't consistent with just being dumped there after being dragged in from the kitchen. It does fit with the body sliding onto the floor from the sofa. Eva found fibres on the back of the sofa, so she must have been sitting there that evening. Of course, it may have been earlier on.'

Moberg interrupted: 'So what she's saying is that Malin was placed on the sofa and then slid off?'

'Eva doesn't think so. She's pretty sure that the body didn't reach the floor by itself. Left alone, the body would have been more likely just to flop over to one side, not forward. Eva believes it's possible that it was handled again and slipped down into the position in which Strachan found it. By the time he discovered the body, rigor mortis had set in.'

'Could the killer have placed it there and then changed his mind? Let the body fall to the floor?' This was Nordlund.

'Eva doubts it. However, she can't be totally sure. Still awaiting more from forensics. Prints et cetera.'

Moberg picked up a cup of water and sipped it thoughtfully. 'We are now certain that the murder took place in the kitchen. The murderer then drags the body through to the living room and puts it on the sofa. Before, it didn't make sense why he'd moved it. But if he set it up like that, it was deliberate. Was he making a statement?'

'The killer wanted the body to be found by Roslyn?' Anita suggested.

'It would be the obvious room for him to go into,' put in Westermark. 'You'd be unlikely to go into the kitchen first.'

'If Roslyn had turned up on time, he would have found the body,' added Nordlund.

Moberg tried to shift in his seat, but there was no leeway for such a manoeuvre. 'It seems that our murderer wanted to create the maximum impact on, we assume, Roslyn. So whatever the motive, someone seems be to trying to get at Roslyn. Given the business he's in, he must have upset a lot of people along the way. We could have a whole cast of bloody suspects.'

'Upsetting egos is one thing,' said Anita. 'Killing is another.'

'If this murder is for his benefit, Roslyn must know the person or, if he doesn't, it's someone who dislikes him more than Malin Lovgren. Maybe she's just the unintended victim in all this.'

There was a further silence as they absorbed this permutation.

'From what Strachan told me this morning, Roslyn was a big hit with the ladies at university.'

'Once a babe magnet, always a babe magnet.' Westermark smirked.

'That's something you won't know anything about then,' said Anita sarcastically. Westermark was about to come back with some smart-alec comment when Moberg cut in.

'If he hasn't changed, then there may be a few infuriated husbands or boyfriends out there as well. Better check his background, too. Let's make sure he was in Stockholm last night.'

'The only other problem,' said Anita slowly, 'is that there may be a second person involved. If Eva's right and the body was disturbed, then someone else was in the apartment that night.'

Malmöhus was a large, squat mass of red brick, low-lying, with grassy ramparts and two circular keeps. Ewan and David made their way in over a moat. It had been an important stronghold in the days when Skåne was part of Denmark. Even today, Malmö had more in common with Copenhagen than a distant Stockholm. Within the castle's walls were a number of museums – too many for Ewan to take in during one visit. He just wanted to get a flavour of the place for his piece. He did visit some of the furnished rooms with an assorted mix of Renaissance, Baroque, Rococo and Neoclassical styles. Downstairs there were lots of stuffed animals, including a gigantic elk. Ewan was staggered to see the size of the beast.

The castle itself, though the interiors were spartan, Ewan

found much more interesting. Here he could sense the history, as he hadn't been able to in the fabricated areas that they had already visited. You could feel the cold strength of the building. The inhabitants would feel secure within these thick walls. And the prisoners would fear that they would never get out. People like Scotland's own James Hepburn, Earl of Bothwell, who was imprisoned here by the Danes between 1567 and 1573. Ewan knew him well from Scottish history: the roguish and unscrupulous third husband of Mary, Queen of Scots. He had been implicated in the murder of the queen's second husband. Ewan knew he had done a bunk when he and Mary had been defeated at the battle of Carberry Hill. After one final embrace, Bothwell and Mary never set eyes on each other again. Not long after, Mary fled to England and what she thought would be the open arms of her cousin, Queen Elizabeth I. Mary was eventually executed, but Ewan wasn't sure what had happened to Bothwell, a swashbuckling but probably highly unpleasant figure. How had he ended up in a Danish prison?

Ewan himself was now feeling trapped in Malmö. He wanted to go home, yet circumstances – and Brian – had condemned him to stay on.

'Let's start with Malin Lovgren's movements. Henrik?' Nordlund was the only one whom Moberg would defer to. He was the most experienced member of the team but hadn't had the ambition to go on to be a chief inspector. He was a cop's cop. Though nearing retirement, Nordlund still showed a commendable professionalism without the corrosive cynicism that many of his colleagues had for a system that they felt didn't support the authority of the police. They often felt exposed to unfair criticism from the media, the public and, above all, self-seeking politicians.

Nordlund took out a notebook. 'Malin Lovgren did her interview on Channel 4 during the seven o'clock national news slot. It was a short piece about her painting; nothing to do with films. She left the TV studio in Södergatan at 7.41 – checked out by reception. She walked up to Stortorget and met an old friend, an Ebba Carlsson, at the Scandic Kramer Hotel for drinks and a meal. According to Carlsson, they left shortly after nine and Lovgren was going to walk home. During the meal, Lovgren did mention that her husband was away, but someone he knew from England was interviewing him next morning. Carlsson was under the impression that Lovgren was just going back to relax and wasn't expecting any visitors.'

'How long would it take to walk back from Stortorget?' mused Moberg. 'Fifteen to twenty minutes at the outside. So she should have been back at her apartment by about half past nine.'

'We can't be sure she went straight home,' cautioned Nordlund. 'Basically, after she left the hotel restaurant, her movements are unknown. We're still asking around. Someone may have spotted her entering the block.'

'Did you ask Carlsson if Lovgren had any extracurricular male friends?'

Nordlund grimaced. 'Yes. She was very cross when I mentioned it. Very protective. She said that once Malin had met Mick, that was it.'

'Mmmm,' murmured Moberg sceptically. 'Keep an open mind on that one. What about anybody who might want to harm Lovgren – or people she didn't get on with?'

'The only person she mentioned was a guy called Bengt Valquist. He's Roslyn's film producer.'

'He came in here with Roslyn when we had that chat,' said Anita.

Moberg frowned at the memory. 'What about Valquist?'

'Not much. Malin didn't think much of him. Too highly strung, apparently. She always referred to him as "Mick's poodle".'

'All right. What about Roslyn?'

Westermark perked up. 'He was booked on the first flight down to Sturup on Tuesday morning. But there is less good news about Jörgen Crabo. Our Stockholm colleagues went to his home and discovered he wasn't there.'

'Shit!' exclaimed Moberg.

'Hasn't been seen for three days. Neighbours don't know where he is.'

'I hope they're going to keep looking.'

'Oh, yes,' Westermark said smugly. 'Once they found out that Malin Lovgren was dead, they were crapping themselves. They'll find him.'

'Unless he's down here.' Anita's reasoning wasn't greeted with any enthusiasm.

'So we can't rule him out. Get hold of his photo and have it distributed. Now, Henrik, what about H?'

'I've got people trawling through the CCTV footage, but that's going to take time. But without the letters or any clue as to his identity, we've nothing to go on.' He paused and consulted his notebook again. 'One thing though. I mentioned to Ebba Carlsson about the letters from this H character, but she said that Lovgren hadn't told her about them. However, she did say that Lovgren had mentioned that she felt she was being followed. Not regularly; just occasionally. One incident specifically. As she was punching in her code to get into her apartment block, she was aware of someone standing behind her. Then, when she turned round, the person was gone. Spooked her.'

'No description?' Nordlund shook his head. 'Well, it might be H. Keep digging. But quickly. Anita, I want you to talk to the journalist again. Find out for definite the position of the body when he entered the living room.'

'He's coming in at three to give a statement. I'll catch him then.'

'And we need to speak to Roslyn again. I want to be in on that. He could well be the key.'

'I'm just off to speak to Lovgren's mother,' said Anita. 'If anybody's going to come out with the truth about Roslyn, it's a mother-in-law.'

CHAPTER 12

He had been flicking between the TV channels. He had all that morning's newspapers strewn around the floor. All the media were full of Malin Lovgren's murder. The great and the good, the celebrities and the nonentities all came out to say what a wonderful person and creative talent Malin Lovgren had been. What a loss, they intoned gravely. Some even managed tears. Where the reports were sketchy, everybody seemed to have an opinion. After asking how this could happen in Sweden, they turned to the theme of Sweden going to the dogs. Where were our traditional values? Nowhere was safe any more. At least Prime Minister Olof Palme and Foreign Minister Anna Lindh had been killed in public places, but this was in the actress's own home. The unspoken implication was that the influx of foreign refugees lay at the heart of this national disintegration. After all, hadn't Anna Lindh been stabbed in the Stockholm department store by Mijailo Mijailović, a Swedish-born Serb?

What had alarmed him was when the Chief Inspector had come on the TV for his press conference. Though he was keeping police findings close to his chest – either that or they had no idea as to who had done it – the large man had mentioned that they were going through CCTV from the Värnhems torget area. He cursed to himself. That was so stupid of him. He tried to think back to his movements on the night. Where were the cameras? Where had he been standing? His palms began to sweat. But

*he was positive that there wasn't a camera at the front of the
apartment block. He went over the other events of the night
and thought whether there were other things he should worry
about – other details that the police could pick up on. Then
they might get on his trail. If they did, he would have to rely on
his training. He knew how to look after himself. Though he was
better with his hands than with a weapon, he always had the
gun. And he knew how to use it.*

Anita stopped at the traffic lights at the interchange. When the
lights flicked to green, she turned the car into Lundavägen,
the wide thoroughfare that she used to travel along regularly
when she had been married to Björn. Then they had had a nice
apartment in Lund. Björn was making a name for himself in
academic circles and, at first, life had been lively in the university
community. She used to drive in every working day along this
road, in the other direction, when she had been Björn's "pretty
little cop". It had taken her a long time to realise that her job
was an amusing curiosity to him. Unlike his colleagues, whose
partners tended to be teachers or in some way connected to the
university, Björn would turn up at parties and functions with a
member of the police force. These occasions had often been fun,
but Anita had never been able to escape the feeling that she was
an outsider. She was never really accepted because academics,
by their very nature, were fighting the system. In their eyes,
however pleasing to the eye she might be, she was still there to
uphold it.

After Lasse was born and her shifts at work became more
erratic, the "pretty little cop" novelty had begun to wear off.
Björn found comfort in the arms of some of his more attractive
students – and Anita had found out. She still had his name. She
had never been bothered to change it back to Ullman.

The car slipped along in the stream of traffic under the
railway bridge. Familiar landmarks flitted by before she turned

right into Östra Fäladsgatan. The road was wide with an avenue of trees running down the middle. She decided to park here and walk round to fru Lovgren's. Next to the 1940s apartments on her right was Rostorp, a group of streets made up of neat rows of pleasant dwellings. All were similar shapes with steep pitched roofs, and each had a reasonably sized garden plot. In the summer the trees in full leaf broke up the military precision of the houses along the straight roads – in winter their regimentation was exposed.

Anita sat in her car. She was reluctant to get out. She hated having to talk to the family of the recently deceased, especially in tragic circumstances. Breaking the news of a death was particularly difficult. In this case, fru Lovgren already knew. The whole of Sweden did. To lose a son or daughter must be the hardest thing for a mother to bear. Think of all the love you've invested in the little person that you've brought into the world. And then the worry never stops, however old they grow or independent they become. How would she cope if anything happened to Lasse? He was her life. There was no one else who could command her utter devotion. After Björn, she'd made sure that she never again got close to any man emotionally, even if she had physically. Bitter experience had taught her to separate the two.

She had taken the precaution of calling ahead first to make sure Lovgren's mother was in. Would there be photographers camped outside the house? Anita hoped for her sake that she would be left to grieve in peace, though her own visit wouldn't help. Fru Lovgren's house was on Beijersparkgatan. It was orderly and well cared for – and there were no photographers.

Anita rang the doorbell and waited. The lady who opened the door was in her late sixties. Her dyed blonde hair was scraped back in a bun. Like her daughter, she was small and had the same high cheekbones. She still had traces of the handsome woman she must once have been. And the piercing blue eyes that must sparkle when she was happy now expressed a deep sadness that words could never adequately articulate.

'Anita Sundström.' She thought it best to dispense with the formal police title.

'Come in.' Without further words, fru Lovgren showed Anita into the living room. Despite its immaculate neatness, it had a homely feel. Anita could never show people into her home at short notice because she would be embarrassed by the mess. She always needed fair warning.

'Do you mind if we talk in the park? I don't think I can speak about my Malin in here.' She indicated the numerous photos of her daughter around the room. A proud mother, indeed. 'Too many memories.'

'Of course not, fru Lovgren.'

'It's Britta.'

She left Anita while she went to put on a coat and hat. Anita took a closer look at the photographs. They covered the actress's life from childhood snaps through to a couple of shots that must have been taken at film premieres. There was her wedding picture, too. Lovgren and Roslyn had made an attractive couple. In her wedding photo Malin looked genuinely happy. As a young girl on a beach, she had a winning smile. In the premiere photos, though she was beaming for the cameras, she didn't seem to be enjoying her moment in the spotlight.

He reached the edge of the park. He tried to get a vigorous walk in most days. Keep in decent condition. He had done five circuits of the park today and felt good. When the weather got a bit warmer, he would start running again. His exercise gave him time to think and he had a lot on his mind at the moment. He was still worrying about the CCTV. The more he thought about it, the more he was convinced that he would have been captured on tape. But so would a lot of others, unless there was

*a camera at the apartment block entrance. He had walked past
there this morning and hadn't spotted one.*

*He waited for the green bus to pass. As he was about to
cross the road, he saw Malin Lovgren's mother. He had seen a
lot of her in the park. She had been accompanied occasionally
by Malin herself. It was in this very park that he had seen Malin
in the flesh for the first time. On reflection, it would have been
better if he had made his move then; out here in the open. Then
he suddenly realised that fru Lovgren wasn't alone. Shit! It was
too late. He was halfway across the road and that policewoman
with the glasses was heading straight towards him. He fought
back the natural inclination to veer away. He held his nerve
and forced his legs to keep moving. And then she was past him.
He kept straight on. He didn't look back.*

Anita didn't think she had ever been in Beijers Park before. It
wasn't as ostentatious as the city's major parks, and the more
appealing as a result. A tree-lined path ran round the edge,
which was used as a track for joggers. One heavily built woman
was doing an impression of running, though her progress was
painfully slow. A couple of dogs were snuffling around the large
open area of grassland in the middle, at the far end of which
was a small lake. Anita and Britta Lovgren had passed a huge
wooden carving of a red squirrel some way from the entrance
before a word was spoken. It was Britta who broke the silence.

'I can't make sense of what has happened. My girl was so
lovely. Why would anyone...?'

Anita instinctively put a reassuring arm round the older
woman's shoulders until she was sure that Britta was OK. They
wandered on towards the lake. Overlooking the water was a
tearoom, which was locked up and deserted at this time of year.
Geese waddled round the grassy edge.

'We're trying to put together a picture of your daughter.
Maybe that will give us a clue as to who might have wished her

harm. I don't really know where to start. Was she happy with her life?'

Britta looked straight ahead as they walked, as though she was by herself. 'I think so. She loved acting. Always did from being a little girl. Not that she was a show-off.' She smiled at the recollection of some long-forgotten incident. She didn't share it with Anita.

'And all the fame?'

Britta shook her head. 'No. That didn't make her happy. Mick loved it. That's why they split their time between here and Stockholm. She didn't like Stockholm. Too many false people, she said. They wanted to know her because of what she was, not because of who she was.' Turning to Anita, 'Does that make sense?' Anita nodded.

'She didn't make many friends up there. A few from her early days when she was a struggling actress. Most of the people they mixed with were Mick's friends.'

'Why did she live in Värnhem? Presumably they could have bought a fantastic house anywhere in Malmö.'

'They had a very expensive apartment in Stockholm. She wanted something different down here. She was more comfortable out of the public eye. I don't think Mick was too pleased, but he was never in Malmö much. It was her sanctuary. She could be herself. Surrounded by ordinary people. Her people. And near her mamma.' Britta stopped. She took out a handkerchief and dabbed her eyes.

Anita waited before asking her next question. 'I've heard, or probably read, that your daughter was at times... temperamental.'

Britta raised a wistful smile. 'She didn't suffer fools gladly. She came across a lot of fools. That's why she escaped into her painting. She could be alone with that. In many ways she was prouder of that than of the acting.'

They had reached the lake. They stood staring at the water

from a little wooden jetty. A couple of ducks disappeared under their feet and emerged the other side.

'I am afraid I have to ask. Was she happy with Mick?'

'He's a charming man.'

'That doesn't answer my question.'

Britta faced her. 'Are you married?'

'Divorced.'

'Did you love your husband?'

'Once.'

Britta turned her attention back to the water and the ripples left behind by the ducks.

'They had their arguments, like any couple. Maybe more than most. I don't know. The things they wanted from life were often very different. But I think she loved him as much as she did when they first married.'

Anita knew she had to stray onto more sensitive ground. 'Was there anybody else in her life? Romantically, I mean. Or in Mick Roslyn's life?'

Anita was expecting anger but none came. 'I don't know. I never asked. Malin's father left us when she was young. Other women. Yet he died lonely. No, I didn't want to know.'

'Do you like your son-in-law?'

'That is very direct.' Britta's eyes were fixed on some point in the middle of the pond. 'Mick has always been good to me. He makes me laugh. He made Malin laugh. And cry. Mothers don't get to choose the boys their daughters marry, so we have to be grateful if we like them. I was lucky.'

'Have you spoken to him?'

'He rang me about... before I heard it on the radio.'

The cold was starting to get to Anita. 'I had better go. Do you want to walk back?'

'No. I'll stay for a while. I love this little park. So did Malin. We often walked here together.' Anita knew that Britta was now holding back the tears. It was time to let them out.

'Thank you, Britta. I am really sorry.'

Britta Lovgren gently put a gloved hand on Anita's arm. Then she gave it a sudden squeeze. 'You will find who has done this, won't you?'

Anita put her own hand on Britta's. 'We will. I promise.'

CHAPTER 13

Ewan and David had taken refuge in Café Simrishamn 3 in Möllevången. This area of town had a real ethnic feel to it. This was where the immigrants mixed with the students to create a vibrant community – it showed that incomers and Swedes could coexist quite happily left to their own devices. But things were changing, warned David, who had lived in the area some years before. The Öresund Bridge connection was bringing in Danish commuters, who were adding to the already-climbing domestic property prices. The effects of the combination were starting to show on Möllevången. It was becoming more desirable, rents were going up, and the old locals were being squeezed out.

Up four steep steps, Café Simrishamn 3 was cosily chaotic. None of the furniture matched and no one cared. The staff were friendly, the coffee was good and the pastries were delicious, particularly the carrot cake. The clientele was mainly young, and many were working on their computers, which looked incongruous next to the traditional tealights on the tables. Ewan decided this would be an excellent spot to come and write up his travel piece. The hotel room was too impersonal. Here the atmosphere might even inspire him to write something above the humdrum stuff he usually churned out.

Despite the worry of going to the police headquarters in a couple of hours, Ewan found himself beginning to unwind. Police stations made him nervous, which is probably why he would have made a pathetic crime reporter. Some people were like that with hospitals. With him it was police stations. And dentists. Here in the café, those concerns had faded, and after Alex had joined them, he relaxed for the first time since his arrival in Sweden. Then his mobile rang. As he took the phone out, he hoped it wasn't Brian pestering him for some update on the murder. It wasn't.

'Hello?'

'Ewan.' He recognised Mick's voice. It still had a hint of Geordie.

'Are you OK?'

'Look, I'd like to see you.'

'Sure. When?'

'Bengt is bringing me back from Lund this afternoon. Can we meet?'

For some reason Ewan found himself lowering his voice. 'I've got to go to the police station at three. Make a statement.'

'After that? Say half four?'

'I bloody hope I've finished by then. Where do you want to meet? A bar or somewhere?'

'No, no.' Mick sounded quite emphatic. 'I have to be very careful. Your hotel?'

Ewan was surprised at this cloak and dagger stuff. Was Mick worried that the press would hound him? Or did he think he was such a big name that he couldn't go anywhere incognito? Ewan gave him his room number and the call ended abruptly. Ewan stared at his mobile before putting it away. David and Alex looked at him expectantly, their excitement obvious at being so close, albeit at one remove, to the biggest story in Sweden since the Boxing Day tsunami disaster. Maybe Mick wasn't being as precious as Ewan had first thought. On reflection, there had been genuine fear in his voice.

Anita was making her way back to the polishus on Porslinsgatan when she decided to call into the apartment on Östra

Förstadsgatan. Luckily, there was a space near the front entrance to park her car. She had bought the five-year-old Volkswagen in Germany a couple of years before. It made a change bringing a car across the Baltic to Sweden. They usually went the other way – to Poland, stolen in great numbers. The joke was that the Polish tourist board slogan was: *Go to Poland. Your car is already there.*

There was a young policeman on guard at the door, who let her in when she flashed her warrant card. He couldn't be much older than Lasse. She hoped that Lasse would never consider the force. She wanted a good look around. On the day the body was discovered, there had been too many people about. She wasn't trying to find anything in particular that would give her a clue as to the murderer, but more to get a feel for the murder scene. And to make some sense of what had gone on in here that night, because the consequences had really hit home as she had left Britta Lovgren.

Anita had looked back to see the small, forlorn figure of a devastated mother, standing alone by the lake. God knows what thoughts were going through her mind. What memories were being stirred. Now she was a broken woman who had been cruelly deprived of the daughter whom she loved, possibly worshipped. Even from some distance, Anita had been able to see that Britta Lovgren was crying. Swedes were not good at showing their feelings. Were they embarrassed by them? Probably, Anita concluded. Yet beneath the national cool, there was a melting-pot of emotions that were keenly felt, yet rarely publicly expressed.

Grief wasn't handled well either. Anita knew that she still hadn't come to terms with her father's tragic death. Nearly fourteen years ago now. When her father was living in Stockholm, after her parents divorced, he had decided at the last minute to take a trip with some fishing buddies to Tallinn. They never came back. All the friends were lost among the 852 death toll in the *MS Estonia* ferry tragedy. Her marriage hadn't lasted much longer after that. Had she tried to turn Björn into a surrogate father figure? If she had, then Björn had been found wanting. Why had men caused her such heartache? And was it heartache that lay behind Malin Lovgren's murder? Someone who loved her too much – or too little? It was certainly someone who knew her, Anita was sure. The mugs in the kitchen pointed to that.

She was now standing in the living room. Like the rest of the apartment, it said more about Lovgren than it did about Roslyn. This was her domain. Her taste. Her things. Her pictures and photographs. There were two of her mother and one of an older man who could have been her father. The whole apartment was more homely than Anita had imagined it would be when she was first called to 35B Östra Förstadsgatan. Fashionable, yes. The furniture was expensive. Yet it wasn't a home, except for the kitchen, that you would see featured in a glossy lifestyle magazine.

Anita wandered through to the studio room. When she had talked to the journalist in here, she hadn't taken in the paintings. She recognised some of the locations. In one were some of the large fishing boats in Simrishamn. And that looked like the little village of Baskemölla, just beyond Simrishamn. It was at the end of Anita's favourite beach. Lilla Vik was a little piece of paradise which had cast its spell over her from childhood onwards. She had taken Lasse there often when her mother was still living close by. Usually without Björn, who was forever disappearing on yet another academic conference. Sadly, Lasse had grown out of beaches. The more she was finding out about Malin Lovgren, the more she liked the sound of her. Beyond the studio was a small bedroom that had been turned into a study. There were two plain bookcases. A lot of art books. Again, this must have been Malin's space, though the computer, fax machine and telephone must have enabled

Roslyn to keep in touch with his projects on his brief trips to Malmö. There was little point in going through the drawers as forensics would have done a thorough job on the contents.

Despite being a spacious apartment, there was only one main bedroom. The adjoining bedroom was used as a dressing room. Obviously they didn't have people to stay here. Stockholm was where they entertained. If the murder had been a crime of passion, the killer probably wasn't going to be someone drawn from their social set. The deed would have been carried out in the capital and would now be Stockholm's headache.

Anita stared out of the window at the modern block opposite. The *Systembolag* was busy. She watched a young couple go into the Värnhems Juveler next door. An engagement ring? A wedding ring? She couldn't imagine Roslyn being seen dead in a jeweller's like that or being happy living opposite the ugly building that housed it. Above were four floors of apartments. No one had seen anything. The curtains or blinds had been closed, but when they weren't, it must be easy to look into this apartment with its big windows. She hoped that the CCTV would throw up something.

Then there was all the building going on beyond the *Systembolag* block. A huge new shopping centre called *Entré* was springing up and was due to open next year. Anita wondered what Malin had thought of that development. It would bring hoards of shoppers and, if successful, turn Värnhem into a more affluent area. Her downbeat bolt-hole would go upmarket. Would she have stayed?

Anita went back into the reception room. On the night of the murder, someone had walked through here and into the kitchen. The person had followed Malin. She was going to make that person a cup of tea. She couldn't have been aware of any danger because she must have turned her back. This person wasn't a perceived threat. Then the murderer had grabbed her from behind, killed her in the kitchen and then dragged her into the living room and placed her on the sofa. Was the sofa significant?

She walked into the small hallway. The door hadn't been forced. Malin must have let her assailant in. Either she knew him or he had talked his way in. If it had been the stalker, Crabo, she surely wouldn't have let him over the threshold. Victims didn't usually let their stalkers get that close, though there had been that strange business with the reclusive Agnetha Fältskog from ABBA and her persistent Dutch fan. This H might be different though. Malin might not have known that he was H.

Of course, the killer might have been here all the time. She had got back home about 9.30 pm. No. That didn't add up. She wasn't killed until at least a couple of hours later, so there would have been other evidence. You wouldn't wait so long to give a visitor something to drink. The killer must have come in later. And that killer knew something about combat techniques. Then there was the problem of the body slipping onto the floor, or being pushed there. Someone else coming in after? It didn't make sense. Then her mobile went off.

'Anita Sundström.' It was Olander. Strachan had just finished his statement and they had taken prints. Olander wanted to know whether they should just let him leave now.

'Keep him there. I'll be five minutes. I need to speak to him.'

Olander was waiting at her desk when Anita arrived back at the polishus. He showed her Ewan Strachan's statement. She glanced over it and saw nothing new that would be useful. But she still wanted a word with him.

'Bring him up here,' she told Olander.

A few minutes later, Ewan appeared at the door with Olander. Anita indicated that Olander could leave them and he shut the door behind him.

'Please, sit down, Mr Strachan.'

Ewan rustled up a smile as he took a seat opposite her desk. 'I hope that's the end of it officially. Did you really need to take my prints?'

'Only to eliminate you from our enquiry. Your prints will be around the apartment and, of course, on the body.'

Ewan grimaced. 'Hadn't thought of that.'

Anita suddenly became conscious of the mess her desk was in. Papers and files everywhere. Two empty paper coffee cups and a half-drunk bottle of water. She picked up the paper cups and popped them into the bin. Moberg had moaned about her untidiness, but as long as she did her job properly, what was the problem?

'I've had a look at your statement. One thing I need to clarify with you is when you entered the living room. This is really important.' She pressed her glasses up against the bridge of her nose. 'Was Malin Lovgren on the floor, or was she sitting up on the sofa?'

'On the floor,' Ewan answered immediately. 'Why?'

'We are just making sure.'

'That's why I knew there was something wrong. You walk into a room and you see someone flat out on the floor; it's obvious, unless they've been drunk from the night before and haven't reached their bed. That's happened to me more than once, I must confess.' The glint had returned to his eye. His amusement caught her off guard and she found herself looking into his eyes. She noticed for the first time that they were deep blue, which was slightly at odds with his reddish hair.

'And you had never met Malin Lovgren previously or had any contact with her before you went round to the apartment?'

'Of course not. She wasn't in Edinburgh with Mick. That other young actress was there. Can't remember her name. Tilda something. Bengt Valquist's girlfriend. The guy who produces Mick's films.'

'OK. That's all.'

'So, officially, I'm not a suspect?'

'I would say so.'

'Good. Then I can interview you in my new capacity as crime reporter for *Novo News*. Inspector Sundström, have you anything to say to the press about your current murder investigation? On or...' with a smirk on his face, he tapped his nose knowingly, '... off the record.'

She wasn't going to fall into that old trap again. 'You'll have to ask Chief Inspector Moberg.'

Ewan put on an expression of mock horror. 'I can't do that. He frightens the shit out of me!'

'I'm sorry.'

'Seriously, we might be useful to each other.'

'How?'

'Well, I can talk to Mick Roslyn in a way that you can't. Maybe he knows something that he's not telling you, or feels he can't. Old friends and all that.' This interested Anita. Maybe she could use Strachan's university connection. She had this strong feeling that Roslyn was the key to the murder, even though he might be an innocent party. She knew that Roslyn hadn't told her the full truth when she had interviewed him. He was holding something back. Could this journalist get something vital out of him? She had nothing to lose, as the investigation was desperately short of leads.

'If you find out anything, talk to me first. Then maybe I can help you.'

Ewan's face lit up. 'I need all the help I can get,' he joked. 'As it happens, I'm meeting Mick,' he glanced at his watch, 'in about twenty-five minutes. If there's anything to report, I'll call you. Better give me your mobile number.'

Anita tore off a piece of paper from the corner of an official memo and wrote down her number. She handed it to him.

'I'll put it in my mobile so I won't lose it. By the way, if we're going to help each other, it might make life easier if you call me Ewan. You seem to have difficulty with Mr *Straak-en*,' he mimicked her pronunciation of his name.

'All right. Ewan is easier.'

'And what shall I call you?'

'Inspector Sundström is fine.' He might be useful, but that was as far as she would let things go. The last journalist she had befriended for professional, mutual, 'off-the-record' information had tried eventually to get her into bed. Sleeping with the enemy wasn't her style. That source of information had dried up immediately.

He grinned broadly. 'I understand, Inspector Sundström. Can I go?'

'Of course.'

He stood up. So did Anita. For a moment she thought he was going to reach across and shake her hand. He smiled at her. 'It amazes me that all your CID people dress so casually over here. Back home, all our detectives wear suits and ties.'

'I know. I found it a shock when I was with the Met.'

'This is better.' He nodded to himself approvingly and turned towards the door.

'One other thing,' Anita said. He turned back to face her. 'Have you ever done military service?'

He laughed. 'Me? You're joking.' He indicated his body with a downward flourish of his hands. 'Do I look the military type?'

Anita watched him standing by the door, a slightly tubby figure. She thought that he had probably been more muscular in the days before he let himself go, but she still couldn't see him in uniform, and she found herself smiling at the thought. 'No, not really.'

'Besides, I'm a professional coward.'

CHAPTER 14

Ewan was glad to get out of the police headquarters. He felt a mixture of relief and suppressed excitement – relief that he wasn't a suspect and excitement because he had got hold of Inspector Sundström's personal phone number. She was a handsome woman and, despite her rather brusque manner, he was warming to her. He tried to imagine her without her clothes on but, disappointingly, he couldn't get further down than her shoulders. When she had allowed herself to smile, her whole face had lit up. The eyes behind the spectacles had sparkled momentarily. The mouth had opened invitingly. And he had realised as they were talking that he wanted to see her again. That was why he had come up with the ridiculous idea that he could get some vital information out of Mick. She had seemed interested by the notion. The trouble was that he thought he had little chance of getting anything useful out of his old friend.

He crossed over the canal and walked quickly down Östergatan. The dark sky above promised more snow, but the weather was having difficulty deciding whether to go all out for proper winter or just to stick to being antisocially cold. It was ridiculous even thinking about Sundström. Why should she be remotely interested in an overweight journalist from Britain who wasn't very good with women anyway? He was sure that she regarded him as little more than an irritant who had stumbled into their investigation. The sooner he was discounted, the better. He knew nothing about her. She was probably married for starters. Someone as good-looking as that was bound to be. Or, if not, probably had some stud of a boyfriend. By the time he recrossed the canal in front of the station, he had convinced himself he was being a berk. He was simply falling for the fantasy of the beautiful Swedish woman; one to which the average British male was highly susceptible. Yet he still felt a tingle of pleasure as he put her name and number into the contacts section of his mobile phone.

Ewan had never seen Mick like this. Admittedly, he had never before witnessed him within forty-eight hours of his wife being murdered, but he was really agitated. Bengt Valquist wasn't helping either. Here really was a nervous man. He continually played with his spectacles. Ewan wished he would stop it. Ewan had ordered up a bottle of whisky in the hopes that it would calm them down, but that hadn't helped either of them. Valquist didn't touch spirits. The two men had slipped in through some back entrance of the hotel to avoid been seen, which Ewan thought was a tad melodramatic.

At first, Mick had apologised again for hitting him. But that wasn't the reason that he wanted to speak to him. Mick took a gulp of whisky and then proceeded to pour himself another glass. Ewan wondered whether Brian would pick up on the bottle when he handed in his expenses.

'I want your advice, I suppose,' said Mick.

Ewan was taken aback. Hardly anyone had ever asked for his advice except on which real ale was worth a try. And Mick wouldn't have lowered himself to ask anything of him when they were at university. In those days, Mick had known all the answers.

'If I can help,' was the only reply Ewan could come out with.

'I, or we, really,' Mick said glancing across to Valquist, who was fiddling with his damned spectacles again, 'need an outside view on something. Something that may be behind Malin's murder.' Ewan was intrigued. He sat on his bed and listened as Mick wore out the wooden flooring.

'Malin thought she had been followed recently. There was this guy who kept sending her love letters, signing himself H. When she didn't reply, they got a bit more threatening.' Ewan wanted to take notes because this was useful to his story for Brian, but that wouldn't have looked right. It was not that sort of conversation.

'I've told the police about him, but we think it might be someone totally different. Someone connected with a documentary we were putting together.'

'Is this the hush-hush project you hinted at in Edinburgh?'

'Yes. But then I didn't know that it would be this dangerous.' Mick took another drink of whisky from the glass Ewan had found in the bathroom. 'How much do you know about the murder of Olof Palme?'

'Nothing really. I remember vaguely that the Swedish prime minister was killed, but that's about it. Can't even remember when it was.'

'Olof Palme was shot in a Stockholm street late on February 28th, 1986.' This information was presented by Valquist, who had now put his spectacles back on. 'He died from his wounds shortly after he was taken to the hospital. He had been to the movies with his wife. She was wounded, but she did not die.'

'Did they catch who did it?' asked Ewan.

'That's just it,' answered Mick. 'They didn't. It was a lone gunman who attacked them. They had no bodyguards at the time. The strange thing is that the visit to the Grand Cinema was fairly last minute, so whoever was behind it couldn't have planned the assassination in that location in advance.'

Valquist took up the story. 'The police arrested a right-wing extremist called Victor Gunnarsson, but he was let go. After three years, they arrested Christer Pettersson. He was a small criminal. Not an important one, I mean. Alcoholic. Palme's wife identified him. He was tried and... what's the word in English?'

'Convicted,' Mick supplied.

'Yes. Convicted. But after three years he was let go from the prison.'

'Pettersson's appeal succeeded because they never found the murder weapon,' continued Mick. 'There were doubts over Lisbet Palme's evidence and, most importantly, there didn't seem to be any motive. I don't think anybody seriously thinks it was him.'

'But someone must have done it.' Ewan was enjoying this. He could feel a conspiracy theory coming on. And a conspiracy theory would give him plenty to write about.

'Over the years the finger has been pointed in all sorts of directions. There was a Kurdish group called the PPK; the Baader-Meinhoff group; and not that long ago a book came out claiming it was do with trade links between the Indians and the Bofors armaments people over here. But the most convincing theory seemed to be the one that it was the South Africans. Palme had quite an international reputation for supporting causes like the Palestinians; he spoke up about Nicaragua and El Salvador. However, his strongest connection was with the anti-apartheid movement. He was an outspoken critic of South Africa and knew many of the officials from the ANC, like Oliver Tambo. In fact, Tambo and lots of other activists attended a keynote speech given by Palme at an event in Stockholm called the Swedish People's Parliament Against Apartheid. It was exactly a week before he was killed. A number of years later, a South African policeman called Eugene de Kock said that Palme had been killed because he was an opponent of apartheid and Sweden was backing the ANC. De Kock even named the killer. A guy called Craig Williamson. That opened a can of worms and at least another two South African-connected names were thrown into the melting pot. Swedish police investigators did go over to South Africa but couldn't substantiate de Kock's claims.'

'So it's still a mystery?'

'Well, we thought so until Bengt was approached last year. It was known that I was interested in making a new movie on the subject. I had come up with some idea based on the Russians trying to get rid of him. A Cold War version. When no one knows who did it, you can come up with virtually anything.'

Ewan watched Mick intently. He was utterly intrigued by the story now. 'So who approached you?'

Valquist took off his spectacles again. 'I got a phone call. Mysterious at first. He had heard about Mick's plans. He says he can tell Mick the real truth. But he would only speak to Mick.'

'So I spoke to him. Then I met him at a secret location in Stockholm. He was all very cagy. After that, we had a number of meetings, all in secret. He claimed he had worked for Säpo in the 1980s.'

'Who are... whatever?'

'Säkerhetspolsen. Säpo for short. The Swedish security police. According to our informant, it was a far right-wing element within Säpo which was behind the killing.'

'You mean Palme's own police?' Ewan whispered incredulously.

'Basically. Despite its reputation for being a liberal country, Sweden has a strong right-wing tradition. Sweden may have been neutral during the war, but there were an awful lot of Nazi sympathisers around. A number even joined up and fought with the Germans, especially on the Russian front.'

'I never knew that.'

'Oh, yeah. Norwegians and Danes, too. Anyway, this rogue group were horrified by Palme's stance on a number of issues, particularly backing black South Africans and supporting left-wing regimes around the world. They thought he was a real liability. He was taking Sweden in the wrong direction. So they decided he had to go. And who better than Säpo to monitor the prime minister's every move? They could react quickly to any situation. Palme played into their hands because he had no bodyguards that night. That's the sort of thing they would know about immediately. And who better to cover their tracks than the people put in charge of trying to catch the killer?'

'It sounds incredible.'

'I thought so, too. But the more I talked to him, the more it made sense. It was such a bombshell that Bengt and I decided it had to be made into a documentary and not a movie. That would carry real weight.' Mick reflected for a moment. 'Malin wasn't keen on the idea.'

Ewan stood up to stretch his legs. 'But I don't understand what this has to do with– '

'My contact said that some of the group were still around. He was pretty sure that included the man who had actually carried out the killing. We think they may have got wind of what we're doing. We were talking about it all last night and we believe that maybe they got to Malin to warn me off. Who knows, they may even have been after me and she was just in the wrong place at the wrong time. She certainly thought she was being followed. Were they monitoring her movements?'

Ewan poured himself a whisky. 'It's a funny thing. That woman inspector – the one with the nice arse – she asked me if I had been in the military.' Mick and Valquist exchanged glances. 'So maybe the strangulation was done by someone who knew how to kill quickly and efficiently.'

Mick sat down and held his head in his hands. 'Christ.'

This was too much for Valquist, who disappeared into the bathroom.

'Why are you telling me all this?' asked Ewan.

Mick looked up. The strain was evident in his features as

he rubbed his unshaven chin. 'I needed to talk to someone who had no connection with Sweden. I know we have... a history. But we go back a long way. You can look on as an outsider. Bengt's too close. He wants me to tell the police.'

'I would have thought that was obvious.'

'I don't trust them. Some may have connections with these ex-Säpo guys. I'm not sure what I'm dealing with.'

Ewan offered Mick a top-up. This time Mick held up his hand in refusal. 'I don't think you've got a choice. The most important thing is to find out who... you know. And if there's even the remotest possibility of some loony ex-secret service guy out there, you might not be safe. You've got to tell them.'

'You're right. They want to talk to me again anyhow.'

A thought came into Ewan's head. 'The lady cop. Sundström. I can't believe she's some Swedish Eva Braun. Now the big bugger who's leading the investigation – I can see him in jackboots. He's fatter than Hermann Goering. Look, why not speak to her first? I'll ring her and see if I can get her to come over here. Explain everything. Then let her decide what's best.'

'OK,' said Mick, but without any conviction.

Ewan got out his mobile. He keyed in the name *Sundström*. This was fantastic. He was killing two birds with one stone. He had an excuse to be very useful to the attractive Inspector Sundström – and he had just been handed a great story.

CHAPTER 15

Moberg had exploded. He raged that she knew damned well that he wanted to be there when they next talked to Roslyn. Instead she had slunk off to the journalist's hotel behind his back. It was totally unprofessional. He was running the investigation and he wouldn't tolerate any maverick behaviour. She was amazed that he didn't add 'particularly by a woman.' But he did throw in a threat. 'Do anything like that again, and I'll have you processing parking tickets down the road!' Anita waited for him to calm down.

'Roslyn thinks you might be a Nazi.'

She knew it would set him off again, but she enjoyed the moment. After he had called in Nordlund, Anita went through Roslyn's story before telling them that she had Roslyn in her office because he was probably safer off in the polishus than wandering around Malmö or Lund. At least the tale had silenced Moberg, whose expression had become more incredulous by the minute. He didn't speak until well after she had finished.

'It's a load of horseshit, isn't it?'

'I don't know,' replied Anita. 'One thing for sure is that Roslyn seems to believe it. He thinks his life's in danger.'

'It has a ring of truth,' observed Nordlund. 'We've all had our suspicions.'

'I know. Christ, every crackpot has had a theory, and

a lot have made money out of it. Why should Roslyn be any different?'

Anita shrugged. 'The problem is, whatever we may think, can we afford to ignore it? If we dismiss it and then Roslyn gets killed, then we're all in the shit. If people had done their job properly, then Mijailovi wouldn't have been on the streets to be able to murder Anna Lindh.'

Moberg pulled a face. He could see his career going down the toilet faster than a flushed fag. 'Has he come up with the name of his informant?'

'"Deep Throat".' Anita smirked.

'You're taking the piss!'

'No, honestly; that's how Roslyn referred to him. He thinks he's uncovered something bigger than Watergate.'

'For fuck's sake! Well, I'll get the name out of him even if I have to bounce the wanker off the cell walls to get it. If there is a grain of truth in this, then we've got some very experienced guys out there to deal with.'

'Erik, there are a couple of things that might add weight to his story.' Nordlund had Moberg's full attention. 'The method of killing certainly fits. Quick, clean operation. No mess. An execution by gun would have at least given us more to go on than we have here. No bullets, no blood, no sound.'

'And secondly?'

'If the body was left sitting on the sofa, as we now suspect, it was deliberate. We've come to the conclusion it was a message – or, if not a message as such, certainly a startling way for Roslyn to come in and find his wife. Presumably, it was meant to be him who found her.'

Moberg scratched his stomach. Anita realised that this was a nervous gesture and not a sign that he was hungry yet again. He turned to her. 'And the journalist definitely found the body on the floor?'

'According to his statement.'

'Right, Henrik, we'll go and have a little chat with him and, if I believe him, then we'll have to sort out a safe house or hotel room and keep him under wraps. This case is not getting any better.'

'Brian, you're not going to believe it, but I've got an amazing story here.' Ewan was astonished at his own excitement.

Brian's response was a mixture of cautious disbelief. 'Really?'

'Yeah. Dropped into my lap by Mick Roslyn.'

'Something we can print?' The scepticism still hadn't left his voice.

'Not yet, because he's only just told the police, and they'll probably keep it under wraps for the time being.' Inspector Sundström's threat was still ringing in his ears: *If a word of this gets out before we've investigated, my boss will have your balls for breakfast. He's very big and very hungry.*

'Can you tell me?'

'It's complicated, but Mick thinks it's tied up with a documentary he's doing on the assassination of Olof Palme. He thinks–'

'Who?'

'Olof Palme, the Swedish prime minister. 1986. You must remember?'

There was a pause at the other end of the line.

'Yes. That's right. I remember. Dead liberal guy.'

'Well, he turned out to be a dead liberal after some bloke shot him in a Stockholm street. They never found the killer. Anyway, to cut a long story short, Mick thinks that his digging into the story has led to his wife's murder. It's all tied up with the Swedish security police. We can't go public yet, and we'll need confirmation first. But it could be a massive international story.'

'God, yes. Could be huge. Brilliant! Keep me in touch.'

'Will do.'

'Oh, by the way. Have you done that travel piece for Henry?'

'I'll finish it tomorrow morning and email it to him by lunchtime.'

Of course, he hadn't even started the travel piece yet, but he would go back to the café in Möllevågen and write it over a couple of coffees. And now Brian was happy and would leave him in peace for a while.

After he put the phone down, he went over to the nearly empty bottle of whisky and poured himself the remains. It had been quite a couple of hours. First he had phoned Inspector Sundström. She had been surprised to hear from him and wasn't sure whether he was serious at first. However, she had come across. Valquist had left before her arrival, saying that his girlfriend, the actress Tilda Tegner, was coming back to Lund from Stockholm to be with him during this difficult time. The conversation between Inspector Sundström and Mick had been in Swedish. Despite having no idea what they were saying, Ewan had watched Sundström in fascination. She was a striking woman. The voice that had virtually no trace of an accent when she was speaking English seemed to be guttural when speaking in her native Swedish; quite harsh to the ear but, from her lips, rather sexy. Or maybe it was just that he had a thing about women in glasses speaking in a foreign language.

When Mick had gone to the bathroom to freshen up before heading off to the police headquarters with the inspector, Ewan pointed out to her that it was he who had been responsible for making Mick go to the police. And that it was his idea that Mick talked to her first.

'It was a sensible suggestion.'

'So I've done you a favour. If you have any information that would be useful to me, then...' He handed her a piece of paper on which he had written his mobile phone number in anticipation of just such an opportunity.

She took the paper without looking at it and popped it into her pocket. He wanted to take advantage of the favourable impression he hoped he had created and find a reason to see her again. And he really *did* want to see her again. 'Would it be out of the question to meet? Maybe for a drink. I don't know. Give me a chance to fill you in on some background stuff on Mick.'

'If we need to talk further, we can do that at the polishus.'

'Is that a "no" to the drink?'

Moberg lumbered grumpily towards the commissioner's office. After a long discussion with Roslyn, he wasn't sure whether it was all fantasy or all for real. But, as that bloody Anita Sundström had said, they couldn't take a chance on getting it wrong. He needed to give the commissioner the facts and decide on somewhere to put Roslyn for the next few days while they checked out his story. At least he had forced the name of Roslyn's "Deep Throat" out of him without resorting to throttling. The only problem was that Roslyn had no idea who this whistleblower's real identity was – he had called himself "Henrik Larsson", presumably after the famous footballer – or where he lived. He might not even live in Stockholm.

'Chief Inspector!'

Moberg turned round and saw Klara Wallen clutching a piece of paper. 'Yes?' he growled.

Wallen flinched before nervously thrusting the paper in his direction. He snatched it from her and glanced over it. 'That's something.'

Wallen scuttled away before Moberg said anything else to her.

Moberg knocked on the commissioner's door. 'Come!' came a call from the other side. He entered a far plusher office than his own. This was where the politicking took preference over proper policing. The commissioner was sitting behind his desk, which had the day's newspapers strewn over it. 'Ah, Erik, tell me that you've brought me some good news.' He cast a hand over the newspapers. 'This lot aren't being very patient. They want results.'

'Well, Commissioner, I have some good news and some bad news.'

The commissioner fiddled fretfully with his expensive watch.

Moberg held up the piece of paper Wallen had just given him. 'Crabo, the stalker. He's turned up. He'd gone north to visit his sister. His alibi checks, so we can rule him out.'

'And the bad news?'

Anita was pleased that Lasse had rung. She had kicked off her shoes and was seeking solace in a glass of Rioja. Even though she was tired and troubled by the case, she could always relax when chatting with her son. They had a good relationship. They had had very few rows over the years, and most of them were caused by her untidiness. Sometimes she felt that their roles were reversed and that Lasse was the mature one. He was far better at making decisions than she was. Above all, Lasse made her laugh. Björn always had until he made her cry more often. Not many males made her laugh these days. Too caught up with themselves, too Swedish.

'How's the investigation going, Mum?'

'Not getting very far.'

'The telly is full of it. I saw your boss the other night. He's even fatter than when I last saw him.'

'It hasn't improved his temper either.'

'Is he giving you a hard time?'

'No more than usual. I can handle him. It's just that he doesn't think that women should be involved in murder investigations. We should be doing traffic or child abuse cases. To him, murder is man's work. Anyway, how's student life?'

'Good.' There was a pause. There was always a pause when

Lasse had something important to say. It was usually a request for money.

'I've got a girlfriend.'

Anita tried to sound upbeat. 'What's her name?'

'Rebecka.'

Was this the moment she had dreaded? She had always wondered how she would cope when Lasse found someone more important than herself. Would there be a feeling of rejection? Since Björn's betrayal, she had channelled her unconditional love into her relationship with Lasse. There may have been occasional visitors to her bed, but no one had been allowed to stay in her heart. She had worried that Lasse's leaving home for the first time would loosen the umbilical cord that had linked them since his birth. Was her real fear that she would be left alone?

'That's a nice name. What is she studying?'

'Politics.'

'Not politics! Haven't we got enough politicians?'

'Oh, Mum! She's fun.' There was another pause. 'She's special.'

'I'm pleased,' she lied.

'You'll really like her.' He was almost too insistent, trying too hard to convince.

'It'll be lovely to meet her.' She knew she would have a battle not to be too judgemental.

'Mum, can I bring Rebecka with me when I come down next?'

Anita's heart sank. She had been so looking forward to spending some time alone with Lasse. Someone to talk to – she loved their cosy chats. Doing those things they enjoyed doing together. Now she would have to share him. She knew young love. It was all-consuming. He would only have eyes for this girl. It wouldn't be the same. And she'd also have to make a real effort to tidy up the apartment.

'Of course. But I might not be around too much if we're still heavily involved in this case.' She didn't want to put him off, but he might think twice about bringing his girlfriend if he thought she was busy.

'I thought it would be over by then. The county commissioner was on the telly an hour or so ago and he said you had some strong leads.'

'Dahlbeck's an idiot. He's just worried that he'll get persecuted by the press. By sounding too positive, he just piles more pressure on us.'

'Don't worry. If you're busy, I can show Rebecka round Malmö. She's never been before.' It wasn't the reaction she wanted.

Afterwards, she chided herself for being so petty-minded. It was his life and she would make a positive effort to like the girl, even if she was awful. The Rioja bottle was more than half-empty. She poured another glass. She had more on her plate than Rebecka. She hadn't known what to make of Roslyn's story. It could be true – or he certainly believed what he had been told. No one really knew who was behind Olof Palme's murder. An ultra-right-wing group within Säpo was as plausible as any other conspiracy theory. If it was true, then they really had their hands full. It might be twenty years since the assassination, but these people had been highly trained. That made them efficient, elusive and dangerous. The method of death and the deliberate positioning of the body would fit Roslyn's theory. And he had seemed genuinely agitated. Of course, it could be that he was a very good actor and for some reason was pointing them in the wrong direction. There was an off-the-wall thought! No, it didn't add up. Roslyn was in Stockholm anyway.

Yet why would Malin Lovgren get herself in a position to offer a professional killer a cup of tea? Anita was still sure that the murderer had been known to Lovgren. And where was the starfish pendant? If it was a professional hit, why bother removing the pendant from the murder scene? There had been no attempt to make it look like a burglary gone wrong. Had it been taken as a trophy? Or was it to be produced later as a warning to Roslyn if he decided to carry on with his controversial documentary? *We've got your wife's pendant, so we can do to you what we did to her.* Or was Roslyn the intended victim? Given what they had discovered about the glamorous couple, he must have had more enemies than she had. People seemed to like Malin. But Mick? Anita had a feeling that all was not what it seemed between the director and his supposed friend, Strachan. Did that really matter, or was it worth digging a little deeper? She couldn't make her mind up, so she drank some more wine.

CHAPTER 16

Ewan was starting to get a taste for Swedish coffee. It was the sort of drink that put hair on one's chest. He had never been able to grow chest hair, which irked him. As a student, Mick had always enjoyed telling him that the 'birds love running their fingers through mine.' Needless to say, Mick's chest was like a demented doormat. In fact, Ewan could never grow hair in all the right places and now he had reached an age when it was growing in all the wrong ones. He sipped his coffee and glanced round the other tables in Café Simrishamn 3. It was half full, and nearly everybody had a computer in front of them. The atmosphere was warm and unhurried.

He looked at the blank screen, then typed: *There's more to Malmö than meets the eye.* He sighed. It was rubbish, though the sentiment was probably true in that in mid-winter it didn't do itself justice. With all the beautiful parks, this was undoubtedly a summer city. Without a green canvas to break up many of the functional buildings, it was difficult to judge its true character. His walk round Kungsparken, the city's oldest park, had been pleasant. The canal ran through it, with the city library on the other side. He had crossed over the canal on an elegant bridge with art nouveau designs and lampposts like obelisks at each end, and made his way down to what was now called the Malmö Opera. It was the main municipal theatre of the town and had built up an enviable reputation under Ingmar Bergman, who had been the director and artistic adviser in the 1950s.

Ewan had stood on the expansive forecourt outside the theatre's large glass frontage and classically crisp concrete elevations. But as he peered through the glass into the foyer, he felt oddly uncomfortable. This building had celebrated its opening in September 1944 with a performance of Shakespeare's *A Midsummer Night's Dream*. While the citizens of Malmö were taking their seats in their stylish new theatre, chatting quietly away before the curtain went up, just over the water, a mere few kilometres away, the world was ripping itself apart. In the same month, the Allies were battling their way through France; the Arnhem parachute landings were proving a bridge too far; in neighbouring Norway the mighty German battleship *Tirpitz* was being attacked by the RAF; and across central Europe trains were still trundling inexorably towards the death camps. How had the Swedes reconciled what was happening all around them with the normality of their own lives? That was something he would ask Inspector Sundström if he got the chance.

He sipped at his coffee. He had thought about the detective a lot since she had left his hotel room the previous day. He used mental pictures of her to drive out the recurring image of the dead body of Malin Lovgren. His fascination with Sundström – he wished he knew her first name – was making him see Malmö in a different light. He typed: *It's all go in Malmö*. That was shite, too.

There was something different about the place. A tension. A suppressed excitement. The moment Anita and Olander came through the front entrance, they knew something had happened. Their routine enquires around Värnhem had yielded nothing. An increasingly desperate Moberg had insisted on their revisiting the crime area in case something had been missed. Anita hadn't expected to turn up anything new because she was covering ground that Nordlund had gone over already. And Nordlund was very thorough. If it had been the slapdash Westermark, then it would have made sense.

Klara Wallen intercepted them before they reached Anita's office.

'Moberg wants to see you.'

'What is it?' Anita asked; she could see that Wallen was caught up in the prevailing mood.

'CCTV. Something's come up.'

When Anita and Olander entered Moberg's room, Nordlund and Westermark were already there with one of the technical people whom Anita knew vaguely but whose name escaped her. They were huddled round a TV monitor and there was some CCTV footage on the screen.

'Ah, Anita, come and see this. Edvardsen has got onto something.' Moberg pointed to the figure on the screen. Anita could see a tall man with his back to the camera. Smoke could be seen rising from in front of him. Then his gloved hand appeared and in it was a cigarette. He stamped his feet, but his gaze never wavered.

'This is taken from the *Systembolag* side. He's looking across the street,' said an evidently pleased Edvardsen.

'Towards the apartment block,' added Moberg.

The continuous time code was running just after midnight on the night of the murder. The time had just tipped over into Tuesday. The man, who was wearing a blue winter skiing jacket and a dark-red baseball cap, took one last puff of his cigarette, then threw it down on the ground. He half-turned so that the side of his face could be seen in profile. Anita wasn't sure what age he was, but he was certainly under forty. He glanced at something across the street – the time code twirled onto three minutes past twelve. He was about to step forward, then he dodged back into the doorway for a moment. He waited for another thirty seconds before stepping out of the frame.

'Night of the murder,' Moberg announced triumphantly. 'And clever old Edvardsen has put together a compilation tape which shows the same man at the same spot every night for the last two weeks. In fact, every night that Lovgren had been back in Malmö after her return from Stockholm.'

'Hit man?' wondered Nordlund.

'Possibly. Or H?' said Moberg.

'Unfortunately, we don't have a full face because of the cap,' said Edvardsen, 'but this is the best we could do.'

On the screen came a nearly full face of the man, but his features were obscured by the shadow cast by the peak of his cap. Anita now put him at about thirty.

'Is it possible to go back to the last bit where he gets rid of his cigarette?' asked Anita.

'Why?' Moberg sounded irritated.

'Just something.'

Edvardsen ran the tape back to the position Anita had asked for. He ran it again. The man threw down his cigarette.

'Stop!' Anita said quickly. The frame was frozen. Anita looked closely at the screen. Then she pointed to the ground. 'That. Can you zoom in?' The pavement moved towards them until the screen was taken up with a large screwed up piece of wrapping paper next to the still-glowing cigarette stub.

'Is that a discarded kebab? Yes,' said Anita with some certainty now. 'There are a number of kebab places around that area. So what?' Westermark was trying to score points.

'If he had been there for a while, then that might be his kebab. He's standing next to it. If someone else had dropped it, he probably would have stood in another place, not virtually on top of it. And if it's his kebab, he would have bought it at one of the shops close by. They might recognise him. He might even have gone in regularly over the last fortnight.'

'Print off this guy's picture and get down there, Olander. It might turn up something.'

Just then Eva Thulin came in.

'That's timely,' said Moberg. 'Have we got a precise time of death?'

'It was probably about midnight. But could be half an hour either way. It's impossible to be totally exact.'

'That would fit in with our friend here.' Moberg was trying to control his exhilaration. Anita knew that feeling. When there doesn't seem to be answer in sight and then suddenly there's a breakthrough, it buoys the team, giving them a focus that was missing before. It might be early days, but it was something to cling onto. Something concrete to investigate.

'That your suspect?' asked Thulin, glancing at the screen.

'Could be.'

'Well, the body was touched by Roslyn and by Strachan.'

'We know that!' Moberg was under pressure but his man-management skills were always dreadful, even on a good day.

'I thought you might like to know,' Thulin carried on defensively, 'that the body was definitely touched by a third party.'

Now Moberg was all ears. 'Touched?'

'Yes. Or held closely. We've got fibres that don't belong to either of the two other men. Strachan had a black woollen coat and Roslyn a brown leather jacket.'

'I thought it odd that Roslyn was only wearing a leather jacket when he had come all the way from Stockholm. Must have been freezing up there.' Anita was impressed that Olander had the courage to contribute his thoughts in front of Moberg and the team. The confidence of youth.

'Because he's a trendy arsehole. Olander, I thought I'd told you to fuck off and do something,' Moberg barked. The young man vanished.

'Anyway,' continued Thulin, 'the third one could be from a

weatherproof jacket. Blue.'

'Bingo!' Moberg smashed the desk in delight with the palm of his hand and pointed at the man who was back on the screen.

The doubtful look on Thulin's face showed she didn't share Moberg's enthusiasm. He sighed impatiently. 'Well?'

'It could be the killer. Or the person who disturbed the body.'

'Couldn't they be one and the same?' asked Nordlund.

'Possibly. But why go to all the trouble of dragging the body in from the kitchen, setting it up on the sofa and then letting it slide onto the floor?'

'I can't believe that there's a second person involved,' Moberg said firmly. 'No.' He swivelled round and pointed at the screen. 'That's our man. Let's bloody find him!'

CHAPTER 17

Ewan clicked on *send/recv* and the email and attached article winged its way to the office in Newcastle. He had to admit that, after a sticky start, he was now quite pleased with his effort. He had given Malmö a very positive write-up, despite his adverse personal experiences since his arrival. Maybe the glow that he had bathed Malmö in had more to do with his feelings for Inspector Sundström. At least they had enabled him to look beyond the cold, drab time of year and see the city's potential as a very pleasant summer destination for British visitors.

He had plundered some history to put the city in context. It had been Hanseatic merchants, enticed by the plentiful herring, who had established Malmö as a commercial centre. Malmö had then come under Danish rule and was the second city of Denmark. Malmöhus had even housed the Danish royal mint. The Danes were driven out of Malmö by Swedish King Karl X in 1658 and it had remained Swedish ever since, though the city still had a strong affinity with its Danish neighbour.

20th-century wealth had been built round the huge Kockums submarine and shipyard. With its decline in the 1970s, Malmö faced difficult times. Isolation from Stockholm hadn't helped, but now the Öresund Bridge had opened up a whole new world of opportunity. Malmö was a vibrant town. He had mentioned the parks, the castle, the theatre, the football club (essential for Geordie consumption), the shopping – and had made a point of namechecking The Pickwick and Café Simrishamn 3. He had included a warning about the strength of Swedish coffee, but he had finished off by encouraging people to come and see Malmö, and southern Sweden, for themselves.

Ewan ordered another coffee and some rich-looking carrot cake to celebrate. Now he would have to turn his attention to Brian's scoop. At least he had the makings of a great story. In fact, he couldn't believe his luck; ruthless, right-wing secret service agents bumping off their own prime minister. And Mick seemed quite convinced that these very same assassins were behind the murder of his own wife. It was manna from heaven and he would push it for all it was worth with Brian. He started to type in some notes, but he would need a lot more information before he could allow Brian to print anything – inside information. That brought him back to the lovely Inspector Sundström. How could he inveigle his way into her confidence? He must have gained some sort of kudos with his Mick manoeuvre. She should do well out of that meeting. A fresh line of enquiry delivered on a plate. Yet she hadn't shown the appreciation he thought had been his due. Playing hard to get or just not remotely interested? Ewan stuffed a large piece of cake into his mouth and concluded it was bound to be the latter.

Anita made her way over to the water cooler. She took out a plastic cup and filled it with the cold water. As she turned, she was trapped by Westermark. His reptilian gaze always made her feel ill at ease. His ice-blue eyes always seemed to be boring into her. Visually molesting her. Like Roslyn, he held his looks in high esteem. He assumed that all women would agree. He was more rugged than Roslyn and his short-cropped, fair hair was in stark contrast to Roslyn's dark plumage. But they were both cut from the same cloth.

'How's the love life?'

A typical Westermark conversation opener. Couldn't he think of anything sensible to say? But that would have been asking too much.

'Too busy trying to catch a killer to worry about that sort of thing.'

'So you're going through a barren patch? I can help you out.'

'Just give it a rest, Karl. And even if I get really desperate, you'll still not get a call.'

She took her plastic cup.

'The boss thinks we're onto something with the CCTV footage,' said Westermark, changing tack.

'Worth following up. It's all we've got, except for the Säpo connection.'

'That could be very tricky. Moberg has got the commissioner to pull strings to get photos of Säpo operatives around the mid-eighties. Maybe Roslyn can recognise his "Deep Throat". Otherwise we're pissing in the wind.'

Anita nodded agreement as she managed to move away.

'One funny thing.' Anita stopped. 'I checked up on that meeting that Roslyn was meant to be having on the evening of the murder.'

'And?'

'And he didn't make it. He wasn't there.'

'Does Moberg know?'

'Didn't think it was worth mentioning because he's so sure he's got the man we want. It's probably nothing, anyway.'

'So why is Roslyn lying then?'

'I'll put money on a woman.'

It confirmed what Anita had always thought: Westermark could only think with his balls.

The phone went as soon as Anita had made it back to her office. It was Olander. He had news from the kebab shop.

It wasn't the closest one to Malin's apartment but over on Lundavägen.

'You were right. The guy on the CCTV had been in a few times recently to buy a kebab at the Värnhems falafel shop. Always pretty late. Trouble is, they don't know his name, but they're fairly sure he's not from round Värnhem. He's not a regular, anyway.'

'That's a start. Well done. I'll let Moberg know.'

A breakthrough of sorts? She put down the phone and noticed that a copy of the CCTV photo of the "kebab man" had been put on her desk. She picked it up. She had a feeling that there was something familiar about the man's profile but couldn't put her finger on it. Besides, she was distracted by what Westermark had told her. So Roslyn hadn't been at the meeting. Were they a hundred per cent sure that he had *been* in Stockholm on Monday night?

Anita still had the photo in her hand when she put her head round Moberg's office door. 'Olander rang in. The man in this photo has visited the Värnhems falafel shop a few times lately. But they don't know his name and they don't think he's local.'

'Good,' grunted Moberg without glancing up, his hands below the desk.

'Anything on the Säpo front?'

Moberg did look up now and his hands appeared above the desk. He held a large bar of chocolate. Had he been hiding it?

'Our beloved commissioner has, amazingly, come up trumps and Säpo are – reluctantly it has to be said – going to furnish us with photos of their operatives. But they won't be for general consumption. They're scared stiff that they'll fall into the wrong hands, even though most of the guys who were operating at that time are long retired. Good job too. They couldn't protect our Prime Minister.'

'Unless they killed him.'

Moberg unwrapped his chocolate bar. 'Do you buy that? I

mean Roslyn's theory?'

Anita leant against the doorframe and tucked the photo under her arm.

'We've all thought it, even if we've then dismissed it.'

'Could this guy,' said Moberg, lifting up his own copy of the photograph, 'be their hitman? He's too young to have been around at the time of the assassination. Whoever he is, I don't think Roslyn was the intended victim. This guy was watching the apartment regularly, so he'd know that Roslyn wasn't in residence.'

Anita stared at the photo as Moberg held it up, face on. She was about to mention Roslyn's absence from his meeting when she suddenly moved towards Moberg's desk – and towards the man in the photo.

'That's it. Something was nagging at the back of my mind. I'm sure I've seen that man recently. The other day. In the park. In Beijers Park.'

Moberg stopped in mid-bite. He quickly ate the chunk of chocolate before he spoke.

'He must live nearby. It's not the sort of park you make a special trip to.'

Anita held her own copy of the photo in front of her. 'It was the cap that alerted me.' She was casting her mind back to her visit to the park. What was it about him? She spoke slowly as she tried to put the missing images in place. 'I was crossing the road with Britta Lovgren. This guy was coming the other way. I wasn't really paying attention. I was just aware of someone. Yes, he was wearing a sort of a skiing jacket.'

'Colour?' Moberg demanded excitedly.

'Can't be positive, but it could well have been blue.'

Moberg shot to his feet and nearly overturned his desk in the process.

'Right, I want everybody in here in five minutes. This is it!'

127

*

He was coming back from the centre of town. He wasn't sure what had motivated him to get on a bus that morning and head off to Sankt Petri Kyrka. He had hardly been to church since he was a boy growing up near Skanör, just down the coast from Malmö. Yet when he entered the church, he found it calmed him immediately. He hadn't slept properly since that night, and the whole experience had just added to his anxieties. Seeing the woman detective had unnerved him. At first he had wondered how she could have found the park he frequented so quickly then he realised that it was only natural that the police would want to speak to Malin's mother. He knew exactly where she lived – he could almost see her home from his apartment. Even if the policewoman had noticed, why should she connect him with the murder?

Yet doubts remained, and in the middle of the night his imagination had run riot with the awful possibilities of being spotted. He had nearly rushed upstairs to his storage cage in the attic where he had hidden the gun. It was an illegal firearm, which he thought would be harder to find if it was stored away among his junk. But if they searched his apartment, they wouldn't find anything. Except the photos of course. He had nearly taken them down, but couldn't bring himself to. Not yet. If it all blew over, he could leave them.

The great church was tall and narrow inside. He sat down in a pew and found his gaze soaring heavenwards. Its white walls and columns could have made the space seem stark and sanitised, but he found it uplifting. And reassuring. In here he felt safe. Safe from his demons, which were waiting for him outside. And safe from any Muslims, who had helped distort his life. He heard the door open behind him and he turned round. An elderly woman came in and as she passed, gave him a beatific smile. She slipped into a pew nearer the altar and started to pray. He did the same, bending down and resting his head on the back of the pew in front. He prayed for Malin's soul. He prayed for himself. And he prayed for protection.

He must have dozed off for a few minutes, for when he raised his head again the woman had gone. He felt better. If there was a God, then he must be looking after him. After leaving the church, he went off to the Hamrelius Bokhandel on Södergatan and bought himself a couple of thrillers. He loved books. They were the only things that had kept him sane on active service during that scorching heat. Besides, though the detectives in his purchases were fictional, he might gain an insight into their thinking, their methods.

His flimsy sense of well-being was quickly shattered when the bus turned into the pencil-straight Beijersparksgatan. He couldn't help but spot that parked near the park entrance were two police cars.

It had only taken half an hour. Moberg had flooded the area with police armed with the photo of the "kebab man" to get a positive identification. The little oriental man behind the counter in the baker's in the small shopping complex on the other side of Östra Fäladsgatan recognised him, but didn't know his name. Across the way, the owner of the video shop proved more useful. The man in the photo was called Halvar. Where did he live? In one of the apartments over the road in Smedjekullsgatan. He would have his details as he was signed up for their video club. While the owner was going through his records, the constable called the chief inspector, who reached the shop within minutes, having come from co-ordinating the operation from his parked car in Östra Fäladsgatan. He was accompanied by Westermark.

'Here it is,' said the shop owner. 'Halvar's surname is Mednick.' He then gave Moberg the address. The block was directly across the main road. Mednick lived on the far side of the block.

Moberg turned to Westermark. 'Get onto headquarters and see if we have anything on a Halvar Mednick. Constable, whip along to the park and get Inspector Nordlund and Inspector Sundström back here. Now!'

The startled constable rushed out.

'What's Halvar been up to?' asked the owner.

'Up to no good,' said Moberg as he left the shop.

Ten minutes later, they were gathered outside the baker's shop awaiting Moberg's instructions. On arriving, Anita had noticed that Moberg had just finished off a bun. Maybe food helped him think.

'His apartment is over in that block, but before we go in I want to know what to expect. Westermark is checking. What we do know is that he's called Halvar Mednick. That gives us our H.'

Westermark came off his mobile phone and pulled a face.

'He's on our radar. He was arrested in November for getting into a fight with a couple of immigrants in Möllevågen. Let off with a caution.'

'So he has a record of violence.'

'Not surprising really – he's ex-army.'

'That could make him a possible hitman,' ventured Nordlund.

'Not so sure,' answered Westermark. 'He had a breakdown after serving with the Nato Security Assistance Force in Afghanistan in 2006. Not exactly hitman material.'

'Anything else?' Moberg asked.

'That's about all we've got so far, but they're digging for more.'

All eyes turned to Moberg. He pulled up his coat collar to ward off the cold. 'I don't want to go in mob-handed. Henrik, Westermark, you come with me. Breakdown or not, he'll have been trained to look after himself. He knows how to kill quickly and efficiently, as we saw with Malin Lovgren. You both armed?'

Nordlund and Westermark nodded. Anita felt annoyed that she was being overlooked. She was the one who had recognised Mednick. It was she who had got them to the right area.

'Shouldn't we keep the apartment under surveillance first?' she asked.

'Fuck procedure!' Moberg roared. Glory was within his reach, and he wasn't going to let the opportunity slip. The commissioner and the press wanted a quick result, and that was exactly what he was going to give them.

'Inspector Sundström, make sure everyone else is out of sight, but be ready to come in if there's any trouble. We don't want to alert him.'

'He may have seen all this police activity already.' It was meant as a timely warning, but Moberg was in no mood to listen to her.

'Just do as you're told.' Anita glared at him angrily, but she could see the tension in his face. 'Let's move it.'

Smedjekullsgatan was a narrow street that had several apartment blocks stretching down one side and the pleasant Rostorp residences on the other. There were cars parked in front of the first block, which was where Halvar Mednick lived. From the road, the block was shaped like a flat-bottomed U. Built in the 1940s, it was constructed from a faded yellow brick, which made it less drab than many found throughout Malmö. Facing the road was a small communal garden with a seating area that ran down the middle of the block's two arms. Beyond was a wooden building for the dustbins and bicycle storage. Mednick's apartment was accessed through the first entrance on the left. It was on the top floor.

While Moberg, Nordlund and Westermark made for Mednick's entrance, Anita and Olander went to the entrance exactly opposite. The names of the residents of the six apartments on each stairwell were displayed next to their respective bells. Anita pressed K. Geistrand and, after a few moments, a voice answered.

'Police,' Anita said. 'We need to come in.'

A buzzing noise followed almost immediately and Anita pushed the heavy glass door open. Olander followed. They took up a position behind the door and had a clear view across to the other block, where they could see Moberg, Nordlund and Westermark disappearing inside.

CHAPTER 18

The bus passed the two police cars. He couldn't see any policemen. Maybe they were in the park. But why? Or could they be visiting fru Lovgren, who lived on the street? If that was the case, why two police cars? Surely it didn't take that many cops to interview an old woman.

The bus reached the end of Beijersparksgatan and turned left into the wide avenue of Östra Fäladsgatan. His stop was coming up. He was now wary and glanced around for any signs of police activity. He couldn't see anything suspicious, but he couldn't quell his growing unease. Everything appeared normal, yet he was sure that things were different. Or was his mind just playing tricks?

He stood up and made his way to the middle of the bus. The bus came to a standstill and the doors whooshed open. The only people to get off were himself and a woman, who had difficulty manoeuvring a pram. She was black, so he didn't offer to help. She must live over in Segevång. On the spur of the moment, he decided to pop into the video shop and pick up something to watch tonight. He fancied an action film. Stefan would recommend something good. He knew his movies.

By the time he left the video shop, he really was feeling anxious. Stefan had acted strangely. They usually exchanged a bit of banter. In fact, Stefan was one of the few people he knew round here. In the twelve months since he'd moved into Smedjekullsgatan, he hadn't made any friends. Not that he had actively sought any. Like most Swedes, he didn't go out of his way to be friendly. He didn't know any of the five other people on his staircase. Two he had never even seen. The only one he had spoken to properly was the strange, overdressed, over-dyed and over-bejewelled woman below, and that was to complain about her fluffy, yappy dog crapping outside the front door. They hadn't spoken since. But the dog had stopped crapping there. Stefan had been offhand and had avoided eye contact. In Afghanistan he had learned to sense danger, to register facial expressions and body language and immediately assess if they were a threat. Even with the kids out there. Let your guard down, and you might be standing next to a human bomb.

He stood outside the video shop clutching his DVD. He had picked it out himself as Stefan had been so uncommunicative. He decided against going into the mini-mart. If they were after him, he would be trapped in there. Only one entrance/exit. He needed to get back onto home ground. He needed his gun.

It was Olander who spotted him first. His telltale red cap was pulled down over his eyes. The blue ski jacket.

'That's him, Inspector!'

'Hell! Moberg expected him to be in the apartment.'

Anita could tell immediately that Mednick knew that something was up. His movements weren't those of someone casually making their way home. He was furtive. Had he seen one of the policemen who were dotted around the area? She cursed. They should be out of sight. She realised she had to make a quick decision. Moberg must already be in the apartment by now. Knowing him, he would have kicked the door down when there was no answer. If Mednick had a gun, then he might catch the three officers unawares – and there wasn't time to ring them. She had to distract Mednick.

It was instinct that drove her through the door and across the garden as she ignored Olander's despairing call. Mednick was already inside the building opposite, but the heavy glass door hadn't quite clicked shut when she reached it, and she was able to slip inside. The concrete steps in front of her rose up to the first set of apartments on the left and right at either end of the short landing. The steps then continued up. She could hear Mednick right above her, so he must be approaching the next storey. The three officers were on the landing above that. She heard him stop. She froze. She held her breath. He must have been alerted by noise coming from his own apartment. Would he come back down? If he did, she was in trouble because she hadn't brought her pistol with her. When they'd set off from the polishus, it hadn't been that sort of operation. But what if he had a gun and was desperate? She didn't have time to think that one through.

Suddenly, she heard Mednick move. He leapt up the stairs quickly. She was about to call out as she herself moved forward, but he bolted past the open door of his apartment, which was wobbling on its hinges, and up the steps beyond. Anita realised that he probably wasn't armed, otherwise he would have tried to escape down the stairs or burst in on the police intruders. She knew he was heading for what must be the apartment block's storage cages in the attic. He must have something up there that he desperately wanted to get hold of. She stifled a call as she rushed past the open apartment door because she didn't want to alert Mednick. If she was quiet enough, she could surprise him and avoid the inevitable shoot-out, with her in the middle.

Anita reached the upper landing. She fought to control the gasps of breath that would give her away. In front of her was an open door. A Hamrelius Bokhandel plastic bag lay on the floor in front of her. She eased herself forward. She could hear the rattle of a key. He was unlocking his cage door. She peered in, but it was semi-dark. He hadn't wasted precious time by switching on the light. All she could see from the light cast through the open door was the metal mesh which separated the storage areas and the jumble of unidentified objects behind – the assembled rubbish, heirlooms and unused items collected from six different lives. She could hear Mednick breathing as he rummaged around in the gloom. In that moment, she decided to dash across the floor, shut him in his cage and try and lock him in – or hold him there while she called out for reinforcements. The theory may have been a good one, but she hadn't made allowance for Mednick's swift reactions. Though he had been taken by surprise by her sudden appearance, the instant Anita reached the cage door, he was pointing a gun at her head.

Her mind had gone blank. She must have had some thoughts, but none of them registered. Anita stared at the hole at the end of the barrel of the gun that was aimed straight at her. It was almost hypnotic. The closest she had ever been to another person holding a weapon was on the police shooting range. She was aware that they were both panting. Nervous gulps of air. Anita managed to tear her gaze away from the gun and look up into Halvar Mednick's eyes. Not that anything was revealed – the lack of light and the shadow cast by the peak of his cap ensured that. What she could sense was that he didn't know what to do next. That indecision was a good sign. If he had been decisive, she would already be dead.

'I didn't do it,' he whispered.

Now she heard someone coming up the stairs to the cages. Olander would have followed her and alerted the others in the apartment. Mednick lifted his head.

'Don't come any further,' he called out. 'I'll shoot her.'

'No need for that.' Moberg kept his voice calm. 'Just come out. We won't shoot.'

As Anita glanced towards the door to see where Moberg was, Mednick's left hand grabbed her shoulder and spun her round so that her throat was lodged in the crook of his arm. She was now facing the door. The gun nuzzled against her temple. The cold metal sent a shiver through her. She couldn't move. This was a strong man who could throttle her in an instant. Just as he had done with Malin Lovgren?

At last she found her voice, but it didn't carry any conviction.

'Please, let me go. Hand yourself over.'

His breath in her right ear was almost deafening.

'I didn't do it.' His whisper was hoarse and strained. 'I didn't kill her.'

'Come on, Halvar,' Moberg called from just outside the door. 'Kill a police officer and you'll never see the light of day again. They'll throw away the key.'

She could have spat at Moberg if he had been within range. She didn't want him throwing around threats while she was in the grip of a nervous gunman.

'You can't get away. You'll only make things worse for yourself.'

Shut it, Moberg! You're closing down all his options. Anita tried to keep the mind-numbing panic that had enveloped her out of her voice as she spoke to her captor.

'Halvar.' There was no moisture left in her mouth and the words came out in a dry croak. 'If you didn't do anything, then you have nothing to fear.'

If Mednick hadn't been holding her, she would have collapsed in a heap on the floor. Her legs had lost the ability to support the rest of her body.

'Shut the door,' he shouted. 'Shut the door, or she's dead.'

'Anita, are you OK?' Moberg called back.

'Yeah. But do as he says.'

There was a moment's hesitation outside the door. Moberg's huge frame came into view and blocked almost any light from coming into the room. 'Harm her, and I'll personally rip your balls off.'

Anita would have been touched by Moberg's concern, but maybe it was just another opportunity to threaten Mednick.

'Switch the light on and then shut the door.' Mednick issued his instructions to Moberg confidently.

Moberg leaned in and flicked the switch by the door. Now he could see the difficult position that Anita was in – and the potential problems his team faced with a hostage situation. Reluctantly, he closed the door.

Mednick released his grip. Anita gingerly caressed the front of her neck, nursing the bruised muscles. She slowly turned and faced him. Mednick was tall and well built. A good physique for the army. Anita put him in his early thirties, though he had the gaunt, sallow features of someone older. He didn't feed himself properly, she concluded. Then she chided herself for thinking like a mum when she should be thinking like a cop.

'Sorry.'

She couldn't make him out. He was frightened. Was that because he knew he had been caught for murdering one of his country's leading personalities? Or was it because he found himself in an impossible position? At least he had choices again. He could give himself up. He could shoot her. He could shoot himself. He could shoot them both.

'You know it's best to give yourself up.'

'They'll say that I killed her. But I couldn't have.'

He was almost pleading with her. He wanted her to believe him.

'Why couldn't you?'

He shook his head as though he couldn't understand why she had even asked. 'Because I loved Malin Lovgren.'

She could hear murmurings outside the door. Moberg was deciding what to do. *Please don't burst in with all guns blazing.* Surely even he wouldn't be that stupid. Mednick didn't seem to notice the activity outside. His thoughts were elsewhere. Anita held out her hand. She spoke gently: 'Halvar, give me the gun.'

When Anita and Mednick emerged, Moberg, Nordund, Westermark and Olander were standing on the stairs. Nordlund and Westermark's police pistols were pointing at the door. They put their weapons away when they saw that Mednick wasn't going to put up any resistance. Moberg gestured to Westermark, who whipped out a pair of handcuffs and clamped them onto Mednick's wrists. Then he took Mednick roughly by the arm and led him down the stairs. Olander followed. Moberg watched Mednick leave then turned to Anita. She handed him Mednick's gun.

'What the fuck do you think you were doing putting yourself in that position? It was utterly unprofessional.'

'I was trying to stop you from getting shot,' she spluttered in fury. She pointed viciously at the broken door. 'And you call that professional? That alerted him.'

She saw his fist tighten. Was he going to hit her? Then he suddenly smiled. 'Well done, Inspector.'

She couldn't believe it. The bastard. It took the wind out of her sails.

'You'd better have a look,' he said, waving a massive hand in the direction of the apartment.

'He said he didn't do it.'

'Oh yes he did.'

Anita followed the lumbering Moberg down the steps. As she passed Nordlund, he laid a reassuring hand on her shoulder. His expression asked whether she was OK. She nodded that she was fine. Her fury at Moberg had buried her fear. The realisation of what she had been through would hit her later.

The apartment was neat and tidy. Or maybe everything was just shoved out of sight from inspecting eyes; the soldier's way. The wooden floor was beautifully polished. Lasse would approve. Moberg led the way from the hall straight into the bedroom. The sight that met Anita's gaze was incredible. The walls were plastered with photos of Malin Lovgren, taken from magazines and newspapers. They were all shapes and sizes. The beautiful actress stared out from every wall, every nook and cranny, with summer clothes, with winter clothes, with no clothes. There was even a poster of her stuck to the ceiling, so that he could lie in bed and gaze up at her. This was obsession. This was sickness. It was a shrine to a goddess who didn't want to be worshipped.

Anita was having difficulty getting her head round how any rational human being could hit such a psychological rock bottom. Would it turn someone into a murderer because the object of their passion, their desire, their every waking thought can never really be theirs? Because they can't get close, does it mean they feel rejected? Malin Lovgren hadn't answered his first letter. Had he found that hard to accept? He had supposedly threatened her, according to Roslyn. Had that threat turned into actual action? Mednick had held Anita in the same grip that had killed the actress. It was the natural reflex of a highly trained man. Halvar Mednick fitted the bill for their murderer.

In the opposite corner of the room was a TV and DVD recorder. Below it was a row of DVDs, which Anita assumed would all be Lovgren films. Moberg squeezed round the side of the bed. 'And the final proof.'

He leant over a table on which there was a bedside lamp. Next to the lamp was a framed photograph of Lovgren. Moberg bent down and picked something up. He came back round the bed and stood in front of Anita.

'Remember what you said at the end of our first briefing? You said if we found the pendant, we would find our murderer.'

Moberg opened his paw and there was the Lotta Lind blue starfish pendant.

CHAPTER 19

He was in the sports bar on Östra Förstadsgatan when he heard
that a man was helping the police with their enquiries. Ewan
had gone to the bar with Alex to watch a mid-week FA Cup
replay. English football was big in Scandinavia, and all the
Premier League matches were shown every weekend in Sweden.
The place was almost empty. The freshly falling snow had put
off the punters. The bar was sparsely furnished, with only the
TVs passing for decor. There were no fripperies, no stylish
touches, no imaginative flourishes. Beer and football were the
only reasons for customers to come in. And warmth. Ewan
had just bought in their second beer and the Swedish pundits
were still giving the viewers the benefit of their knowledge
and score forecasts when the broadcast was interrupted by a
newsflash. An earnest female newsreader came on. Behind her,
Ewan recognised a picture of Malin Lovgren. He put his glass
down and strained to understand what was being said. Then the
cameras went over to a reporter standing in the swirling snow
outside the police headquarters. It didn't last long, and he had to
ask Alex to enlighten him.

'The police have taken someone in for questioning.'

Ewan smiled. 'Blimey, that's quick.'

'Doesn't mean they've got the right one. They've cocked
up before.'

They turned their attention to the match, which was just kicking off. But Ewan couldn't concentrate. Before coming out, he had had a call from Brian asking whether there were any fresh developments. He was keen. A bit too keen. He was putting the pressure on. Ewan had managed to fob him off with some scraps of information on Olof Palme that he had found on the internet. That had only whetted Brian's appetite further. He had already run upstairs to the managing director and promised him that a massive scoop was in the offing. The bloody halfwit! Ewan had tried to impress on him that there was nothing concrete yet. Now had come this piece of news. Ewan wondered who on earth it could be. Could they have tracked down some ex-secret service operative so quickly? If they had, could they make a murder charge stick? It was puzzling.

At half-time Ewan went to the toilet. When he had finished, he took out his mobile and made a call. 'What about that drink?'

It had been another long day by the time she answered her mobile. Anita was sitting at her desk going over the events that had shaken her then got her mind racing again. The aftershock of her experience in the loft of Mednick's apartment block only hit home when she was sitting in her car near the park. When she had got into the vehicle she had been fine. Calm even, given the near-death situation she had just been through. Then she had begun to tremble. She couldn't control her limbs. Then bile had gushed up from her stomach to her throat and she had been sick. All over the passenger seat. Fortunately, she had been alone. Then she had cried. Uncontrollably. A man had walked past and hurried on. He hadn't stopped to ask her if she was all right. The sight of a woman sobbing had caused him embarrassment. She could tell by the way he pretended not to notice her.

Anita had done her best to mop up the mess, but the car stank all the way back to the polishus. Moberg had told her to go home. Relax. Open a bottle of wine. But she knew that if she did that, then she would just keep replaying the whole horrible scene over and over again in her mind. And in one of those replays, she might not come out alive.

She had cleaned herself up in the ladies' before reporting back to Moberg who, though pleased with himself, was smarting at the bollocking that the public prosecutor, Sonja Blom, had given him for rushing in to make an arrest without a warrant or her say-so. Moberg had explained that it wasn't an arrest but simply a matter of asking Halvar Mednick nicely if he would like to come down to headquarters and answer a few friendly questions. Then he had lost his temper and told her that they had just caught a 'fucking murderer' and hadn't had the time to wait around for her 'fucking permission' to do his job. Moberg knew he would pay for his outburst later, but it had made him feel good at that moment. Sonja Blom was not the best person to cross. He told Anita that he and Nordlund would do the initial interview, and he was certain it wouldn't take long to get a confession. Anita was not so sure.

'Tell you what you could do,' he said like a teacher who can't think of what task to give a persistent student who has finished their work too quickly, 'You can go over to see our Mr Roslyn and tell him that we're making progress with the case. You can even tell him we've arrested someone and that his theory about Olof Palme is a load of bollocks.'

'Do you want me to let him leave the safe house?'

Moberg scratched his stomach. 'Better not. Forget the Palme stuff, but I think I prefer him out of the way for the moment until this is all tied up. He's the sort of guy who'll rush off to the press with his bleeding-heart story.'

Anita knew exactly why he didn't want Roslyn running around free. Moberg didn't want any of the limelight taken off himself. Besides, Anita had her own reasons for talking to Roslyn. She wanted to ask him a question.The car still stank horribly all the way to the farmhouse outside Vellinge, south of Malmö on the E22 to Trelleborg. The sky was threatening snow and she wanted to get back to Malmö before it started. Right now, she knew that Moberg would be piling the pressure on Halvar Mednick to get him to confess. He was such an intimidating presence that she had seen a number of suspects and non-suspects crumble under his aggressive interrogations. She hadn't much sympathy for Mednick, but she had this nagging feeling that they had got the wrong man. So much pointed to him, yet the way he had said 'I didn't kill her' had the sound of truth.

The farmhouse was long, low-slung and narrow, like so many in Skåne. It stood by itself at the end of a track surrounded by dark fields waiting for new planting. No fences or hedges broke up the landscape around it. There were a few winter-weary trees behind the farm buildings, which needed a lick of paint. So did the farmhouse itself; its once brilliant whiteness now grubby and peeling. That was why it didn't attract attention. That was why the Skåne County Police had squirrelled Mick Roslyn away here.

She asked the policeman who met her at the door how Roslyn was getting on. 'Pain in the arse,' was his succinct reply. Mick was watching television when she came into the main room. He had the remote control in his hand and was idly channel-hopping. When he saw Anita, he threw away the remote but left the TV on, which immediately irritated her.

'What's happening?' he asked without bothering to get up. He had let himself go in the twenty-four hours he had been at the farm. The artfully dishevelled appearance had descended into the merely dishevelled. The designer stubble was sprouting into a fledgling beard, which went neatly with the black rims under his eyes. Mick Roslyn hadn't slept much recently.

Anita went straight to the television set and switched it off to make sure she gained his full attention. She knew that she should just tell him about the arrest and get out of there. But she couldn't. In fact, she knew that what she was about to ask would probably come back and haunt her. Certainly get her into trouble with Moberg. After what she had been through today, she no longer cared what anybody thought.

'Monday night?'

'What about Monday night?' Mick's eyes narrowed as though the light in the room was too strong.

'You told us you were in a meeting.'

'Yeah.'

'But you weren't, were you?'

She could see he was about to bluster, but he realised that it was a waste of time. They must have checked. So he didn't say anything.

'That means you have no alibi for the night your wife was murdered.'

'I shouldn't bloody need one.' His anger was instant, just as it had been in the interview room in the polishus. He wasn't used to being challenged. She had riled him, and that was a positive sign. Nordlund had once told her that getting a suspect to lose their temper was a great way of getting them to drop their guard. Then they might let something slip out as their carefully prepared thought process had been thrown out of the window.

'We have to look into every possibility. You wouldn't expect us to do otherwise.'

'I was in Stockholm. I was nowhere near Malmö.'

'All we need to do is confirm you *were* in Stockholm when you said you were. You certainly weren't at the meeting you said you attended. You lied,' she said pointedly. 'So I'm going to need you to provide us with proof that you were up there that night. And this time, the truth please.' She knew Moberg would have a fit if he knew what she was doing. He was running the investigation and she was prying into an area that was closed to scrutiny. Mick Roslyn was not a suspect. If Roslyn kicked up a fuss, she might even be hauled in front of the commissioner. Even talking their chief suspect into handing over his gun without a shot being fired wouldn't shield her from official wrath.

'I was working on the Palme documentary. I told you that.' He avoided any eye contact. He was flustered.

'You're saying no one can vouch for your whereabouts all afternoon and evening until you got your flight first thing in the morning?'

'I suppose so.'

'By my reckoning, if you had a fast car – and I assume you have at least one – you could have got down here to Malmö and back up to Stockholm in that time. Just.'

'You're not seriously suggesting–'

'I'm only saying that it is physically possible.'

Mick was out of his seat. He glared at her. 'This is bloody unreal. I can't believe you're even asking me this.'

'You've lied once. Why should I believe you now?'

He shook with fury. 'Because I was with her!'

Anita let the silence settle on the room. Mick stormed over to the window and stood transfixed. The first feathering of snow was descending from a darkened sky.

She addressed his back. 'Who is she?'

'I loved my wife, you know.' The anger had abated. 'I wouldn't have done her any harm.'

'Who is she?' Anita repeated. Gentler this time.

'Tilda. Tilda Tegner. She's an actress. She was in my last film.'

'And you spent the evening with Miss Tegner?'

He half turned. 'Yes. I'm not proud of what I did.'

Anita nearly screamed at him. Björn had said the same thing to her, more than once. Men seemed to use it as a get-out clause in their fidelity contract. It made everything OK.

'Would Miss Tegner corroborate this?'

Mick looked genuinely appalled. 'This won't come out, will it?'

'I don't know.' She knew it wouldn't because he now had an alibi and therefore would never be considered a suspect. But she wasn't going to let him off the hook just yet. 'We may have to speak to her. For corroboration.'

'Bengt mustn't know.' He played distractedly with his wedding ring. Anita wondered how long he would go on wearing it. While it remained on his hand, it would be a constant reminder of his unfaithfulness. Ewan Strachan had been right: Roslyn was "a ladies' man" and he hadn't changed his ways. He had a beautiful wife yet he still couldn't keep his hands off a younger model.

'Bengt Valquist?' Mick nodded. She could see that might not go down too well with his close associate. Bedding his girlfriend. It wouldn't look good if it came out in the press, either. Public sympathy would soon dissipate.

'What makes you think he doesn't know already?' She let that little grenade explode. 'All right, that's it.' Anita bent down and turned the television back on. 'I don't have to interrupt your viewing any further.'

Mick appeared bewildered. Anita headed for the door, which she opened. 'Oh, by the way, we're interviewing a suspect at headquarters. He was arrested this morning. Chief Inspector Moberg thought you might want to know.'

She didn't wait for his reaction.

She had no idea why she had agreed to meet Ewan Strachan for a drink. She didn't really want to see him; she was incredibly tired and she wanted to wash away the day in a hot shower. But the bathroom was half-painted. She had started it three weeks ago. The initial burst of enthusiasm had quickly gone down the plughole and now the project had turned into a pain. She couldn't face the lonely apartment by herself. Not tonight, or not yet anyway. If only Lasse were at home, she could talk things through with him. He would cheer her up. Reassure her that everything would be all right. She had left the farmhouse on a high. She had felt good. She had made the confident Roslyn uncomfortable. But it was a cheap victory.

By the time she had got back to Malmö, she was starting to worry about Roslyn making a complaint of harassment against her. She was a natural worrier. Lasse had often said that she could worry for Sweden if it ever became an Olympic sport. Lasse could always sense when something from work was bothering her. He would sit her down with a cup of something or a glass of wine and let her pour out her worries. And once they were out, they didn't seem so bad. She had often felt guilty that he had to do the job of a husband or a partner. At his age he shouldn't have to listen to his mum moaning on. But he did. An old head on young shoulders. Now that he was gone, there was no one to speak to.

So now she was sitting in the Mellow Yellow bar in Lilla Torg nursing a glass of red wine, with Ewan Strachan sipping a beer opposite her. She was too weary to feel self-conscious about the fact that they were easily the oldest customers there that evening. She had been expecting him to try and pump her for information on the case, but he hadn't. She had mentioned that they had a suspect who was helping them with enquiries, though he had already seen that on the TV. She didn't reveal how the suspect had come into police custody.

'Was that stuff that Mick told you of any use?' Ewan asked when the first conversational exchanges had run into an awkward silence.

'We're looking into that. The only thing I can tell you is that the suspect at the polishus doesn't seem to be connected with Mr Roslyn's documentary.'

Ewan looked disappointed. That was a good story gone for a burton. Never mind, he wouldn't tell Brian just yet.

'Are you married?'

The sudden question took Anita by surprise.

'Sorry, that just popped out. None of my business.'

'You're right. It's none of your business.'

Ewan flinched at the brusqueness of the reply. Yorkshire folk were meant to be blunt, but they had nothing on Swedish women. To his inherently polite British sensibilities, it was a bit of a shock. Coming from such an attractive woman, it was even weirder. Ewan retreated into his beer.

Anita realised that he had been taken aback. Maybe it was a chance to take her mind off the case for a while and talk about something else. After today she was even more confused. The dramatic arrest of Mednick and the revelation of Mick's affair had only raised more questions rather than providing much-needed answers. Maybe she would shove the case to the back of her mind and re-examine it when she walked back to the quiet of Roskildevägen. She had left her stinking car in the polishus car park as she couldn't bear the smell any longer. She took off her glasses and put them next to her drink.

'Divorced.'

Ewan came out of his beer.

'I believe there's a lot of divorce in Sweden. I mean, more than in a lot of countries.'

'It's a national pastime. Now, I haven't time for a husband,' she lied. 'I've got a lovely son to look after.'

'How old is he?'

'Lasse. He's coming up for nineteen. Away at university.'

'Letting go. Can't be easy. My mum died just before I went off to Durham, so I don't know how she would have reacted. My father was delighted to see the back of me.'

Again Anita didn't know whether he was being facetious or not.

'It's very hard for a mother.' Anita put her glasses back on. Ewan thought she was just as beautiful with as without them.

'And where's your husband now?' Ewan was feeling more relaxed in her company now. He was trying to get her to unwind because he could sense that she was tense and preoccupied.

'He's at the university in Uppsala.'

'Obviously an academic.'

'Professor now. He was just a lecturer when I met him.'

'So how did a cop meet an academic? Not exactly the same line of country.'

'I arrested him.'

Ewan looked at Anita blankly. Then he guffawed. 'That's fantastic.'

She was taken with his delight. His face lit up when he smiled. She thought that many things in life must amuse him. That was a good way to view things. Not the Swedish way.

'So how come you arrested him?' he said, still laughing.

'We were called out to a rowdy party in Lund. That's where I started after the National Police College in Stockholm. The neighbours complained. Parties with Björn were always noisy.'

'Did he spend the night in the cells?'

'Yes. He was drunk, so he needed to sleep it off. It hadn't helped that he had insulted the neighbours for complaining, but he came quietly enough.'

'Not surprising. I'd happily be arrested by you.' He smiled.

'I don't think you would.' Though she said it seriously, she couldn't help but be flattered.

'So how come arrest led to the altar?'

'When we released him the next day, he asked me out on a date. I was so surprised that I said "yes".'

'But it obviously didn't last?'

'Being surrounded by beautiful students was too much of a temptation.'

'From lecturer to lecher?'

Anita smiled wearily. 'Something like that.'

'I won't pry any further. Another drink...? Sorry, I can't

keep calling you Inspector.'

She finished her drink with an unladylike swig. 'Another wine would be nice.' She handed him her glass. 'And it's Anita.'

He took her glass. That twinkle was in his eye again. 'Red wine...' he let his tongue linger over '... Anita.'

While Ewan was over at the bar ordering the drinks, Anita was trying to work him out. He was pleasant. Funny even. She was beginning to relax, which she didn't often do socially in the company of men these days. She wasn't so unaware that she couldn't detect that he seemed smitten with her. He was no pretty boy, but she had been seduced down the handsome route too often for comfort. Yet something nagged at her; she had no idea what. She could see that he covered his loneliness with humour. But there was a hidden sadness. Swedes were good at detecting melancholy. They knew all about what they called *svårmod*, that blackness of the mind that came from the long winter nights. That was why the country went crazy at midsummer.

'*Skål!*' Anita said, raising her glass.

'Skoll!' Ewan replied, not quite getting his pronunciation right.

After a deep sip of beer, he put down his glass. 'So where have you hidden Mick?'

Ah. Was this the reason for the drink? Just when she was thinking it was because he wanted to be with her. Now it made her think again about Mick's revelation.

'Out of harm's way.'

'I hope I was useful to you. I mean, getting Mick to talk to you. He wasn't keen until I persuaded him that he could trust you.'

It was her turn to smile. 'Are you trying to say that I owe you a favour?'

'No, that's not what I'm after, honestly.' He appeared genuinely horrified. 'I just...' but he seemed unable to complete the sentence.

Anita delved into her bag to try and find her tin of snus. The bag was like a black hole, and she was forever losing things in there. Had she left the tin in the office or the car? Oh, there it was. She pulled it out. She opened the lid and offered the tin to Ewan.

'What's that?'

'Snus.'

'What is it?' he asked, pulling a face. 'Looks like miniature teabags.'

She picked out a small sachet and held it in the palm of her hand. 'It's tobacco. You put it up here,' she said putting her finger in her mouth between her gum and upper lip. 'It has minute fragments of fibreglass inside to puncture the gum so the tobacco gets in the bloodstream.' Ewan pulled a face. 'It's good. It has helped me stop smoking. Snus is very popular in Sweden.' And she popped a sachet into her mouth.

'It sounds disgusting. I'll stick to fags.'

Anita felt herself switching back into cop mode. 'Actually, I was going to ask you about when you met Roslyn at the Edinburgh film festival.'

He smirked. 'Are you interrogating me again?'

'We're just chatting in a bar,' she said holding up her glass, letting the light catch the richness of the red liquid. He hadn't bought her the usual rubbishy wine she was used to on her occasional social outings.

'Fair enough.'

'Roslyn was there with Tilda Tegner and Bengt Valquist?'

'Yeah.'

'How was Roslyn with Miss Tegner?'

Ewan twirled his beer glass and puckered his lips. 'Has he been playing away from home?'

Anita knew the expression from her time in London. She had also learned how to say "get lost" to over-amorous colleagues who saw the words "blonde Swedish woman" as a green light for an easy shag.

'I am not saying that. It is just he's a successful man and Miss Tegner is a young actress making her way in the business. He might be a mentor.'

'I think Bengt Valquist assumes that role. To answer your question, there didn't seem to be any untoward body language between them. In fact, it was Valquist who was the attentive chaperone. Possessive almost.'

'And you've met Valquist since?'

'A couple of times. Very nervous bloke if you ask me.'

'Could he easily become jealous?'

Ewan contemplated his beer. 'A man with so little obvious self-confidence? Definitely.'

CHAPTER 20

Ewan had enjoyed going to bed last night. He had played various scenarios over and over in his mind. They all ended up with Anita Sundström in his arms. On waking, he was disappointed that she hadn't featured in any of his dreams. In fact, the only woman he could remember was Malin Lovgren. He had run away from her but, however far he scuttled, she was still there. Still dead. However, he had a spring in his step this morning. He had got Anita – yes, Anita – to promise him that if there were any new developments, she would tip him the wink. This was only extracted after he explained that he wouldn't print anything unless she had given him the OK to do so. He had no way of delivering that promise.

On returning to the hotel after his drink with Anita, Ewan had phoned Brian at his home and informed him that he had now established a great working relationship with one of the top detectives on the case. A lovely blonde woman, he had added in order to increase his stock with the lascivious editor. She had told him that an arrest had been made. He had made it sound as though he had been the first to know, and Brian was impressed. Maybe Ewan wasn't as useless as he had always assumed him to be. Brian had asked if the arrest was anything to do with the Palme conspiracy theory.

'Keeping that information close to her chest,' Ewan said,

knowing full well that it wasn't, but he wanted to keep Brian sweet as long as possible.

'Has she got a nice chest?'

Ewan had avoided answering the question. He hadn't wanted Anita reduced in his eyes by the usual male banter and innuendo. She was better than that. Besides, despite his best efforts, he still couldn't imagine her totally naked. He would work on it.

He knew he was falling for the attractive police inspector. He hadn't felt like this since... Well, that was a long time ago. But what did she make of him? Was there hope? Or was the whole thing pie in the sky?

As he stood in the shower, he tried to plan his day. If an arrest had been made, he would have to find out more information. He would start by going onto the internet and finding again that useful site that he had discovered yesterday which carried Swedish news stories in English. Things were going well. Sweden might not be so bad after all.

Anita was in early. She had skipped breakfast and had her first coffee of the day in her office. There were other early birds, too. She saw the public prosecutor, Sonja Blom, coming out of Moberg's office. Even at that time in the morning, she was irritatingly immaculate. She was wearing her usual smug expression that seemed to be permanently sandblasted onto her face. She looked straight through Anita, who had decided, against her better judgement, to say good morning.

Coffee in hand, Anita knocked on Moberg's door and went in. Moberg and Nordlund couldn't have had much sleep between them, though the chief inspector seemed happy enough. He was tucking into a sandwich.

'The prosecutor looks pleased with herself.'

Moberg grunted. 'She thinks we've got a result.'

'Have we?' she asked.

'Yes, I think so.' Anita caught Nordlund glancing down at the floor. She wasn't sure he was convinced.

'Has he pleaded guilty?'

'Not yet. But he will. He's admitted he went into the apartment. He says he was infatuated with Malin Lovgren and had plucked up the courage to go up and see her. Wanted to confront her for ignoring him. He knew the apartment combination because he had seen her punch it in.'

'Roslyn thought that incident was ex-Säpo surveillance,' said Anita, who was cupping her coffee to warm up her hands.

'Mednick reckons that the apartment door was open when he got upstairs. He went in and wandered around before finding Malin Lovgren dead in the living room.'

'How did he find her?'

'Sitting up, as Thulin suggested. He claims he went over to her and was so upset that he hugged her, and when he let go, she slid to the floor. He was so horrified by the whole experience that he left her there and fled.'

'Could it be true?' Anita waited for the blast.

'Pigs might fly! The bastard's guilty. He was in the apartment, he handled the body. Forensics matched his prints and fibres overnight,' Moberg said, picking up a file and flapping it down on the desk again. 'He was in the army and he would have been taught how to choke someone efficiently, so that sorts that one out. We've got CCTV footage to show he was outside the scene of the crime at the right time. Anyhow, he's confessed that much. The clincher was that bloody blue starfish pendant of yours in his apartment. You were right there. As for motive, he admits sending letters to Malin, though he didn't think they were threatening.'

'So we've only got Roslyn's word for it that they included actual threats. And we haven't got the letters themselves.'

'Doesn't matter. We've got everything else except the actual confession. He was some poor sod who got sent to Afghanistan and lost his bottle.'

'Mednick was at a place called Meymaneh.' This was Nordlund's first contribution. 'He was with a Nordic group of the Security Assistance Force. It wasn't a good place to be for a Scandinavian because there was all that bother about the Danish cartoons of Mohammed. And to the locals, all Scandinavians are the same. There was a nasty riot and Mednick was in the middle of it. Ironically, there were no Danes in the group.'

'That's why he got caught up with those immigrants in Möllevången,' added Moberg. 'He's got a thing about Muslims. It was while he was out in Afghanistan that he got into Malin Lovgren. They showed a couple of her films out there. No girl at home, so he starts fantasising about the actress. It gets worse when he returns home after he's kicked out of the forces because he's not quite right any more. Malin doesn't answer his letters. He's fixated. He does something about it.' Moberg took a satisfied bite out of his sandwich. He continued, with his mouth half full. 'Throw in the unlicensed firearm which he picked up in Afghanistan, and using it to threaten a police officer, and Blom thinks we've got a very strong case. She's off to court later today to make it all official so we can keep him under lock and key. Mednick is going to be officially charged and the commissioner is going to hold a news conference and announce to the whole of Sweden how brilliant the Skåne police force is, and, by implication, what a bunch of tossers they are up in Stockholm. They cocked up the Palme murder and we've tied up our celebrity case in three days.'

Anita took a sip of her coffee. It was going cold. 'Why didn't Mednick use the gun on Malin if he was seriously going to threaten her?'

'Maybe he had it with him but thought it was easier to strangle her instead,' Moberg said dismissively as he flicked some sandwich crumbs into the corner of his mouth. 'And it's less noisy.'

Anita didn't try and hide her scepticism. 'Did he say where he found the starfish pendant?'

'He said he found it on her lap,' said Nordlund stroking his chin.

'Said he took it as a trophy – something that belonged to her – back to his weird shrine of an apartment. But obviously what really happened was that it came off in the struggle in the kitchen and he took it away because the chain had broken. Clear up the evidence.' Moberg was starting to get annoyed. He had explained everything. She should be pleased.

'And the tea and two mugs?'

'Didn't mention that. He obviously wormed his way in. Mednick was a fan, Malin's a nice girl and offers to make him a cup of tea. She turns her back, and he throttles her.'

'Does he drink tea?'

'How the fuck should I know?' Moberg was furious now. 'It doesn't fucking matter now. The case is closed.' The rest of the sandwich disappeared into his mouth as he stood up. He was still chewing it when he said, 'Must go up to the commissioner. I suspect he'll want to congratulate the team.'

'And are *you* sure Mednick's the murderer?'

Moberg glared at Anita. 'Look, Inspector, you can fanny about with your fucking female intuition and all that shit, but this case is finished as far as you're concerned. We've got our man. Try and enjoy the moment. I am.' As an afterthought, 'And just you remember who's running this investigation.'

Anita stared defiantly at him. 'Remember Olof Palme.'

Moberg lumbered out of the room and left a contemplative Nordlund and a grim-faced Anita.

'When Mednick was holding a gun to my head, he said that he didn't kill her. I thought he sounded sincere.'

'Knew his time was up. Living in denial. Could be any number of reasons to plead his innocence.' Nordlund locked his fingers together on his lap and began to twiddle his free thumbs over each other in a continuous circular movement. 'It all seems to fit.'

'That's not the same as being guilty. He was wearing the same jacket when we took him in as he had on the night of the murder. If he had done it, surely he would have got rid of it. Or tried to hide it. And Moberg's wrong to dismiss the tea as irrelevant. I'm convinced that she knew the person who was in that kitchen with her.'

Nordlund grimaced. 'Anita, you've got to remember that Erik is under enormous pressure from above, from everyone, to solve this case. It makes one very single-minded.'

She was struck by a thought and picked up the forensics file. 'I bet you another thing, Henrik: that Eva's team didn't find any of Mednick's footprints in the kitchen.'

Nordlund stood. 'Well, if I were you, I wouldn't stop digging just yet. That's why I think I'll check out those photos Säpo have sent down from Stockholm.'

'I thought you would like to know. There's a press conference at the polishus at 2.30.' Ewan was dumbstruck. He hadn't really expected Anita to contact him. Now that she had, he was paralysed. As he didn't say anything, she pressed on. 'Commissioner Dahlbeck will be speaking. So will Chief Inspector Moberg. They'll give you something to write about.' Then there was silence. At last Ewan found his voice.

'But I won't understand what they say.'

'Take along one of your Pickwick friends to translate. I'm sure some of the other journalists will fill you in. Most have reasonable English.'

'Thanks.' Then he suddenly blurted out, 'Will you be there?'

But the connection had gone dead. She had finished the call. He cursed himself for not taking advantage of the situation. Say something about how much he had enjoyed his drink with her. Keep the conversation going a bit longer. The truth was that she had caught him on the hop while he was walking past the station on the way into town. It was an opportunity missed, and he now felt utterly deflated. All that had gone right last night was ruined by his inability to think on his feet. Maybe Anita would be at the press conference and he could grab a word with her then.

Nearly all the snow from the night before had gone. The ground was wet; but there were streaks of blue sky, the first he had seen since his arrival. Ewan stared at his mobile. He was still putting himself through the mental flagellation that men go through when they've cocked up the chance to enhance their relationship with a woman they seriously fancy. He was still in that frame of mind when he called David.

The call to Ewan had only been one of a number that Anita made from her office that morning. She felt that she owed him at least some help after he'd passed Roslyn on to her. Besides, he might still be a useful source of information concerning her own enquiries, which had been encouraged by Henrik Nordlund.

She had more respect for Nordlund than any other officer she had come across in her time in the force. He had taken the unofficial role of mentor when she had joined the department and was feeling constantly out of her depth. She liked the fact that he wasn't an over-ambitious career cop like so many of the younger ones. Steady, clear-headed, if a little cautious. But their department needed his calming influence when characters like Moberg and Westermark were forever bulldozing their way through investigations and rushing into situations without thinking. And though he was an old-fashioned policeman, he had no hang-ups about her being a woman in the force. Quite the opposite; he respected women.

His own wife had been in the police before cancer had taken her some years before. His sadness was deep-seated, yet he never let it affect his work. Nor did he hold it against Anita that she didn't have a Scanian accent (which the rest of Sweden derided as ugly). Her detractors viewed her voice as snobby, though she had spent a lot of her youth in Skåne. But the family had moved around – including spending time in England – and her accent was neutral. It meant she had something in common with Olander. They were both seen as outsiders.

If Henrik Nordlund advised her to keep on digging, then she would do just that. Certainly Nordlund didn't appear to have Moberg's solid belief in Mednick's guilt. Or maybe even Moberg was only convincing himself because he was under pressure. Of course, she hadn't been involved in Mednick's interrogation. Often in that claustrophobic situation, she had found herself forming an opinion of a suspect that flew in the face of the facts. Their body language was under the microscope. Their every utterance could be swiftly interpreted. Lies and truth could be disseminated. Above all, your instincts were always heightened by the close proximity of those in the interview room. More often than not, you could sense whether the suspect was guilty or innocent.

Yet sometimes – and she had been culpable herself – one had gone into an interrogation so convinced of someone's guilt that your instincts were banished from the room. Nothing that was said would change that view. Nordlund had often spoken about keeping an open mind, even in what appeared an open-and-shut case. Had Moberg gone into the Mednick interrogation with his mind already made up, or was there something about Mednick during the questioning that had convinced him that this was their man? She feared it was the former.

Anita had called Eva Thulin about the footprints. And, no, Mednick's size forty-threes hadn't shown up in the kitchen. Or any fingerprints. She had also put a call into Roslyn's production company in Stockholm to find out the whereabouts of Bengt Valquist. The girl at the other end of the line, Agnes, had told her that Bengt was at his apartment in the house he had bought his parents in Lund. That was where he stayed when he wasn't working and schmoozing in Stockholm. He had been there since before the unfortunate murder, as he did some occasional guest-lecturing at the university. She gave Anita his address and mobile number. Anita asked whether she knew where Tilda Tegner would be. Agnes said she didn't know, but she assumed she would probably be with Bengt. Anita also enquired if Agnes remembered the fuss about the letters from H to Malin Lovgren. She did, but most of them had been delivered by hand to Malin's Malmö apartment. She said that Mick had been upset by them more than Malin.

'I believe they contained threats against Malin Lovgren's life?' Anita had hazarded.

'I don't know about that,' answered Agnes. 'I misplaced the first one. She got lots of fan mail. Stuff disappears in a busy office. There's only me here full-time.'

'That first one. Can you remember whether it was from Afghanistan?'

'Goodness me, yes it was,' Agnes said in surprise. 'How did you know?'

'We found a connection.'

'But I probably wouldn't have passed it on anyway because it wasn't properly signed. If her letters didn't carry a full name, then I censored them. A lot came in anonymously. They usually contained filth. Sexual things.' Anita could hear Agnes shudder. 'Very explicit, some of them. Or just creepy.'

'And this one from Afghanistan?'

'I can't remember it being like that, and I probably shoved it in with the others. It only came to light when Mick mentioned the hand-delivered letters down in Malmö.'

'But others came through your office posted from Malmö?'

'A couple, but they didn't have an address on, so we couldn't reply even if we'd wanted to.'

'And the content?'

'Pretty harmless stuff about how much he loved Malin. Nothing sexual. But they must have changed to get Mick so wound up.'

'OK, many thanks, Agnes.' Anita was about to ring off when she remembered something Nordlund had mentioned at an earlier meeting. 'One last thing. What was the relationship like between Malin and Bengt Valquist?'

She heard Agnes snort. 'Uneasy.'

'"Mick's poodle?"'

Agnes laughed. 'How did you know that?'

'Just came up. Were there any serious disagreements between them?'

'Well, I shouldn't really say this, but Malin thought Bengt was too flaky. She could never relax around him. Made her nervous on set. There was gossip...' Anita could hear Agnes stop herself.

'Gossip?' Anita pressed.

'I'm sure it wasn't true, but there was a whisper that Malin was going to push Bengt out.'

Olander came bouncing into the office, a broad grin spread across his face. 'The first murder case I'm involved in, and we get such a quick result! There's a pretty happy bunch of people out there.'

Anita was busy fishing about in her bag, trying to locate her tin of snus. She couldn't find it. How annoying. In her mind's eye, she could see it in the kitchen next to the microwave. Or was it by her bed? She had left the apartment so sharply this morning that she had been more disorganised than usual. And she had forgotten to book her slot on the apartment block's laundry-room rota. She'd soon have no clean knickers.

Her frown quickly punctured Olander's enthusiasm. 'You don't appear too pleased,' he observed, taking his seat on the other side of the office.

'Too many unanswered questions, Mats.'

'What questions?' said Olander, easing his legs under the desk.

'If Mednick killed Malin, why did he place her on the sofa, then let her slide onto the floor? Why take her into the living room at all? Why, if the murder took place in the kitchen, can't we find Mednick's footprints and fingerprints when they are elsewhere in the apartment? They are all in the places he said he went into. Why was he wandering around in the same jacket he committed the murder in? You'd expect him to get rid of that.'

'Yeah, but we can place him in the apartment at the right time. We've got him on tape. The method of killing fits his training; he had a motive of sorts – he felt rejected. Admittedly, we haven't got the letters, but they carried threats. And we found the pendant in his apartment.'

Anita wasn't listening as she had just had a thought.

'And why did he try and resist arrest if he was innocent?' continued Olander. 'The fact that he made straight for his hidden gun shows he was expecting a police visit at some stage.'

Anita was back again. 'He must have known we would track him down eventually. He'd been in the apartment. I think he was just scared because he realised we would jump to the obvious conclusions, which we have. But there's one question we haven't asked Mednick. We know from the tapes that he was watching the apartment for some time. If he didn't kill Malin Lovgren, then he probably saw who did.'

Ewan stood in the car park outside the back of the polishus smoking a cigarette with a local journalist called Kurt Ekholm. He worked for *Aftonbladet*, which was a popular national tabloid. This murder was right up his street. Ekholm had been standing next to Ewan in the crowded room in what turned out to be quite a short press conference. The commissioner had said a few words of introduction. His hardly suppressed grin told its own story. Then he had introduced Chief Inspector Erik Moberg. Ewan didn't understand a word of what the angry policeman was saying, though he wasn't looking as happy as he should have been at that moment. All the following questions were in Swedish, so Ewan had collared Ekholm afterwards to try and get information out of him, as David hadn't been available to translate.

'It is not so much,' Ekholm said between puffs of his cigarette, which Ewan had offered him to break the ice. 'They are arresting this fellow who is helping them with their enquiries. This fellow has a military background. They say they are not looking for any other persons. They must be thinking he is the one. He was brought to this place last night.'

'And you think they have got it right?'

Ekholm shrugged extravagantly. 'Who knows with Swedish police? They not always right. Is good for newspapers,' he said with a wry grin.

Ewan glanced round at the polishus. It was a very large, very modern building. Five storeys high with alternate sections in red brick and beige tiles. Despite the muted scheme, it was more colourful than any other police headquarters he had ever seen. It was topped off with a tangle of antennae on the roof. Due to the surrounding streets and canal, it was triangular in shape, with the entrance and car park at its base. The few gangly, leafless trees near the glass-paned entrance did little to soften the general feeling of functionality. This was a place designed to tackle crime, not to win architectural awards. It was at its most impressive round the other side, where it stood astride the bend in the canal. It reminded Ewan of a latter-day castle or cathedral. He coined a phrase in his head: "the cathedral of crime". He thought he would use it in his next piece, until he realised that it didn't make any sense. He was disappointed that there had been no sign of Anita at the press conference. Was she somewhere now in that mass of offices and corridors?

'This big story in England?' Ekholm asked.

'No. I'm here because I work for one of the top newspapers in the north of England,' Ewan lied to cover the embarrassment that might come out if he had to admit he was working for a second-rate magazine with a third-rate editor. 'Newcastle; that's where Mick Roslyn comes from.'

'Ah, Geordie!' Ekholm laughed.

Ewan nodded. 'Mick Roslyn's a Geordie boy.'

'You know him?'

'No.' He could sense that Ekholm smelt an angle on his story and he wasn't going to provide him with one.

The sun glistened off the cars. It even contained a hint of warmth. As he had assumed that Sweden would be like the Arctic, Ewan was pleasantly surprised.

'What happens now?'

'If the prosecutor thinks the facts is strong against this suspect, she will go in the court no longer than three days and ask for this fellow to be held. The court it must decide to keep this fellow in *häktet* or to–'

'Sorry?'

'*Häktet*. Like prison. Or let him go. If they say prison, the Prosecutor has after two weeks to build the case.'

'Thank you. That's really useful. Doesn't work in quite the same way in Britain. Well, not according to all the detective dramas on TV.'

Ekholm took a last puff of his cigarette, dropped it onto the ground and crushed the dying ember under his foot.

'And Mick Roslyn is famous in Newcastle?' He was fishing again.

'No. No one has ever heard of him. Except his parents,' Ewan joked.

Ekholm gave him a puzzled look. 'So why are you in Malmö?'

'I was doing a travel article when this came up. Thought I'd stay on and find out more when the murder took place. Play up the local connection.'

'Oh, well, we like to give our visitors something special. A good murder, eh?' Ekholm laughed at his joke. 'It sells newspapers. It is sad that there is no sex in the story as well. That sells even more newspapers.' He was still chortling when he left Ewan.

The duty officer unlocked the door and let Anita in. She knew she shouldn't be there, but Moberg was busy with the commissioner after the press conference, so she had time. Halvar Mednick didn't move. He was sitting on the wooden bed, which was attached to the wall. The only other furniture in the cell was the table, also attached to the wall under the barred window; and a chair tucked under the table. It wasn't meant to be homely. It was a place for concentrating minds.

'How are you?' It was a stupid question, but Anita hadn't been quite sure how to begin. Here was a man who had been arrested for the murder of one of Sweden's most famous personalities. Things weren't rosy, and the commissioner, the public prosecutor and Moberg all believed him to be guilty. And so would public opinion once his name appeared in the press, which it would do after Sonja Blom had gone to the district court. When he turned his wounded gaze on her, he didn't come out with the sarcastic reply she anticipated.

'I didn't kill her. I told you that.'

'So you did. It's just that when you have a gun pressed against your head, it's hard to take anything in.' Now she was being sarcastic. Stop it. This wasn't helpful.

Mednick flicked an imaginary object away with the toe of his shoe.

'I was frightened.'

So was I, screamed Anita to herself, but she didn't say anything. She pulled the chair away from the desk and sat opposite the prisoner.

'I need to ask you a couple of things.'

'I've told them everything.'

'I've got a couple of questions that they didn't ask.'

He screwed up his face and shook his head.

'My lawyer says I'm not to say anything without him being present.'

Anita edged her chair a little closer to the bed so that their heads weren't far apart. She fixed his stare. 'You told me you didn't kill Malin. Answer these questions and I might just believe you.'

The natural mistrust in his eyes faltered for a moment. Anita knew she was falsely raising his hopes, but she didn't have time to waste.

'When you entered Malin Lovgren's apartment, did you go into the kitchen?' Anita already knew the answer.

'I told them. I went into the reception hall or whatever you call it. Then into the living room. That's where I found her.' His voice trailed off.

'Did you go into any other rooms?'

He shook his head vehemently. 'Once she slid out of my arms onto the floor, I freaked out. I just ran out. Though I think I shut the front door.'

'But not into the kitchen?'

'Why?' He treated it as though it was another stupid question.

'OK. How long were you watching the block that night?'

'I was there from about eight. She came back around half nine.'

'From half eleven onwards did you see anyone entering the block?'

He thought for a moment. 'Yes.'

Anita suppressed a growing excitement.

'Recognise the person?'

'Yes.'

'And?'

'It was the man who lives on the first floor. Gunnarsson. His name's by the buzzers at the front. I know all the residents by sight.'

Anita couldn't hide her disappointment. Maybe she had been clutching at corroborative straws. If no one had entered, then possibly Moberg was right. She stood up and put the chair back in its place.

'As a matter of interest, why did you go into the apartment?'

'I just needed to talk to her. Tell her how I felt. Tell her that I cared and that I was here to look after her, which is more than her husband did.'

'What do you mean?'

'He was never there. He was married to the most fantastic woman in the world and he was always pissing off.' She looked at the crushed human being in front of her and wondered what mental torment he was putting himself through. The psychiatrists would have a field day with this one. Put together a celebrity fixation with an anti-Muslim complex and throw in God-knows-what sort of hideous childhood experiences, and he could expect to enjoy years of expensive therapy at the taxpayers' expense.

She knocked on the glass pane of the cell door to attract the attention of the duty officer. She felt pity for Mednick. He had probably been fine until his spell in Afghanistan. At least he'd come back alive, which was more than an increasing number of British and American soldiers were able to do. The key rattled in the lock and the door swung open.

'There was something.'

Anita turned quickly. Mednick was rubbing his temple with the fingers of his right hand as though he was trying to squeeze out a memory.

'I went and got a kebab. It was the only time I wasn't

watching the apartment. It was when I was coming back. The entrance door. I'm sure it was swinging back into place. Yes, it was.'

'So you didn't see anybody actually go in?'

'They certainly can't have been coming out. I would have seen them.'

At last, something to go at. They had checked all the comings and goings of the other residents and their visitors that night. No one had come in after Gunnarsson at 11.35, according to the reports she had gone through before coming down to the cells.

'I assumed it was someone visiting one of the other apartments,' continued Mednick, who had stopped toying with his temple.

'And the time?'

'About twenty to twelve.'

'And did anybody come out before you went in?'

'No.'

So, whoever went in at twenty to twelve was still in the building when Mednick discovered the body. Had that person heard Mednick come in? Were they still in the apartment at the time? Or skulking on the stairs? If that were the case, then they were dealing with a cool customer. Maybe the Säpo theory wasn't a figment of Roslyn's creative imagination after all.

'By the way, can I have a cup of tea sent in?'

He looked pathetically grateful at the suggestion. 'Don't drink tea, but a coffee would be... you know.'

CHAPTER 21

'What do you want doing with Roslyn?'

Moberg didn't answer Nordlund. The bar of chocolate he'd bought from the machine after the news conference didn't taste nice. Was it the chocolate, or the doubts that Anita Sundström had put into his mind and that he hadn't been able to dismiss during the press questioning? That was why he hadn't revealed more details, such as the CCTV footage, Mednick handling the body and the pendant turning up in his apartment. The commissioner had been quite short with him afterwards. 'This was a golden opportunity to give the press some real information for a change. It would have made us look good instead of putting up with the shit they normally give us.' Yet something had prevented Moberg from revealing too much. Too many mistakes had been made before.

'Leave him for the moment.'

'What if he wants to go? We can't stop him.'

'Tell him that there may still be a Säpo connection. He'll know from the press conference that we've arrested an ex-military guy. That would fit in with his own suspicions.'

Moberg flung the uneaten chocolate into the bin. 'That fucking woman!' He got out of his seat with surprising speed and glanced out of the window. 'She gets on my tits.'

'She's not stupid.'

'We've got an excellent case against this prick, but she's not happy.'

'Which means you're not happy either.' Nordlund paused. 'Maybe we're so keen to tie this one up, we're not looking at other possibilities.'

Moberg was still gazing outside. 'You mean *I've* rushed into this.'

'There's pressure…'

Moberg pivoted round like a ship manoeuvring into its berth. 'Henrik, you were in there with me in the interview. Mednick was shitting himself.'

Nordlund pulled out a white handkerchief and whisked it briefly across his nose. He knew why Mednick was nervous. A full-blown Erik Moberg interrogation wasn't for the faint-hearted. It was like being gored by a raging bull. 'Erik, maybe we have to take a step back. Our big problem is that we can't place Mednick in the kitchen where we know, or are pretty sure, the murder was committed. There's no evidence in the forensic report.'

Moberg gave a rueful grin. This was the nearest that Nordlund would get to admonishing him. Moberg hadn't read the report right through; he'd just concentrated on the bits that fitted his case. His lips smacked as he pursed them.

'Are you suggesting I stop Blom from going to the district court?'

Nordlund stuffed his handkerchief back in his trouser pocket. 'Too late for that. Anyhow, it would make us look ridiculous after the press conference. At least while Mednick's locked up, it'll stop further press speculation and keep the commissioner off our backs. It'll give us time to gather further evidence against Mednick… maybe another forensic search of the apartment. They may have missed something. We can also pursue other avenues.'

'The Säpo route?'

'I've got the ex-Säpo operatives' photographs. I'll go out and see Roslyn and use them to persuade him to stay put. See if he recognises his "Deep Throat". If Mednick isn't our man, then the killer may have been more concerned with getting at Roslyn than at his wife.'

'OK. But keep this under your hat for now, Henrik.'

'I'd have a word with Anita. She may have another angle worth exploring.'

Moberg snorted. 'Tap into her feminine intuition.'

Nordlund was smiling when he left the office as Moberg threw an imaginary object at him.

Ewan was busy putting his first murder investigation piece together for Brian. Though the press conference hadn't been particularly illuminating, except about the way that the Swedish legal system operated, he had plenty of background. He had painted portraits of the main players in the tragedy. Mick Roslyn, the Geordie-boy-made-good in Sweden. Newcastle upbringing then onwards and upwards in the glamorous world of films. Then there was the victim – his stunning actress wife. He built up the sultry Swedish beauty bit and sprinkled his description with facts he'd purloined from Google. The golden couple whose magical existence was cruelly cut short. A grisly murder on a cold winter's night in southern Sweden. Strangled by an ex-military man.

Ewan was in a good position to fill in some details of the actual murder scene, though he made no mention of his own role in the proceedings. Despite Anita telling him there was no connection, Ewan went as far as hinting that there might even be a link with the Olof Palme murder – he used it in reference to previous high-profile slayings in a country not noted for a huge homicide rate.

And central to the story was the sexy Swedish policewoman who was masterminding the investigation. Not true, though more newsworthy for British readers, who always wanted their stereotypes reinforced. The way he described Inspector Anita Sundström was as a brighter version of Britt Ekland with specs. It all made a merry mix among the mayhem of a murder case that was gripping northern Europe.

Ewan was sitting in Café Simrishamn 3. The staff were beginning to recognise him and the service was now accompanied by a warm smile. Ewan bit contentedly into his cake as he read over what he had written. He particularly liked the way he had set the scene by juxtaposing the dourness of the city in winter with the glitzy world in which the victim had moved. Brian would love it. Not that that could be regarded as a benchmark of quality. The only scoop that Brian had ever come across before was the sort used for digging out ice-cream from a carton. But it *was* a scoop because Ewan hadn't found more than a couple of paragraphs about it in the *Guardian* and the *Daily Mail* among the British nationals he had picked up in Malmö that morning.

He ordered another coffee. He sent off the piece to Brian with a covering email then stretched his arms. Now it was time to go back onto the internet and discover more about the fate of the Earl of Bothwell. How had he ended up imprisoned in Malmöhus? His mind went back to Anita's call this morning. He was still cross with himself. Maybe he should call her and thank her for telling him about the press conference. If they had found someone to pin the murder on, then maybe she would have time on her hands. Could he ask her out for a meal? His time in Malmö might be limited if this man was charged. The trial wouldn't be for months, and he would have to go back to Newcastle. He would have no reason to stay, except the real reason he didn't want to leave Malmö. Inspector Anita Sundström.

Moberg found Anita in the car park. She had gone to her car with the idea of taking it home and cleaning it up properly.

On opening the door, she had recoiled at the smell and slammed it shut. That was when she saw Moberg heading in her direction. She inwardly groaned. She wasn't in the mood for another Moberg blast. So when she was greeted with an unexpected smile, she was immediately on her guard.

'Heading home?'

'Need to clean the car. Bit smelly.'

Moberg shoved his hands in his trouser pockets. 'You OK? I mean, after yesterday. Not a nice position to be in. You could see the police shrink.' Anita shook her head. 'Get off home then and put your feet up.'

'Well, the case is solved, isn't it?'

Moberg shrugged his large shoulders. 'Sort of.'

Anita squinted into the low sun and shaded her eyes with her hand.

'I thought–'

'As there is so much riding on this case, we can't afford any slip-ups. So I think while things are proceeding against Mednick, that we shouldn't discount other routes. Henrik is pursuing the Säpo connection. I was wondering whether...'
He was having difficulty admitting any weakness in front of a female officer. He knew she was a good cop, but he didn't like the thought of a woman standing up to him, questioning his decisions. He had managed to crush the challenges offered by his two ex-wives. He knew Anita Sundström was different. He found the physical attraction got in the way and he couldn't view her as just another one of his detectives. The only way he could cope was usually to dismiss what she had to say or fight her off with sarcasm. But this wasn't the time for either approach. He offered her a cigarette instead.

'Trying to give them up.'

Moberg eased one out for himself, flipped it between two flabby lips and lit it. He didn't speak until he'd exhaled the first plume of smoke.

'Apart from Mednick, what thoughts have you got?'

'I keep going back to Roslyn.'

'And?'

She breathed in the reassuring aroma of smoke and was tempted to ask for a cigarette after all, but fought the impulse.

'He lied to us about his whereabouts on the night of the murder. He didn't attend the meeting he said he was at.'

'Is that significant?'

'Might be. I went and had a word with him.'

'You...' Moberg bit back his rebuke. There she goes again, doing things without his say-so.

'Want me to continue?' He clamped the cigarette back in his mouth and nodded. 'I asked him if he had an alibi. And he produced one.'

'So that definitely puts him out of the picture.'

'Yes. But his alibi raises another possibility. The alibi he was sleeping with happens to be the girlfriend of his business partner, Bengt Valquist. She's called Tilda Tegner. Actress.'

Moberg stopped, mid-puff. 'Those thespian types seem to fuck like rabbits. When do they find time to act? This Valquist – he's the "poodle", right?' Anita nodded. 'Does he know his girlfriend's cheating on him?'

'We don't know. If he did, then there might be a possible motive. Getting his own back on Roslyn?'

'Wouldn't it be more natural to go after his girlfriend or the lover?'

'Maybe he loves Tilda Tegner too much to kill her. And he's certainly in awe of Roslyn, who's his mentor. Could it be his way of punishing Roslyn?'

Moberg shook his head slowly. 'Not totally convinced.'

'There's something else. When I was talking to the girl from Roslyn's office in Stockholm, she said there was gossip that Malin wanted to get rid of him. Valquist, that is. If that was the case, he had a lot to lose. Malin's death would protect his position. And he was in Lund on the night. Just up the road.'

Moberg leant against Anita's car and she hoped it wouldn't roll over.

'That's an interesting possibility. The affair thing raises another one, too. This actress. What do we know about her?'

'She was in Roslyn's last film. Sleeping her way up the ladder?'

'If that's so, then she might be a suspect, too. Getting rid of her rival?'

'I thought you'd dismissed the possibility of a woman doing it.'

Even Moberg had to laugh after he caught the mocking flicker of amusement in Anita's eyes. 'You know me. Always open-minded.'

'It can't be her, anyway. She was in Stockholm enjoying a night of bliss in the arms of our dirty director. Should I follow up Valquist?'

'You were going to anyway, weren't you?' Moberg dropped his cigarette. 'Keep me informed. Find anything, and I'm the first to know.'

'Of course.'

Moberg gave her a sceptical glance as he eased himself away from the car. It was undented.

'I saw your British journalist at the press conference. Surprised he's still about.'

'Ewan's covering the story for his newspaper.'

'Ewan?' Moberg's eyebrows arched. Anita couldn't believe that a hint of a blush appeared on her cheeks. Why? There was nothing in it. She didn't even fancy the man. 'Rule of thumb, Anita. Never trust a journalist.'

'He might still be useful. He knows something about Roslyn that he's not telling us.'

Moberg could see that Anita hesitated. 'And what else?'

'Something nagging. It comes back to the so-called friends.

When Roslyn discovered Malin's body in the living room, he attacked Strachan and the photographer had to pull him off.'

'Only natural. There's someone bending over your dead wife.'

'Even in that instant, Roslyn must have realised that it was his old university friend because he'd asked him to come. Roslyn wouldn't seriously expect Strachan to kill his wife and then hang around. He's got no motive anyway. What sparked his overreaction?'

'It's almost as though he assumed Strachan had killed her,' said Moberg slowly.

'Exactly. Or maybe it was a way of covering up the fact that he already knew she was dead.'

'A bit fanciful. Let's stick to the real world.' The sarcasm had returned.

As Moberg made his way back to the main building, he had his mobile in his hand.

'Westermark. I need you to look into something.'

CHAPTER 22

Mick was anxious to speak to someone of a senior rank when Nordlund entered the room. Though the safe house had been at his own instigation, being confined in some peasant bothy was not his idea of being incognito. At least they could have given him a hotel suite. Were the police trying to save money? And he hadn't been able to contact anyone because they had said that any call might be traced, particularly if he used his mobile. He wanted to speak to Tilda, to warn her that he had been forced to spill the beans about their last night together on Monday. He just hoped she wouldn't be fazed, that she would stick to their agreed story.

The man who came in was in his early sixties, bald on top and what little hair he had left almost totally grey. His presence wasn't threatening like that of Chief Inspector Moberg, nor had he any of the suppressed hostility that seeped out of every pore of Inspector Sundström. Yet, behind the sad expression and deeply sunken eyes, this man was someone he had to be wary of. He was of the age of someone who might have had Säpo connections from the 1980s.

The man could have been reading his thoughts. 'I voted against the euro and I dislike the EU but don't worry, I'm not a neo-Nazi sympathiser.' Before a startled Mick could answer, Nordlund continued courteously in Swedish, 'How are you bearing up, herr Roslyn?' Nordlund's English was too poor to tackle this particular conversation.

'I don't like it here.' Mick was on his fourth beer of the afternoon.

'It's probably best you stay put.'

Mick held out his right hand, which was clutching the Carlsberg Export. 'This guy you've arrested. All they said was that he has a military background.'

'That's correct,' said Nordlund, who sat down on the sofa while Mick prowled about the room.

'Anything to do with Säpo?'

By not answering the question, he let Mick jump to his own conclusions.

'It's about Säpo that I am here.' He put down a file on the plain wooden coffee table in front of him. 'I have here the photographs of a number of Säpo operatives at the time of the Palme murder. I would like you to go through them carefully and see if your "Deep Throat" character is among them, or "Henrik Larsson", as I believe he called himself.'

Mick came and sat down in the chair opposite, placed his bottle carefully on the table and flicked open the manila file. There were fifteen photographs for him to go through. He took each one in turn and scrutinised it carefully, screwing up his eyes as he did so.

Nordlund watched to see if there was any sign of recognition. 'Remember, these were taken over twenty years ago, so your man may have changed quite a lot. Balder, greyer, fatter.'

Mick's gaze never left the photos. Two of them attracted his attention for longer than the rest. Only when he had gone through them did he speak. 'I don't think so.'

'Try again, sir. There were two that you took your time over. What about them?'

Mick took a swig from his bottle before extracting two of the photos from the pile. He laid them side by side in front of him. He must have spent a good two minutes examining them before pushing one aside and staring fixedly at the remaining image. Then he tapped the photo with his index finger lightly. Then the tapping became more forceful. 'I think this could be him. His hair is very grey now, but he has a look of "Deep Throat", I think it's the nose. The shape of the mouth as well.'

'Sure?'

Mick nodded his head vigorously. 'As sure as I can be, given the period of time that's elapsed.'

Nordlund leant over and picked up the photo. He turned it over to check the back. He had numbered each image beforehand – this one was five. He took out a piece of paper, which had names to correspond with the numbers. Andreas Tapper.

'Thank you very much. We'll check this man out.'

'What's his real name?'

'Can't tell you that at the moment. But we'll find him.'

'It's his old colleagues I'm more worried about.'

'Brilliant! I love it.'

Ewan had never heard Brian praise anything he had written before. He was rather chuffed.

'I've had a word with upstairs and they're going to run it across all the group's flagship papers. I've got some great shots of the Malin woman. It's putting some noses out of joint, I can tell you,' Brian said with undisguised relish.

'I'm not sure how much further I can take the story once they've made official charges. Then the process will take months before it hits the courts if their system is anything like ours.'

'Oh.' Brian sounded disappointed. 'Any chance of a Roslyn interview?' 'Don't know where he is. Police hid him away when they thought there was a secret service connection.'

'Surely he'll appear now?'

'I haven't the faintest.'

'Get onto that policewoman of yours. She sounds fantastic. Any chance of getting a photo of her? Sexy Swedish cop sounds even more of a turn-on than a sexy Swedish film star.'

Ewan realised he had gone a bit over the top with Anita's description in his piece. 'Best to leave it to the readers' imaginations. As for Mick Roslyn, I doubt if he'll want to talk publicly just yet.'

'He's in the entertainment business, for fuck's sake! They all want to talk. Normally you can't shut them up. First interview with heartbroken star's husband. I can make a real splash with that.'

Now the first person plural had turned into *I*, Ewan noticed. 'Even if I can find Mick and he agrees to talk to me, he might want paying.'

There was silence at the other end of the line. 'Well, see what you can do.' That meant that there was no money available for an interview.

'How long are you giving me?'

There was another pause. 'If you can't get him over the weekend, then you'd better come back on Monday. Don't want you running up mountainous expenses. I know how expensive Scandinavia is.'

'Don't worry; I'll get another piece out of what we've got even if Mick proves elusive.'

By the time Anita had requisitioned a police car to drive to Lund, the sun was going down. It would be dark soon. She sat in silence while Olander drove. It was a short, 20-kilometre drive straight along the E22. She was relieved that at least Moberg was investigating other options. She was now convinced that Mednick wasn't their culprit, despite running into a hassled Eva Thulin before leaving the polishus. She had just been ordered by Moberg to re-do the whole of Malin Lovgren's apartment.

'I don't know what he's trying to prove,' Thulin said

in exasperation.

'He's trying to prove he's right.' Anita smiled.

'Men!'

'Just think of the overtime. Oh, by the way, have you checked the Lotta Lind pendant for fingerprints?'

'Yes. Strange actually. It had Halvar Mednick's prints all over it but no others. Not even Malin Lovgren's.'

'So someone must have wiped the pendant clean after the murder and before Mednick picked it up.'

The light was fading fast by the time they got into Lund. Anita had little difficulty directing Olander to the house as it was not far from the main university buildings. The door was answered by Valquist's mother; a tall woman with a gaunt face below dyed blonde hair scraped back in a severe bun. She was alarmed at first when she discovered that Anita was from the police, but when it was explained that it was only routine enquiries, she relaxed. Bengt had had to fly up to Stockholm. Something urgent. But he would be back tomorrow lunchtime. Before leaving, Anita asked whether she knew the whereabouts of Tilda Tegner.

Anita got back into the car.

'No luck?' asked Olander.

'He's in Stockholm. Back tomorrow.'

'Back to Malmö?'

'No. We'll wait here. Tilda Tegner should be turning up soon. She's been in Malmö doing a voice-over for a commercial. She'll be walking back from the station. Fru Valquist invited us in to wait, but I want to talk to Tegner with no one else around. So you can pop out and get us a coffee.'

Olander waited patiently as she dived into her bag to find some kronor. On his return, Anita sipped at the coffee, which was as plastic as the container. But it was hot and the evening was now cold.

'Could Bengt Valquist really be our killer?' Olander asked.

'I have no idea. But he's got a couple of potential motives. Malin getting rid of him. That might have finished his career. And then there's his business partner doing the business with his girlfriend.' She took another sip of coffee. 'As our resident movie expert, what do you know about Tilda Tegner?'

'Good-looking lady. She played the husband's lover in *Gässen*. Not a big part, but she was OK. That's the second film she's done for Roslyn. The first was just a walk-on part.'

'Maybe she'll get a lead role in Roslyn's next film after this.'

Olander put his coffee on the dashboard. 'I think that's her, Inspector.'

Anita could see a tall, slim woman walking along the street in their direction. She had on a blue woolly hat and plaid coat pulled tightly round her. When she got closer, Anita got out of the car.

'Fröken Tegner?'

Tegner pulled up in surprise. 'Yes.'

Anita produced her warrant card. 'Inspector Anita Sundström. We'd like a word.'

Panic flitted across Tegner's beautiful face. 'What about?'

'If you get in the car, I'll tell you,' said Anita, opening the vehicle's back door.

Tegner looked about nervously. 'Why don't we go inside?'

'I don't think you'll want the Valquists to overhear this conversation.'

Tegner meekly slipped into the back seat and Anita got in beside her. Tegner kept her hat on and it was difficult to see her face clearly in the darkened car. Maybe that would make it easier for her talk, Anita hoped.

'How well do you know Mick Roslyn?'

'Is this to do with Malin's murder?'

'Just answer the question, please.'

'Of course I know him. I've appeared in two of his films. He's Bengt's boss and business associate.'

'And Bengt Valquist is your partner?'

'Yes, of course he is.' It was either bluster or growing confidence.

'So he doesn't know about you and Roslyn?'

'I don't know what you mean.' There wasn't enough light for Anita to register Tegner's facial expression.

'Oh, I think you do, fröken Tegner. Where were you last Monday night, for example?'

Tegner didn't answer straight away. The pause was too long. 'In Stockholm.'

'And what did you do?'

'Nothing much. I had been here in Lund with Bengt and then drove north. I was tired when I got back to my apartment.'

'Not so tired that you spent the night with Rolsyn.'

She tried anger. 'What makes you think I was with Mick?'

'Because he told me so.'

The instant intake of breath made her sound as though she had been slapped in the stomach. She didn't say anything.

'Are you denying it?'

Tegner's head slumped. 'Oh, God!'

'How long has this been going on?'

Tegner didn't look up. 'A couple of months.' The words were barely audible.

'What I want to know, fröken Tegner, is this: do you think herr Valquist knows about your liaison?'

Tegner tugged nervously at her gloves with her teeth.

'Well?'

'Oh, God, I hope not! I didn't mean...' She started to sob. Anita let her cry gently until she stopped. She wiped her eyes with her gloves. 'Why are you asking me this? What has this to do with Malin?'

'You've given Roslyn an alibi.'

Tegner turned to Anita for the first time. 'Why does he need an alibi? Surely you can't think–'

'We have to check everything.'

'Are you going to tell Bengt?' The worry had returned to her voice.

'That's all.' Anita got out of the car and held it open for Tegner. Despite the situation, Anita noticed that Tegner eased herself out of the car elegantly. The trained actress. 'By the way, do you work out? The gym, martial arts, that sort of thing?'

Tegner was now standing next to Anita. She was a good 10 centimetres taller.

'I work out in the gym most weeks. I started when I got a small part in a German action movie a couple of years ago. I was supposed to be in a terrorist cell so there were a couple of fight sequences. There were stunt doubles, but we still had to run around a lot.'

'Did you kill anybody?'

Tegner laughed. 'No, we were there to be killed by the goody German cops. Anyway, why do you ask?'

'Good night, fröken Tegner.' Anita slammed the back door shut and got into the car next to Olander.

Tilda Tegner watched them drive off before dragging herself slowly towards the Valquist residence.

Anita didn't say anything until they were leaving the outskirts of Lund. 'What did you make of her?'

'She lied about something. But I don't know what.'

'I don't know either.'

CHAPTER 23

It was a rather surreal experience watching a game of indoor cricket in Scandinavia. But here Ewan was, after taking the bus with Alex and David into the suburbs to some faceless sports centre in the middle of a housing estate. Ewan had totally lost his bearings by the time they had reached the building where the shivering teams from Malmöhus and Lund were gathering in the car park. Cricket whites seemed incongruous in a Swedish summer, let alone a Swedish winter. The players were drawn from all over the British Commonwealth with a handful of keen Swedes thrown in. Many had obviously just dragged themselves out of bed on this freezing Saturday morning but appeared jovial enough as greetings were exchanged, complicated rules discussed and last cigarettes smoked.

As he watched the enthusiastic sixteen-overs-an-innings contest, Ewan was starting to chill out. Sweden, so far, had been a disconcerting experience to say the least. Being caught up in a murder within the first twenty-four hours wasn't what he'd planned; but now they had a culprit, he could rest easy. The name of Halvar Mednick was all over the newspapers this morning after Public Prosecutor Blom had successfully applied in the district court for his further detention. Ewan could savour Sweden as a country that he was starting to recognise had similarities to his own Scotland. The only real difference as far as he could work out was that the Swedes weren't as confrontational and they were far healthier. And, of course, the women. Or one woman in particular. He realised that he would probably have to be on the plane back to Newcastle on Monday. That left him the rest of the weekend to try and contact Mick to get some sort of story out of him and, more importantly, contrive another meeting with Anita.

Anita was on her third coffee of the morning. It would be another long day. It was her own fault. If she hadn't raised doubts about Halvar Mednick, she could have had the weekend off. Westermark watched her resentfully as they gathered in Moberg's office. He had a hot date that he had had to put off. Olander was also there but no one else as this was an informal meeting.

'Right,' Moberg began, 'we're here unofficially. The investigation of Mednick continues.' He glanced over to Anita. 'However, doubts have been raised among the team and I think, to protect our arses, that we need to be 100 per cent sure that Mednick's our man. At the moment, we can place him at the scene of the crime but not in the room where the crime was committed. Anita's also raised the question of the pendant and its lack of fingerprints, except Mednick's. Malin's prints should have been all over it.'

'Shouldn't Henrik be here?' Westermark asked. Why should he be dragged in and the old bugger let off?

'I've sent him to Stockholm. Took a plane from Sturup this morning.'

'Why?'

'Because we're following up other lines of enquiry. Roslyn has identified his Säpo contact. Henrik is following that up.'

'Surely we're not taking that seriously.' Westermark was getting annoyed with the whole situation.

'We have to take everything seriously,' snapped Moberg,

who was quickly becoming irritated by Westermark's negativity. He didn't like officers questioning his judgement – and certainly not a slimy fart like Karl Westermark. 'If Mednick isn't our murderer, then we really have to take the method of killing seriously. It smacks of a professional job. No noise, no prints, no witnesses.'

Westermark shut up and sulked.

Moberg turned to Anita, who was leaning against the windowsill. 'And what theories are we getting from you this morning?'

'I think we need to look at Roslyn's inner circle. We know that Roslyn lied to us about being at a meeting. The reason now seems to be because he was having a night of passion in Stockholm with his business partner's girlfriend, Tilda Tegner.' This attracted the huffy Westermark's interest.

'So they have given each other an alibi,' mused Moberg.

'On the face of it, yes. But it does give Bengt Valquist a possible motive to kill Malin. Jealousy. According to Tegner, the affair has been going on for a couple of months, which gives Valquist time to find out and time to plan his revenge. Tegner left Lund on the Monday and drove to Stockholm to meet Roslyn. Valquist was in Lund and he would have known that Malin would be alone. He could have been down here, kill Malin and be back in Lund in an hour. Of course, he might have killed her for another reason. Self-preservation. According to office rumour, Malin wanted to get rid of Valquist. If it were true, then everything he had worked for would be lost. Position, prestige, girls like Tilda Tegner.'

'Have you talked to him yet?' Moberg asked.

'I'm speaking to him later. He was in Stockholm last night.'

Moberg eased his chair away from his desk. 'This Tilda Tegner. She couldn't be covering for Roslyn – or Roslyn for her?'

'I'm sure they spent the night together. Roslyn was reluctant to tell me about it and Tegner seemed genuinely horrified when I brought the subject up. If she'd been in Malmö, I'm sure she would have been capable of doing the murder. She's ambitious enough. She's also tall enough, and she's done combat-type training for some German film she was in. But she was in Stockholm, so that's a dead end.'

'OK. Off you go. Take Olander here. Put the pressure on Valquist. Squeeze the bastard's balls if necessary. Time's not on our side.'

Anita, Olander and Westermark started to move towards the door.

'A word, Westermark.'

They were using the requisitioned car again as Anita still hadn't been able to summon up the required enthusiasm to take her own car back home and clean it. This time she drove. And ignored the mobile call that started off the familiar Samba ring tone in her pocket. She had forgotten about it by the time they met Bengt Valquist at Lund University. The main university building, situated beyond the impressive Romanesque cathedral, was un-Swedishly extravagant, with its white colonnaded façade and two ornate wings. Anita assumed the style was neoclassical, but it always reminded her of a Mediterranean casino. Valquist had wanted to meet there and not at the home of his parents so not as to upset them. They had taken Roslyn's death badly, and his mother had been worried after Anita's appearance at her door the previous evening. What Anita didn't know was whether Tilda Tegner had come clean with him after their talk – or even whether she was in Lund any more. Her guess was that Tegner had scurried back to Stockholm so she didn't have to face the music. If he didn't already know about the affair, then he was going to be in for a shock in the next few minutes.

Valquist was waiting nervously over by the circular fountain. He wore a thick, expensive coat and elegant leather gloves.

He was tall and spindly, and the coat seemed too large for him. He certainly didn't fill it out. He was more the young business executive than Anita's vague idea of what a film producer should look like. As Anita and Olander approached, he pushed his glasses further up the bridge of his nose.

'Thank you for meeting us.' Anita said, trying to physically weigh him up. Was his physique right for the killer they were after? Difficult to tell in that coat, was the answer.

'Where's Mick? He hasn't been in touch.'

'He's safe. We have to make sure that he doesn't call anyone so that he's untraceable, hence his lack of communication.'

Valquist stamped his elegantly shod feet to ward off the cold. Anita wondered why they couldn't have met indoors somewhere.

'It's just I... I mean the company needs decisions making on a couple of ongoing issues.'

'I'm afraid they'll have to wait.'

As if they had been given a signal, they all began to walk slowly away from the university. The destination was unclear.

'This man you've arrested: Henrik Mednick–'

'Halvar Mednick,' Olander corrected.

'This man is connected with the secret service?'

'We haven't established that yet.' Anita remained non-committal.

'But he is ex-army?'

'Yes.'

Valquist was now looking over towards the cathedral. 'So how can I help you?'

'We're still exploring other lines of enquiry. Other possible suspects.'

He turned his head towards Anita, who was walking by his side. 'And you have others?' he said in some surprise.

'Yes. You, for example.'

Valquist stopped dead in his tracks. His mouth opened, but

he was too flabbergasted to say anything.

Anita pressed home her advantage. 'Where were you last Monday night?' She cut short his protest. 'Just tell me your movements.'

He clasped his gloved hands together. He was starting to fret. 'I was... I was here, in Lund.'

'Times, please?'

'Well, I gave a talk to a group of students about film production at 7.30.' He started to nibble anxiously at the gloved index finger of his right hand as he reminded himself of his whereabouts that night. 'I had a quick drink with some of them afterwards then went back to my apartment at... well, it must have been around ten.'

'Anybody vouch for your movements after that? Your parents?'

'No. My mother goes to bed early each night. Usually about 9.30. Dad was with a friend over in Landskrona until late. Though we share the same entrance, my apartment has a separate staircase. I converted it about three years ago for when I'm down from Stockholm. I do some part-time lecturing at the university, and I can keep an eye on my parents.'

'So what were you doing between eleven and one that night?'

'Erm... I was reading some scripts that some of the students had given me. Checked emails. Then watched a movie I had on DVD. Must have gone to bed about half twelve.'

'No alibi?'

Anita stared at Valquist, which only increased his nervousness.

'Why should I have an alibi? I'm hardly going to kill off the business's main asset.' It struck Anita as a funny way to describe Malin.

'Did you ring fröken Tegner when you got back?' asked Olander. The attack was now coming from two fronts.

'No. I got an SMS from her when she arrived in Stockholm, but it said she was tired and wanted to go straight to bed. I didn't want to disturb her.'

'She went straight to bed.' Anita paused. 'But not by herself.'

It took a few moments for the implication of what she had said to sink in. 'What are you talking about?'

'I'm saying she wasn't in bed alone.'

'This is fucking stupid,' Valquist burst out furiously. 'What are you trying to do?'

'Don't you want to know who she was with?'

The mouth was open again. Confusion, agitation and anger fought for a place on his face. 'You're talking rubbish. You're trying to get me to say something. To incriminate myself.'

'Herr Valquist, your girlfriend was in bed with Mick Roslyn on the night that his wife was murdered. If you knew about their affair, then you had a motive for killing Roslyn's wife. Getting your own back.'

'I'm not going to listen to any more of this shit!'

'Or was it because Malin was going to have you sacked?'

Valquist stared at Anita in disbelief. 'Why would she do that? Mick would never—'

'That would have ruined your reputation in the film business. Get rid of Malin and you might save yourself. You had opportunity. It's easy to get to Malmö and back quickly from here. And you knew that Roslyn was out of the way in Stockholm. It appears that Malin let her murderer in because she knew him. Her business partner, for example? No one can vouch for your movements before, during, or after the murder. And, finally, you have the means. You're tall enough. So I think it's not unreasonable for us to ask – did you kill Malin Lovgren on Monday, the 11th of February?'

'Should we have brought him in?' asked Olander, who had taken over the driving for their journey back to Malmö.

'We can't arrest someone on the basis of office tittle-tattle,' Anita answered distractedly. She had remembered the call that she hadn't answered before and discovered it had come from Ewan. For some inexplicable reason, she felt too self-conscious about ringing him back in front of Olander. She put her mobile away.

'Do you think he could have done it?'

'Quite possibly. I can't work out whether his nervousness is just his natural state or a sign of guilt.'

'I'm not sure he looks strong enough. Bit of a weakling.'

'It's amazing the strength you can summon up when you're spurred on by jealousy, or you think you're about to lose everything you've worked for.'

They were clear of the houses on the outskirts of Lund. 'He seemed quite shaken when you told him about Tegner and Roslyn. You certainly didn't break it to him gently.' He laughed.

'Always best to put them on the spot. You're more likely to get a genuine reaction.'

'I'd love to be a fly on the wall when he next talks to Tilda Tegner.' With that he put his foot down.

The debriefing with Moberg was short. The upshot was that they would return to the CCTV footage and see if they could find a sighting of Valquist. They would also check the multistorey car park at the back of the *Systembolag* to find out whether his blue metallic Volvo had been in there that night and to cross-reference the forensics with any prints. Anita felt the latter was a waste of time as Valquist must have been a frequent visitor to the apartment. However, she couldn't be bothered to argue the point. At least Moberg was widening the investigation.

As she was leaving, the phone rang.

'Moberg. Ah, Henrik.' Moberg motioned with his plate-like hand for Anita to stay while he took the call.

It didn't last long and consisted of Moberg saying 'yes' a

dozen times. 'You do that, Henrik. Speak tomorrow.' Moberg
put the phone down.

'Well?' Anita asked expectantly.

'Roslyn's contact, Andreas Tapper. He's dead.'

CHAPTER 24

The noise in The Pickwick was rising, and Ewan nearly missed hearing his phone go off. The Malmöhus boys were celebrating their victory. One more drink and they would be off to an Indian restaurant just off Möllevångstorget. Ewan was in the process of passing drinks from the bar when he heard the call.

'Sorry. Bit loud in here. I'll just go outside.'

As he pushed his way towards the pub entrance and down the steps, his excitement was mounting. Anita was on the other end of the line.

'Are you in a bar?'

'Yes. Sorry about that. I've been watching a cricket match. Out having a few drinks with the winners.'

'A cricket match!' Anita sounded incredulous. 'In Malmö? In this weather?'

Ewan laughed. 'Fortunately, it was indoors, but it was still bloody freezing.' There was a pause as he didn't know how to go on.

'You called,' Anita said uncertainly.

'Yes. So I did. Erm… two things really. Business and pleasure.'

'OK,' came the guarded reply.

It was glacial out in the street and Ewan had taken off his coat inside the pub. 'The business. Is there any chance of seeing

Mick Roslyn? For a quick interview before I leave on Monday?'

'No. I am afraid there is no chance of that at the moment. Once everything is cleared up, he is free to speak to anyone he chooses.'

'Ah, it was just a long shot. My editor won't be pleased. I'll just have to make something up.'

'I thought that was what journalists always did.'

'That's harsh.' He smirked. 'Only crap journalists, like me, who can never be arsed to search for the facts.'

He heard her laugh and it made him feel good. This was an opportune moment to put the question he really wanted to ask.

'I'm booked on a flight out of Copenhagen on Monday morning.'

'I'm sorry your first visit to Sweden has caused you so much trouble. We're really a nice country.'

'As tomorrow is my last day, I was wondering whether we could meet up. For a drink, a chat or something...' The words petered out as his confidence ebbed away. He suddenly felt like a teenager asking out his first date. For the record, Mary Young had turned down his offer to watch a film at the Lyceum in Lothian Road.

After an agonising pause at the other end: 'OK. Tomorrow night.'

Anita was starting to have second thoughts almost immediately. After her last experience, she had sworn never to socialise with another journalist unless he could be of use in terms of the job. But this wasn't really a date. Besides, he was leaving the country, and she doubted she would ever see him again. There was nothing to lose. It would give her a chance to find out about how much Durham had changed since her childhood. They had a place in common. He also amused her. And if she was honest, she was quite flattered at his obvious attention. His embarrassment when asking her out was endearing – it had sounded like a case of hope over expectation. With most of the Swedish men she had come across, it was usually the other way round.

She was now standing outside her apartment on Roskildevägen. She had her car doors and boot open as well as having wound down all the windows. The short drive back from the polishus car park had been extremely smelly. She had scrubbed the passenger seat down and sprayed around the inside of the vehicle with two different types of air freshener she had found under the kitchen sink. They were ancient, and she wondered whether cans of air freshener had sell-by dates. Their combined odours didn't make much difference. In fact, they nearly made her gag. They seemed to attack her throat in the same way that ladies' toiletry sections did in smart department stores, where all the scents fight each other to attract the customers' attention but cumulatively are a rather nauseous combination. She decided to leave all the windows open and to keep an eye on the car from the living room while she phoned her mother. She doubted whether the car would be stolen, as any thief would be overcome by the pong.

She had been feeling guilty about her mother. She hadn't visited her in Kristianstad for weeks. They talked regularly on the phone, but there was always the unspoken rebuke about lack of filial visits. She loved her mother, but they drove each other mad, which was why she always found excuses not to invite her across to Malmö. Her parents' break-up had hit her hard because she adored her father. He had stayed in Stockholm while she had gone back with her mother to Simrishamn to live with her maternal grandmother. Her teenage years had been difficult, and she had been glad to escape to the National Police Academy in Stockholm and spend some time near her father. And then his drowning severed that side of her life. After her grandmother's death – Anita had left home by then – her mother had moved to Kristianstad to live with her sister, Aunt Fanny. Both had been unlucky in love and enjoyed their mutual moaning about men, life and the price of fish. Anita's visits to Kristianstad only depressed her, and she always rushed back to Malmö at the first excuse. The horrid truth was that she feared that she would turn into her mother.

Inside her living room, she could see the car a short distance away. Passers-by would get a whiff, and assume some occupant had been sick after too much booze. God knew what her neighbours would think. Not that it mattered as there was only one other person in the block she ever talked to. It was time to ring her mother. As she stared at the phone, her mind went back to Nordlund's call to Moberg earlier.

Andreas Tapper was dead. He'd died six months before in a road accident. Taken to drink after being shoved out of Säpo and was drunk at the wheel when he drove off the E4 north of Norrköping, where he was living at the time. That was the official version. So "Deep Throat" couldn't be Andreas Tapper because Roslyn claimed to have seen his contact in recent months. Did "Deep Throat" exist or was he a figment of Roslyn's fertile imagination? Moberg had wondered, not unreasonably. Nordlund said that he had tracked down a brother, Linas, who lived in Västerås. He would get out there tomorrow, snow permitting. But Anita was now more interested in Bengt Valquist. She would plump for an emotive murder over a cold conspiracy killing every time. She picked up the phone and rang the familiar Kristianstad number.

CHAPTER 25

There weren't many people standing alongside Henrik Nordlund as he waited on the platform at Centralstationen on a bitterly cold Sunday morning. Stockholm was a city that suited all seasons, and snow suited its fine buildings best of all, Nordlund had always thought. As Skåne had escaped heavy snow so far this winter, he enjoyed the visual freshness that it brought to the capital. The locals were less enthusiastic as they had endured it for some weeks and were praying for signs of spring.

By the time the train left the dreary suburbs behind and the snowbound countryside took over, Nordlund had lost interest in the view out of the window and thought about how he was going to tackle Linas Tapper. He couldn't decide whether this was a complete waste of time or whether they were onto something genuine. On hearing about Andreas Tapper's death, he had flirted with the idea that such an accident could have been staged. The car Tapper was driving hadn't hit another vehicle. It had veered off the motorway because, it was alleged, he was drunk at the time. They had found a huge amount of alcohol in his bloodstream.

Nordlund had managed to establish that Tapper had been stationed in Stockholm at the time of the Palme assassination, so he could have known what had gone on behind the scenes. But the timing of his death didn't seem right. Six months ago.

Did that fit in with Roslyn's documentary timetable? Even if it did, would his brother know anything? Brothers often didn't get on. Would he even speak to him? Would he even be there? Or was he looking into the wrong man? Nordlund acknowledged that he had rather pushed Roslyn into identifying Andreas Tapper in the first place.

Nordlund reached Västerås at mid-morning and took a taxi out to Råbykorset, an area of faceless apartment blocks that were made grimmer by the unrelenting winter weather. He crunched his way to the entrance of Linas Tapper's block and made his way up to the first floor apartment. The plate by the bell only had Linas Tapper's name on it, so he wasn't married or certainly wasn't sharing his apartment with anyone. He had to wait for the door to be answered. When it was opened, he could hear a television playing loudly in the background. The man standing in front of him had a vague resemblance to the photo of Andreas that Nordlund had in his pocket. He was unshaven and bleary-eyed. Maybe the fondness for drink ran in the family. He had a head of thick, dark brown hair above restless blue eyes. From his mouth hung a half-smoked cigarette. He wore a black T-shirt and old jeans.

'Yes?'

'Inspector Henrik Nordlund.' He held up his warrant badge.

Doubt immediately crept across Tapper's face.

'Police? What do you want?' Tapper was about to close the door.

'It's not you,' Nordlund put in quickly. 'I want to talk about your brother.'

Tapper's demeanour changed. He opened the door wide to let Nordlund in.

The unfavourable impression that Nordlund had formed on seeing Linas Tapper's appearance at the door was challenged on entering the living room. The blaring telly was large and brand new. So was the sound system near the window which opened onto the small balcony. Beyond the balcony were snow-laden pine trees. Out of the other window, Nordlund could see the next block of apartments. The furniture wasn't as new. It was more local flea market than IKEA.

Linas Tapper appeared behind Nordlund. The cigarette was gone, but he had a mug of coffee in his hand. He didn't bother to offer Nordlund a drink but did wander over and turn the television off. He then slumped in an old armchair. Neither did he invite Nordlund to sit down, so the inspector sat in a wicker chair opposite.

'I suppose you've been sent to warn me off.'

'Warn you off about what?'

'Andreas, of course. I assume you're connected to Säpo.'

Nordlund adjusted his coat, which had got ruffled up under his thighs when he sat down. 'No. I'm from Malmö. Skåne County Police.'

Tapper smirked. 'I should have recognised that daft accent. So what brings you up to this civilized part of the world?'

'As I said, your brother. He died in a car accident six months ago?'

'Yes. And the bloody authorities reckon he was drunk. He was a good driver even when he was pissed. No other vehicle involved. They did it!'

Nordlund didn't take his eyes off Tapper. 'Who did it?'

Tapper flashed Nordlund an incredulous glance. 'Säpo, of course. Shut him up. So nothing would come out. That's why I went to the local police, down in Norrköping. Asked questions. I was fobbed off. It was like an official iron curtain came down.' He stared into his mug: 'They did it.'

'But why would Säpo want to kill him?'

'He knew about the Palme murder. He knew what really took place. Not all the shit they said that happened.'

Nordlund could feel the hairs rising on the back of his neck.

'How do you know this?' he asked cautiously.

'Andreas got kicked out of the service four years ago. After twenty-three years. Said he was no longer performing to a high enough standard. Become a liability.' Tapper almost spat the words out. 'Drinking too much. I know Andreas liked his liquor, but he could control it. Always had. The bastards didn't even give him a full pension. No wonder he was bitter.'

'I can understand that. But what I can't understand is why Säpo would want to kill him.'

Tapper gave a dry, mirthless laugh. 'I told you; he knew who was behind Palme's killing.'

'How do *you* know?'

'Because he told me one night. Right here, in this room. We'd had lots to drink and he opened up. When he was working for Säpo, he never spoke about his work, so I was surprised when he started talking about it. It all came flooding out. Or some of it, anyhow.'

'Exactly what came out?'

Tapper was about to launch into his story when he pulled himself up short. Suspicion suddenly distorted his features. 'You still haven't told me why you've come all the way from Malmö to talk about my brother.'

'We're looking at the possibility of a connection between your brother and an on-going investigation.'

Tapper jumped out of his seat and spilled coffee in the process. It spattered across the wooden flooring, but Tapper ignored it. 'I fucking knew it! The Malin Lovgren murder. Mick Roslyn.'

'I can't say.'

'You don't bloody have to.' Tapper paced the room in some agitation.

'Why do you think there's a connection between your brother and the Lovgren murder?' Nordlund asked pointedly.

'Because...' He stopped moving.

'Because you're the one who's been talking to Roslyn. You're his "Henrik Larsson", or what he likes to call his "Deep Throat".'

Tapper's face lit up in delight. 'Really? "Deep Throat?"'

'Herr Tapper, I think you need to tell me everything.'

Anita got out of the shower. She felt better for the long dousing. She even found that she was looking forward to her drink with Ewan Strachan. She had got to the office about nine to see whether there had been any developments. She had interrupted a conversation between Moberg and Westermark. They had stopped talking when she came into Moberg's office and she assumed Westermark had been telling the chief inspector about his exploits the night before, which were bound to include lurid details of his latest conquest.

Moberg hadn't any positive news. Forensics hadn't been able to place Mednick in the kitchen, so there was the possibility that they would have to let him go. They could charge him with possession of an unlicensed firearm, resisting arrest and threatening a police officer, but the murder charge wouldn't stick unless they unearthed something new in the next few days. There was no sign of Valquist on the CCTV, but that didn't mean he hadn't been to the apartment that night. He was becoming their prime suspect. As for the Andreas Tapper connection, Roslyn had confirmed that the initial contact with "Deep Throat" has been about five months ago – a month after Tapper's death. 'So unless he's contacting Roslyn from beyond the grave, I think that link is dead,' joked Moberg. But he was hoping to hear from Nordlund later, and then that end of the investigation would be cleared up.

Before she left, Moberg had asked just in passing if she knew whether "her journalist friend" was still around. She told them that Strachan was flying back to the UK tomorrow morning from Kastrup. Moberg and Westermark exchanged glances, which she had interpreted as the usual pathetic boys' reaction to anybody they thought she might currently be connected with emotionally/romantically/sexually. Normally, she shrugged off their innuendo-laden reactions, but this time she felt embarrassed. And that disconcerted her. There was nothing going on, she had thought defensively.

Then she and Olander had headed back to Lund to establish Valquist's movements before he went back to his apartment in his parents' home. This entailed dragging some disgruntled students out of bed and getting them to confirm, between yawns, that Valquist had given his talk and that a few of them went for a drink afterwards. He left at ten, so that story held up.

Now she caught herself in the semi-steamed-up mirror. Her body wasn't that bad for her age. She twirled round to see her bottom. Then laughed at herself. That was still nicely shaped. She still had a *snygg rumpa*, as Björn had called it in the days when he was still interested. As she dried herself, she wondered how long it had been since she had last had a man. Ages. And she had tried hard to forget that occasion as he had been a definite mistake. Too much drink at a midsummer party in Simrishamn.

Though she had Lasse, she had often found it difficult to be on her own with no other half. No mutual support. He was always sympathetic, but there were certain things she didn't feel it was right to burden him with. And now he had gone away to university, there was no one to confide in after a bad day at the office. No one to take her frustrations out on or to share the funny moments that had happened at work. She had spent the last few years being strong for Lasse. That strength she had had to take into the workplace, too. The police might be changing and the number of women joining the force was now substantial; but in the upper echelons, female officers still had to prove themselves to some of their sceptical male colleagues.

They had to be twice as good just to be judged on the same level as the men, especially in serious crime. It had made her harder, more abrasive sometimes. It wasn't really her. It was a front.

In her early days, she had broken down and cried in front of a senior male officer. His pitying look was seared on her memory. She had sworn it would never happen again. It hadn't, though she had retreated into a cubicle in the ladies on the odd occasion to sort out her feelings, with a hanky stuffed in her mouth to stem the tears of frustration or humiliation. She was aware of her vulnerability and, to her shame, believed it to be a weakness and not a sign of her humanity.

In front of the mirror, she rubbed her wet hair vigorously with the towel. Well, sod Moberg, sod Westermark, sod the lot of them; she was going to enjoy her drink tonight.

Nordlund had a coffee in his hand now. He had made it himself while Linas Tapper had gone and had a quick wash and brush-up. Nordlund watched the kids playing in the snow below. Most were immigrants; many from war-torn Iraq. How did they exchange their warm climate for the cold of Sweden? At least they no longer had the fear of being blown up every time they went shopping. Not that they were receiving a warm welcome from many native Swedes, who regarded them with suspicion. Some with downright hostility. Tapper was smarter and more alert when he returned, though he had a glass of whisky with him. He took a sip before he started his story.

'It began that night, last April. Andreas suddenly turned up. I hadn't seen him for months. He'd been drinking. He was drinking more after he left Säpo. His wife left him after he lost his job. Silly cow. He was really down. So I helped him polish off the bottle of Absolut he'd brought. Suddenly he came out with it. "We did it, you know", he said. I didn't know what he was talking about until he mentioned Palme. He didn't go into detail, but he implied that members of Säpo were behind the killing. It was a set-up. A right-wing element in the security police thought Palme was getting too pally with the communists, blacks, lefties, you name it.'

'Was Andreas one of these right-wingers?' asked Nordlund.

'I never thought so. I was under the impression he actually admired Palme. But he didn't like the flood of immigrants coming in. They're bloody everywhere. These apartments are full of them. Most can't speak Swedish.'

Nordlund let it pass. 'So, if Andreas knew about the murder, why didn't he come out and say something? Especially after he was chucked out.'

Tapper shook his head and forced a smile. 'I asked the very same question.' He took a swig of his whisky. 'He said he was scared shitless. "You don't mess with these guys." His very words.'

Tapper stood up and went back into the kitchen. He re-emerged with the bottle of whisky. Nordlund noticed it was Bells. 'Were there any details?'

Tapper pursed his lips. 'Not really. Wasn't that enough?'

Of course it wasn't, but Nordlund wanted to get as much information out of him as he could while he was talkative. 'So your brother's death…?'

'It was them, of course,' Tapper said bitterly. 'Couldn't afford to let him get out of control. He might blab something. They must have set it all up. Shut him up for good.'

Nordlund surveyed the room again, the faded furniture and the new electronic equipment. He had got money from somewhere very recently.

'Where do you work, herr Tapper?'

Tapper gazed over the rim of the raised glass. 'At the Willy's supermarket. Other side of the road into town. Why?'

Nordlund gestured towards the television. 'Nice and new. Expensive?'

'I can afford it,' Tapper said defensively.

'I didn't think shelf-stackers at Willy's were paid so much.'

'What makes you think I stack shelves?'

'If you had been a manager, I'm sure you would have said so.'

Tapper sullenly sank back into his whisky.

'Right. What about Mick Roslyn? How did that happen?'

Tapper refreshed his glass from the bottle, which was disappearing rapidly. It was not Nordlund's idea of a Sunday breakfast. 'I saw an article in *Expressen* about a film company that were doing something on Olof Palme. So I thought they might be interested in what my brother had said and what had happened to him.'

'So why all the cloak and dagger stuff with your "Henrik Larsson" bit?'

This time Tapper laughed. 'I phoned up Roslyn's company and got someone called Valquist. As soon as I said I knew who had killed Palme, I could hear he was getting all enthusiastic. So I thought there might be some kronor in it for me. He was wetting himself with excitement by the time I'd finished. That's why I invented all the "Henrik Larsson" shit. Arranged to meet Roslyn in a dark car park in the centre of Stockholm to add to the sense of mystery. I pretended to be Andreas, without giving a name of course. I reckoned if I told Roslyn the truth about my brother, he might have second thoughts and bugger off. He was impressed by the titbits I gave him. I said he could have more if he paid me. He agreed, so the next time we met up he gave me some money, and I gave him some more information. We met a few times. Nothing wrong with that,' he finished off defiantly.

'But you didn't have much to give him.'

'I gave him enough to pay for these.' He chuckled as he nodded towards his recent acquisitions. 'I may have elaborated a bit, but there was truth in there.'

Nordlund picked up his coffee, which had gone cold. He put it down again.

'I've seen your record. The Stockholm police were very helpful. When you ran that car bodyshop in Hammarby, some pretty dodgy vehicles came out of your workshop. All sorts of lethal combinations. One bit of a car stuck to another. The judge described them as "deathtraps". And that's not the only dubious dealing you've had over the years. You were bullshitting people then. You could be bullshitting me now.'

Tapper pointed the glass at Nordlund. 'If I'm bullshitting, why are you here? I'll tell you why. Because they're trying to shut up Mick Roslyn just like they shut up my brother.'

CHAPTER 26

Anita laughed at Ewan's well-rehearsed anecdote about his father's embarrassingly prehistoric attempts to explain the facts of life. She was really having a good time. Ewan had already made her laugh at a number of his stories. Nearly all were told at his expense. She liked that. When he laughed, he was better looking than she had thought. Lose a bit of weight and he might be quite presentable. It was the blue eyes that kept catching her attention. They were playful. He had probably been a mischievous kid, which made her think of her own childhood.

'Do you get to Durham often?'

'Occasionally. Sometimes I cover a cultural event there.'

Anita twisted the top off her snus tin and popped a sachet into her mouth. It was when having a drink that she most missed a cigarette. They were sitting in Perssons, a small and intimate bar at the end of Storgatan.

'It is a beautiful city. I was very happy there.' She smiled at the recollection. 'My father used to take me for a walk round the river banks. In the summer we sometimes went on the river... in those old rowing boats. There were punts too, but Dad never had the nerve to try one of them.'

'I'm not sure if they're still there. I'll look next time I'm through.'

'I would like to go back. See if it still has that magic.'

'It's changed. The university is even bigger and it's taken over many of the green spaces. But the castle still looks as dramatic as ever. And the cathedral, of course.' He paused as though caught up in recollections of his own. 'You should come over. Visit. I'll show you around.'

She watched him closely. He really meant it. It was tempting. She hadn't got anything planned for a holiday this year. Lasse probably had his own plans, which would involve Rebecka and not her.

'I don't know. They say you should never go back to a place you have been really happy in. Were you happy in Durham?'

The cheery expression he had worn most of the evening disappeared. 'Part of the time. Another drink?' He pointed to Anita's empty glass.

Perssons still only had a smattering of customers. The weather and the back end of the weekend were keeping the drinkers away. As she watched Ewan at the bar, she realised she had hit a nerve. She would steer clear of Durham because he was being so nice to her. And attentive. And polite. On his return, she noticed he had changed from Czech beer to a glass of rum.

'There's no real ale here like in The Pickwick,' he said by way of explanation. 'Rum was my old man's drink. He was in the navy in the war. Actually, it was the Swedish navy that gave us our expression "pissed as a neut". It came about after some British naval officers had had a night's drinking with their Swedish counterparts. Afterwards, they said that they had got as "pissed as neutrals", which was then shortened to "neuts".'

She put on a mock-serious face. 'I am glad that Sweden's contributed to British cultural life. There's more to us than Abba, IKEA and Björn Borg.'

'And Sven-Göran Eriksson. Pornography as well. Don't forget that.'

'I think you will find that most of that horrible stuff comes from Denmark,' she said with some distaste.

Ewan smirked. 'I apologise. British males prefer to think of Swedes as being the sexy ones. It doesn't quite work with Danes for some reason.'

'Sweden offers so much more,' Anita said indignantly. She had had many an argument defending Sweden during her time in London. The British couldn't see beyond the obvious. Much as she loved them, it was their sense of superiority that struck her as one of the nation's least appealing traits. They always seemed so arrogant when it came to history, architecture, culture, music and sport – and so condescending about what they saw as lesser nations. It made her patriotic, which surprised her as she had never thought of herself as being remotely nationalistic.

Ewan was taken aback at this sudden turn. 'I didn't mean to–'

'Ingmar Bergman, Greta Garbo, Carl Linnaeus, Alfred Nobel...' She stopped herself in mid-rant. She was sounding petulant.

'Great design, too,' said Ewan, breaking the awkward silence that followed. 'And buildings. Just look at the Turning Torso. It's very Scandinavian. Who designed it?'

Anita's eyes widened. 'The Turning Torso was designed by a Santiago Calatrava.'

'That doesn't sound very Swedish.'

'No, he's Spanish!' Then they both laughed.

Moberg picked up the phone in his office. It was late, but he had much on his mind. He had had another conversation with Westermark, which he had decided to act upon. And he was still awaiting news from Västerås. And the truth was that he was avoiding going home. His third marriage was going the way of the first two. The only thing keeping it together was the fear of paying out three lots of alimony. Nordlund was on the other end of the line.

'Linas Tapper is our "Deep Throat",' Nordlund explained. 'Doing it for the money he can get out of Roslyn.'

'So we can forget him and that line of enquiry?'

'Not entirely. He claims that Säpo were behind his brother's fatal car accident. There were certainly no other vehicles involved. No witnesses. And he believes that they probably got to Malin Lovgren, too.'

'He sounds like a fucking fantasist,' Moberg said dismissively.

'I thought so at first, but his brother was in Stockholm at the time of Palme's murder and claimed, albeit after a lot of booze, that he knew who had killed the prime minister. He indicated that it was an inside job.'

'So what do you want to do, Henrik?'

'Give me another day – or a couple at most. I'd like to check out the brother's death. If there are question marks over it, we may have some rogue ex-Säpo operatives on the loose.'

'OK. But time isn't on our side. And don't piss off the local cops, because I'll get it in the neck from the commissioner.'

'By the way, is there anything more on Valquist?' Nordlund asked.

'No. But something else has cropped up.'

Anita threw her coat over the sofa and flopped down next to it. She was tired but happily mellow. The evening had been good. Fun actually. She hadn't been that relaxed for quite some time. She had tried to persuade Ewan to go up the Turning Torso before he left because she had a contact at the building who would let him up onto the roof. He said he would love to, but his train was early. Their parting had been awkward. Neither had known what to do.

'I didn't have time to tell you about the Earl of Bothwell,' Ewan said, turning up his collar against the cold. 'Interesting story. Maybe next time?'

'You think there'll be a next time?' she teased.

'I hope so.' His eyes locked onto hers. She glanced away, unable to match his gaze.

'Thanks for a lovely evening.' He leant forward as though he were going to kiss her on the cheek but ended up holding out his hand for her to shake.

She, too, turned up her collar. 'I hope it's not so cold next time you come. It's lovely here in the summer.'

He smiled. 'It must be nearly freezing now.'

'Zero degrees Celsius.' Then her face creased into a wide grin. 'Anders Celsius was Swedish.'

Anita zapped the television on. She put it on mute and flicked through the channels. There was nothing worth watching, so she switched it off again. She got up and went into the kitchen. She was too weary to eat. A cup of tea would have to do as a nightcap. As she waited for the water in the pan to boil, she found herself wondering what Lasse would think of Ewan. Would he like him? Would they have interests in common? Football maybe? Why was she thinking these things? She hardly knew Ewan, and yet she was worrying about how her son would react. It was stupid. She might never see him again, let alone contemplate getting close to him.

Her mobile interrupted her confused thoughts. She went back into the living room and found the phone in her pocket. It was a work number. She groaned. 'Anita Sundström.'

'Anita.' It was Moberg. 'I don't think you're going to like this.'

CHAPTER 27

Ewan packed up his overnight bag. It was fuller than when he had arrived. He'd had to buy some extra clothes as he'd only enough with him for the original two nights. He shut down his computer and packed that up, too. Last night, after he had left Anita at about half-nine, he had completed his follow-up article on the murder. He had quoted Mick, using things he had said before he went into the safe house. He wrote as though he had had access to Mick after he had gone into hiding. As the piece was concentrating on the capture of Halvar Mednick, he wasn't able to overdo the Olof Palme assassination theory, which was the best angle. However, he did again hint at the dark machinations of a secretive government organisation. It was too vague to pinpoint, but had enough clues to sound interesting. The fact that Mick had been hidden away helped the mystery quota. And, as before, he had built up Inspector Sundström's part in the story. Anyway, Brian would be pleased.

He went to the window. It was another cold day, though the sun was trying to heave its way over the horizon to spread a little light. The locals had said that it had been a mild winter so far. He could see the distorted white blocks of the Turning Torso. If he made it back to cover the trial, he would take up Anita's offer and get himself up to the top. His feelings about Malmö were split. Half of him was glad to be escaping; the other half yearned to stay and be close to Anita. He had relived their evening together many times already. He had so wanted to kiss her when he was saying goodbye, but his nerve had failed him. The handshake seemed pathetic. So bloody British. However, two positives came out of it all. He had got the impression that she would be happy to see him again if he could ever get back to Malmö; and he had also managed to get her email address. The first thing he did when he returned to the hotel was to put her details in his email contacts. He had even started to compose one to her, thanking her for a great night. On reflection, he decided it might be best to wait until he got back to Tyneside, and that would give him an excuse to write – back safely, thanks for help, fun evening, etc. This was a woman he had only met six days ago – at a murder scene – but he knew that he was in love with her.

For the last time he made his way to the station. It took five minutes. He wanted to be early as he had a fear of missing trains, flights, ferries. His train was at twenty past nine. He was twenty minutes early. He took a free copy of the *Metro*. There was nothing on the front page about Malin Lovgren that he could see. After days of full coverage, the Swedish media were waiting for the police to release further details on the case. All speculation had been used up over the weekend. He checked the platform for the Copenhagen train before wandering into the book booth in the middle of the station concourse. He still had ten minutes left when he walked through to the platform. His train was already in and people were boarding. Some late commuters, early Copenhagen shoppers and a few people dragging huge suitcases heading for the sun via Kastrup airport. He didn't blame them.

He was about to get on board when he noticed a familiar figure coming along the platform. He couldn't believe it – it was Anita. This was fantastic. She had come to see him off. 'Anit...'

He didn't get her full name out because he had just noticed that she was not alone. She was with a man who looked suspiciously like a policeman, despite the leather jacket, the jeans and the expensive shoes. It was the supercilious sneer below the blond cropped hair that alerted Ewan.

'This is Inspector Karl Westermark,' Anita explained rather formally when they reached him.

Westermark whipped out his warrant card for a moment and then casually put it back in his inside jacket pocket.

'We would like you to accompany us back to police headquarters.'

Ewan thought he had misheard. The noise around him suddenly vanished. He could see Anita repeating the request, but he couldn't hear her. Why was the woman he had fallen in love with asking him to go to the police station? This woman had laughed at his jokes only last night. At least she had the grace to look embarrassed.

'I can't. I've got a plane to catch,' Ewan managed to get out between gasps of air. He felt as though he had just been winded by a well-aimed punch to the solar plexus.

Westermark sneered again. 'I am not thinking that you understand. If you refuse, we will arrest you here.'

Anita switched on the tape machine and leant towards it: '*Klockan är sju minuter över elva. Närvarande är herr Ewan Strachan, kriminalinspektör Westermark och kriminalinspektör Sundström. Samtalet kommer att hållas på engelska.*' Turning towards Ewan, 'We will speak in English.'

She had found it difficult to order her thoughts from the moment she had received the phone call from Moberg. It had disconcertingly turned her world upside down, yet in many ways it vindicated her first instincts. There had been something wrong about the relationship between Ewan Strachan and Mick Roslyn. She knew both of them had lied to her. Even now, the reason wasn't obvious. What was clear was that Westermark – at Moberg's prompting – had unearthed information about the British journalist, which had resulted in their sitting in a stark interrogation room at seven minutes past eleven on Monday morning, 18th February. She knew she should have told Moberg and Westermark that she had been out for a drink with the suspect – twice. That compromised her official position. The fact that she hadn't mentioned it when she'd had the opportunity now made her nervous that it would come out in the interrogation and cause her serious embarrassment. So why hadn't she spoken up?

She realised that she desperately wanted to be part of this case, to find Malin Lovgren's killer. And she knew she had been onto something when the rest believed Mednick to be the murderer. She had asked the questions they hadn't – or most of them. She had come to believe that Mick Roslyn was the key to the murder, and not Malin Lovgren. And she was damned if Moberg and Westermark were going to bugger it up when she was the one who had been right. Only this was a twist she hadn't foreseen.

What was adding to the pressure was conducting this particular interview with Westermark at her side. She could sense that he was enjoying her discomfiture. Moberg had insisted that she should lead the interrogation because of her fluent English. Westermark was there to intimidate the suspect.

'Can you state your name and address? For the tape.'

'I can't believe you've brought me here,' Ewan started to protest once more. He had done nothing else since they had picked him up at the station.

'Your name and your address,' Westermark came in sharply. Anita couldn't think of anyone else she knew on the force who could make a straightforward statement sound so much like a threat.

'Ewan Strachan. I live at Etal Court, North Shields, Tyne

and Wear.' Then, with pointed emphasis towards Westermark: 'That's in the United Kingdom, of which I am a citizen.' Turning to Anita. 'Why am I here?'

Anita ignored the question. 'We need you to tell us again your exact movements from late Monday afternoon.'

'For God's sake! It's all in my statement.' There was real frustrated anger in his voice.

'Just answer the kriminalinspektör,' commanded Westermark.

Ewan glared at Westermark before he spoke. Then, slowly and deliberately, he began. 'I went out for a meal in Lilla-thingy square. Had a drink and a bite to eat. Then I went to The Pickwick pub. After that, I went back to the hotel.'

'And what time was that?' Anita asked before Westermark did. She wasn't going to let Westermark wrest control of the interrogation.

'About 9.30. Wanted to prepare myself and get a good night's sleep before the big day. Well, it was a big day, but not in the way I was expecting.'

'Did anybody see you return to the hotel?'

'There was a girl on reception. I gave her a smile. She didn't smile back, but I'm sure she'll vouch for my movements.'

'And you didn't leave the hotel after that?'

'Of course not.' He was having difficulty reining in his temper.

Anita opened a manila file and Ewan recognised the statement he had signed. 'And you say that you had never had any contact with Malin Lovgren at any time. You had never seen her or talked to her.'

'No. Never.' Ewan was becoming increasingly irritated, even though it was Anita who was asking him these questions. He was the prey and she was the beautiful hunter. 'I've already said so.'

Anita picked up another piece of paper, which contained

long lists of numbers. 'We've got a record of all the calls that came in and out of Malin Lovgren's apartment, including on the night she was murdered.' She pointed to the last figure on the page. 'The last call she had came in at 10.49. It lasted nearly four minutes. The strange thing is that it was from *your* mobile.'

She could see Ewan was stunned by this snippet of information. She had known the number was his because she had been able to double-check it on her own mobile. She hadn't mentioned that to Moberg either.

The man who had been so relaxed last night was obviously fighting to regain his composure. 'OK, I did talk to her.'

'And why didn't you mention this when you were asked originally?'

'I don't know. Didn't seem that important.'

Westermark let out a snort of derision.

'I would have thought it was very important.' He squirmed under her gaze; it was not a gratifying sight. 'Why did you call her?'

'I… erm… I wanted to make sure everything was still on for the next day. I've interviewed a lot of luvvies and they're not the most reliable species.' His flip remark didn't elicit a response. Neither Anita nor Westermark knew what "luvvies" were.

'And you spoke to Malin?' He nodded. 'What did you discuss?'

'Arrangements. She said that everything was fine. And that Mick–'

'That Mick was still in Stockholm.'

'Yes.'

'So you knew she was alone,' Westermark butted in.

'Big deal,' Ewan countered off-handedly.

'And you didn't arrange to go round and see her for a nightcap?' said Anita, taking the interrogation back into her hands.

'No. Why should I?'

Anita put the telephone list back in the file. 'When I saw you at your hotel, you said that you only drank tea at night.' Westermark turned quizzically to Anita. 'Malin was about to make two cups of tea moments before she was killed.' Anita didn't ask for an answer and let the implied suggestion hang in the air. 'You say that at the time of the murder, you were asleep?'

Ewan shifted in his seat. 'Trying to, anyway.'

'So you have no alibi.' This was Westermark.

'I assume I'd have been seen by the receptionist if I had tried to sneak out.' The hostility between Ewan and Westermark crackled.

'You can get out at the side and the back of this hotel. I have checked,' Westermark added with a smug grin.

'This is all so fantastic, it's… it's unbelievable!' Ewan was now appealing to Anita. 'A phone call. A cup of tea. It's ridiculous.'

'The next day,' Anita continued. 'Can you go through what you did on the Tuesday morning?'

Ewan sighed theatrically and moved his backside again. 'I didn't fancy breakfast at the hotel, so I went out to that modern shopping centre. Triangle or whatever. I had a coffee,' he said with exaggerated emphasis. 'Spent a bit of time there and then went back to the hotel to get ready. Have a piss and brush-up. Then I headed off to Mick's apartment.'

'You were knowing the way?' asked Westermark.

'I can read a map,' came Ewan's sarcastic reply. 'Shall I go on?' Anita nodded. 'I was there in time. I pressed the buzzer a few times, but there was no reply. I was getting annoyed because it occurred to me that Mick might have forgotten I was coming.'

'You knew that Malin would be there. You had already talked to her.'

'That's right. It was all a bit weird. When a young woman

came out, I managed to get in. By the time I'd staggered up four flights of stairs, it was eight minutes past eleven.' Staring at Westermark: 'I checked my watch.'

'Why didn't you go up in the lift?' asked Anita.

'I get claustrophobia.'

'Or was it to be seen?'

'I don't understand.'

'Carry on, please.'

Ewan's puzzled expression changed as he thought carefully before filling in the details up to the point where he was holding the body and Mick and the photographer came in.

'Why did you touch the body?' asked Westermark. 'Strange, no?'

'I don't know why. I think at first it was to see if she was OK. And when she obviously wasn't, it was as though she needed comforting. People don't always do rational things when faced with totally unexpected situations.'

'Inspector Westermark has a suspicious mind. He thinks you were being very clever.' They had talked through all the possibilities and scenarios – Moberg, Westermark and herself – when she had come in at half past five that morning. 'He thinks that you killed Malin the night before and used the opportunity the next morning to cover her body with your prints and fibres so there would be a natural explanation for them being there.'

Ewan had regained his composure. 'Well, you can tell Inspector Westermark that he's an even bigger fucking idiot than he looks.'

Westermark was out of his seat in a flash and made a grab across the table at Ewan. Ewan had anticipated such a move and lurched back in his chair, evading the policeman's outstretched hand.

'Karl!' Anita shouted.

Westermark checked himself and angrily sat down. Ewan's lips creased into a hint of a smile. A victory of sorts.

Anita waited for a simmering calm to descend. 'The kitchen?'

'What about the kitchen?'

'Did you go into it?'

'Erm... yes, I did. After Mick hit me. I needed to spray water on my face. I didn't know where the bathroom was.'

'That puzzles me.'

'What does?'

'Roslyn attacking you. He saw you bending over his wife. He couldn't have known she was dead in that first moment. Did he think you were molesting her? But he must have known it was you because he had invited you there in the first place. Did he *assume* you were...?'

'I have no idea. He just lost it for second.'

Anita said ruminatively, 'I wonder whether he attacked you, not because of Malin, but because it was you.'

'Sorry, you've lost me, Inpsector Sundström.' She had no idea what Ewan was making of this turn of events, but he was playing the game and not giving away the fact that they had been in danger of becoming friends, or even something more, only yesterday. Westermark fidgeted and she was aware that he was growing impatient. She knew where he wanted her to go next.

'You know how Malin Lovgren was killed?'

Ewan nodded his head slowly. 'I know she was strangled. That's what the papers say and, remember, I did see the body at very close hand. Unless she had died of a heart attack, there couldn't have been any other way.'

'Malin was grabbed from behind. She was caught in what is called a chokehold. The airway was blocked at the front of the neck. She was throttled.' Anita paused. 'But you know all about that. Inspector Westermark has been investigating your police record.'

'Northumbria Police were helping me very much.'

Westermark smiled, his lips curling maliciously. 'They say you tried to kill a man.'

'But I didn't kill him.'

Anita opened up the file again. 'December 20th, 2004.'

'I was drunk. It was another journalist.'

'And the circumstances?'

'It was a Christmas get-together. He was winding me up.'

'What is "winding up?"' Westermark queried.

'Taking the piss. Ollie was making fun of me. We had worked together on the sports desk and, when I moved over to *Novo News*, he thought it was a pathetic comedown. Sports reporters like to think they're a bit harder than the rest of the hacks. He was mocking me for covering crappy craft fairs and vacuous social events. He was right, actually, but I didn't want to hear that at the time. Not after a lot of drink.'

'So you lost your temper,' Anita suggested.

'He just pushed me too far, and I snapped.'

Anita made a play of studying the file again. 'According to the report, you grabbed an Oliver Turner round the neck. A chokehold, in fact.' Ewan contemplated the table. He said nothing. 'The same as Malin Lovgren.'

Ewan raised his eyes. 'I didn't kill her. And I didn't kill Ollie either. He dropped the charges. I got a bollocking from the management but wasn't given the bullet.'

Anita closed the file again. 'Why round the neck? Why did you grab Oliver Turner round the neck?'

'I don't know. Heat of the moment. Just instinctive. It's better than punching someone. You might get punched back. Ollie's quite a big bugger.'

'When I asked you before, you said you hadn't done any military service. But have you done any sort of combat training? Or martial arts?'

Ewan licked his dry lips. 'Is this going to incriminate me?'

'You need to tell the truth.'

He sighed. 'Yes. At university. In my first year I did judo.' Anita and Westermark swapped glances. 'I joined up with Mick. We thought it would be a laugh. It wasn't, actually, because he was far better than I was. He kept throwing me all over the place.' Anita stared at Ewan. He couldn't read her thoughts. Westermark was smiling smugly to himself. 'These things don't prove I killed the woman. Why should I? I haven't got a motive. More to the point, you can't find one.'

'That's all for the moment,' said Anita leaning over to turn off the tape.

'I can go?'

'No,' smirked Westermark as he eased himself off his chair. 'You will be our guest,' he mocked. 'Now I'm going to be examining your computer. What secrets are you are keeping there?' He left the room. Anita hung back.

'Anita. Honest to God, I didn't kill her. You've got to believe me.'

Anita was having difficulty keeping it official. 'We can keep you here for the moment while we carry out further investigations.'

'This can't be happening to me.'

'You can have a lawyer present. Shall I arrange one for you?'

His laughter was hoarse. 'I don't trust them. My brother's one!'

'Ewan, I advise you to get one.'

'No. I'm not guilty. Getting a lawyer smacks of desperation. I'll get out of this because I'm innocent.'

'It is your decision. But I will inform the British consul in Malmö.'

A young policeman came into the room to escort Ewan to the cells.

'Can I make a phone call? I had better ring my editor. Now he *really* has a story.'

Anita nodded to the policeman. '*Telefon.*'

'Thanks.' Ewan sounded grateful. 'Anita. Do you think I'm guilty?'

She didn't give an answer. She hadn't got one.

Anita took off her glasses and squinted at the mirror. The ladies' washroom was empty. She was thankful that she didn't have to pretend to pass the time of day with one of her colleagues. Was it because she had begun to warm to Ewan Strachan that she was finding it difficult to believe that he could have cold-bloodedly murdered Malin Lovgren? He had a temper, which she had witnessed flashes of at their first meeting in the apartment and now in the interrogation room. But the slaying hadn't been carried out by someone who had lost control. The opposite, in fact. There had been nothing frenzied about it. Ewan's attack on his fellow journalist had been caused by a combustible combination of drink and derision. A moment of macho madness. Malin's death appeared more calculated, which brought her back to Nordlund's investigations in Stockholm. Ewan had the means – his judo experience would have equipped him for such a murderous manoeuvre. Yet the clinical nature of the act and the lack of compelling forensic evidence suggested a professional hand at work. Only Mednick's intervention had muddied the waters and distracted them from finding the real killer.

Anita doused her face in cold water. It was bracing, without banishing the tiredness she felt. She had hardly slept before dragging herself out in the pitch dark to get to the polishus for half five. She slowly dabbed her face with a paper towel before slipping her glasses back on. She wondered how Ewan would be feeling. Shocked? Bitter? Bewildered? If he was innocent, then he would hardly forgive her for arresting him. Strangely, that made her feel sad. But she must remain professional. She fished a brush out of her black hole of a bag and ran it through her hair. All they had was circumstantial evidence against Ewan.

He was right; they had no motive. And he certainly couldn't have planned it. It was only at Roslyn's suggestion that he was in Malmö in the first place. So why had he lied about the call to Malin? There was no obvious reason to keep it quiet.

Was Ewan their man? Their fledgling personal relationship complicated matters and only succeeded in kick-starting her natural instinct to worry. It was inextricably linked to the self-doubt which had haunted her throughout life. She could only grudgingly admire the total self-belief of colleagues like Moberg and Westermark, who took it for granted that they were right, even when they were proved wrong. Anita's lack of confidence both helped and hindered her in the job. It acted as an internal check on her assumptions on the one hand, while becoming a corrosive force that undermined her thoughts and actions on the other. Whether that helped to make her a decent cop, she wasn't sure. She certainly didn't fall into the maverick, Miss Marple or menopausal boozer categories that most female detectives found themselves pigeon-holed in in popular crime fiction and on TV shows.

She put the brush away and stared at the mirror. The person looking back wore a confused expression. She frowned, but it didn't make her appear any more decisive. She wondered whether Westermark's trawl through Ewan's computer would throw up any new clues. Though she felt the urge to flop into bed and try and catch up on some sleep, she knew she had to do something positive. She would go back and see Mick Roslyn. Now the woman in the mirror looked like someone who had made up her mind. She was going to find out once and for all what it was that Ewan and Roslyn had been unwilling to tell her. What had gone wrong in Durham?

CHAPTER 28

Distraction. That's what he had read. Deep breathing was also meant to help. It didn't. His mouth was dry, his palms sticky. He felt nauseous and his heart was thumping and the panic attack was almost upon him. The moment the cell door had slammed shut, all his claustrophobic fears began to run amok. This small room with its barred window, wooden bed, table clinging to the blank walls – and smell of oppression – was the nearest he had come to hell on earth. He wanted to scream for someone to let him out. He would go mad if he had to remain in here for more than a few minutes.

Distraction techniques. Think of something positive, the article had advised. Something that had brought you pleasure or happiness. A birthday celebration, a moment of personal triumph or picturing a loved one. He had given up on the first, there had been precious few of the second, and the third only kept producing Anita. Her laughing face from last night. The image grew stronger. The shimmer of light on her glasses giving way to the delight in her eyes. His breathing became more controlled. Why was he thinking of her when she was the one who had put him in this hellhole? Had she been suspicious of him all along? Was she so calculating that she could impassively spend an evening drinking with him when she thought him capable of murder?

Or was it that shit Westermark who was behind all this? There weren't many people he loathed at first sight, but the weaselly Westermark hit his hatred spot instantly. Ewan cursed himself. His instinct had been to get out of Sweden as soon as he knew the police had finished their initial enquiries and he was no longer needed. He had ignored it and had let himself be seduced into staying so he could be near Anita.

How could all of this have happened? It was the classic nightmare of the little man caught up in the big situation. Whom could he turn to? Brian had been no bloody use. After congratulating him on the two murder pieces, Brian's excitement hadn't allowed Ewan to get a word in edgeways until he bellowed down the phone, 'They've fucking arrested me!'

'What for?'

'Murder.'

A stunned silence followed. Ewan waited for the recriminations, the vilifications and the inevitable sacking.

'That could make an interesting angle.'

'What?' Ewan choked incredulously.

'Reports right from the epicentre of the case. What it feels like fighting to clear your name, battling for justice.'

'I don't believe this.'

'You didn't kill her, did you?'

'Of course I bloody didn't!'

'There you are. I'll get things moving this end. I'll get onto upstairs. They love what we've done so far. Put the weight of the group behind it. Massive exposure. Will you be able to send reports out?'

'I don't bloody know. As soon as they realise they're barking up the wrong tree, I'm out of here for ever.' Ewan had slammed down the phone. Now he was in the cells. Maybe he should let Anita bring in a lawyer. Then again, if he didn't, they might conclude that he really was innocent. Show he wasn't hiding behind the law. Or was he just being damned stupid and naïve? At least he still had one card left to play. It was just a matter of picking the right moment to use it.

'Ewan? For real?' Mick was staring out towards the field at the back. He had been outside the farmhouse when Anita arrived. Wrapped in a thick coat, he was smoking a cigarette. He hadn't accepted Anita's invitation to talk inside as he was sick of seeing the walls of what he now regarded as his own prison. 'He's in custody?'

'Yes. This morning.'

'I can't believe it. Are you sure?'

'No.' Anita could see her breath. Her eyes were watering from the raw chill. It made her realise that she wanted to go home, put a duvet on the sofa and snuggle up under it with her book. 'We know he called Malin on the night of the murder. He lied about that. He has no alibi for the time of the killing. He could have carried it out because he told us that he did judo at university.'

Mick flicked away his cigarette. It glowed momentarily on the rock-hard ground. 'So did I. We both joined the judo club at the same time.'

When she was detailing the main points of evidence to this third party – albeit the most interested party in the case – she could see how flimsy it all appeared. The case against Ewan Strachan was not strong.

'We can't find a motive,' she said, almost apologetically.

Mick took out of his coat pocket an expensive silver cigarette lighter and absently flicked it on and off. Little shoots of flame reared up and then were immediately extinguished. Anita had no idea what was on his mind.

He put the lighter away. 'I can provide you with one.'

CHAPTER 29

'Debbie Usher.'

It was as though Anita had given Ewan an electric shock. All colour drained from his face. For a moment, his eyes bulged and he looked around the bare room wildly as though he was trying to find an escape route. There wasn't one. The huge figure of Chief Inspector Moberg sitting opposite him was the most obvious obstacle

'How do you know about her?' His question was barely audible.

'Tell us about Durham and Debbie Usher,' Anita urged.

The fact that Moberg was sitting in on the interrogation was a bone of contention with Westermark. He had done the background checking on Ewan Strachan and felt he should be in there. Moberg brusquely overruled him at the meeting they had had an hour before. Once Anita had told them about her conversation with Roslyn, Westermark was even more convinced that the journalist was their killer. He didn't bother disguising his venom when discussing him. He had reported that the search of the computer hadn't thrown up anything significant. 'Hasn't even any porn on there, so he's probably a poof,' he said with a knowing glance at Anita.

Afterwards, by the coffee machine, Westermark had collared Anita.

'I saw the articles Strachan had written about the case. He makes it sound like you were the only one working on it. He must love you,' he said nastily. 'Trying to get into your knickers?'

Anita was feeling uncomfortable, but it didn't stop her hitting back. 'Not likely if he's a poof!'

That reptilian smile appeared again as she was attempting to move away from the machine with a coffee in her hand.

'I found something else. Your email address.'

'What of it? I suspect your email address book is full of journalist contacts. I'm sure that bimbo on the *Sydsvenska Dagbladet* is in there.'

'I bet you're better in bed than she is.'

'Were you born a creep or did you have to work at it?'

'But your *boyfriend* started to write you an email last night. It was in the *draft* section. Thanking you for the "wonderful evening".'

This wasn't something Anita had expected or wanted to hear, and definitely not from a snake like Westermark.

'Is that why you were soft on him in the interrogation?'

Anita was furious that her professional integrity was being questioned.

'I did my job properly in there. Just because you were acting like a testosteroned tosser.'

Westermark ignored the insult. 'I don't know what you got up to,' the insinuation was clear, 'but it puts you in a difficult position, Anita. You're interrogating someone who you've just had a "wonderful evening" with. If the boss gets wind of this, you'll be straight off the case.'

'And will he get wind of it?' Anita challenged.

'That depends. Maybe if you were more accommodating? I wouldn't say no to having a "wonderful evening" with you.'

'Karl, you are the biggest piece of shit I've ever come across.'

She stormed off to her room. When she shut the door behind her, she was breathing heavily. She knew she had made a real enemy.

Ewan had retreated into his mug of coffee before he spoke. 'You must have got that from Mick.' Anita nodded confirmation. 'It was the first time I'd been away from home. At Durham. It was all so exhilarating.' He manipulated the mug with his fingers. 'And Mick was exciting. Women flocked to him. He was very handsome. Still is.'

'What is this having to doing with this girl?' interrupted Moberg exasperatedly. He was anxious to get to the detail. Anita wished he would belt up for a change: they'd get what they wanted if they were patient.

Anger flared in Ewan's eyes as he regarded the massive chief inspector. 'Because you will not understand.' He spoke the words with fierce deliberation. 'You will not understand unless you know things.'

Moberg held up his hands in acknowledgement.

Ewan's gaze returned to the mug. 'The girls loved him. He loved them... then left them. I fed off the scraps from the great man's table. When Mick entered the room at a party, every head turned. I trotted along behind. Don't get me wrong, I didn't mind in the least. I basked in his reflected glory. For two years. After the first year, we lived out of college. We moved into a house together. We shared it with another guy. Trevor from Bristol. Have no idea where he is now. Bristol probably.'

Anita could feel Moberg growing fidgety beside her. Though his English wasn't very good, he could understand more than he could speak. Yet some of what Ewan was saying would be going straight over his head.

'It was the end of our second year,' Ewan continued. 'Summer term. Amazingly, I found myself at a party without

Mick. But Debbie was there. Oh, she was. Even in my inebriated state, I could see she was something special. Not in an obvious way. She wasn't drop-dead gorgeous. But she was pretty. Long, rich red hair. Real red; not ginger like mine.' Ewan suddenly glanced up at Moberg. 'Ever fallen in love at first sight?' Moberg was taken aback at being put on the spot. He shook his head, as though Ewan was mad.

Ewan smiled to himself. 'Funnily enough, I can't see Swedes doing that. You're too damned practical a nation.' His eyes caught Anita's. She tried not to flush as she used her notes as an excuse not to engage his stare.

'Love finds you in the most unexpected places. It jumps out and grabs you by the throat.' Ewan turned his attention back to Moberg. 'A bad choice of metaphor in the circumstances. But that is what happened that night in the chaplaincy. And do you know what the most extraordinary thing was?'

Moberg and Anita were both now feeling awkward, for different reasons. Moberg hated men talking about their emotions, unless it concerned football. Anita realised that Ewan's feelings were strong and genuine and that she had been the target of them until the arrest. Neither answered.

'Debbie felt the same about me. I couldn't believe it. She liked me... loved me for what I was. I wasn't smart, or witty. And certainly not sexy. Just average. But that was enough for her. It was so good after that. We had a fantastic summer together. Travelled around Europe on one of those student rail cards. France, Italy, Greece. Best time of my life. The next term we moved in together. It was a horrible little student flat in a grotty terraced house, but I didn't care. Life couldn't get any better. But it couldn't last.'

'Why not?' Anita found herself asking. 'You said you loved each other.'

'Ah, you forget Mick. And no one is allowed to forget Mick.'

'So what did Mick do?' Anita found herself being sucked

into taking sides. Ewan versus Mick.

'Nothing at first. He was fine. I thought he was even pleased for me that I had found someone. But the more he met Debbie, the more he discovered how special she was. She was a genuine person. No side to her.'

'This I am not understanding.' Moberg was struggling again.

'She didn't think badly of people. Unlike the police, she only saw the good in everyone.' Even Moberg had to smile.

'You may find it hard to believe, but I was a bit like that, too. I was just being naïve. Pathetically naïve. Anyway, because Debbie never showed any interest in Mick, he began to see her as a challenge. Men like that do. The thrill of the chase. Suddenly he was always coming round to the flat. Sometimes I'd come back and he was there, talking to her.'

'You were jealous?' Anita was struck by the inevitability of his tale.

'Strangely, not at first. Pride at first. I had something that Mick wanted. But then pride was replaced by irritation, and irritation by jealousy. Deep, gut-wrenching jealousy. Ever felt that? I became nervous whenever Mick appeared. I suddenly became tongue-tied. His jokes were effortless; mine were forced. My confidence drained. It was so corrosive. I got edgy, moody. Debbie and I started arguing about the silliest of things. Stupid stuff.'

Ewan took a gulp of his coffee. It tasted horrible, but he needed something to break the spell of despair he was recreating in his head. He pushed the mug away. 'Then the inevitable happened. I came back from a lecture early because I had forgotten to take an essay in. Debbie and Mick... I'm sure I don't have to paint a picture for you. That was the end.'

'It was not the end.'

Ewan's eyes searched Anita's face for sympathy. He needed help right now. She sat impassively. How could she be so unmoved?

'No. It wasn't the end. Debbie… Debbie moved out and shacked up with Mick. I didn't ask why she had done it. I knew the answer already. But once Mick had made his conquest, he lost interest and dumped her.'

'Did you see her again?'

'Once.' Anita could see he was now close to tears. She hoped he wouldn't break down in front of Moberg. 'Well, I didn't actually see her. Debbie came round to the flat. She wanted to talk to me.' His voice lowered and became ragged as he forced the words out. 'I wouldn't let her in. She cried and screamed outside the door, but I wouldn't open it. She kept saying how sorry she was. I couldn't face her. She had betrayed me, and I could never forgive that. Everything between us had been destroyed.'

Ewan's head slumped into hands. 'God, I should have opened…'

Anita and Moberg watched him fighting his demons. But Moberg wasn't going to give him any respite. 'This Debbie. What happened to her?'

'To Debbie?' Ewan sounded surprised by the question. The answer that came out was very matter-of-fact. 'Debbie jumped off the main tower of Durham Cathedral.'

'And you blamed Mick?' Anita was now back to her most businesslike.

'Of course I did!' His voice was raised and reverberated round the enclosed room. 'Wouldn't you? I blamed Debbie, too, for giving in to him. In some ways her sin was worse. But it was Mick who destroyed us.'

'It gives you a strong motive to kill Malin. His woman for your woman.'

Ewan was startled by the accusation. 'Wait! No. It doesn't. It happened well over twenty years ago. If I was going to do something, I would have done it then. Why wait until now?'

'Opportunity. You admitted to me that you had lost touch with Mick after university. Maybe this was your first chance to get even. You might not have planned it. I'm sure you didn't. But suddenly you get the chance of revenge. Mick was away. Malin was alone, which you established by the phone call you failed to tell us about. You could have slipped out of the hotel at any time. Inspector Westermark has checked out the side door round from Carlsgatan. Maybe she actually invited you round. When you get there, she offers you a cup of tea. You do drink tea in the evening. Even in Newcastle United cups, a team you and Mick support. Suddenly you have an opportunity, after all this time. All that resentment that had been welling up for years. The way that you have described the events at Durham, they are obviously still raw, despite the years. Here was a chance to even the score.'

Ewan's mouth had dropped open as she catalogued the case against him. He couldn't speak but just kept shaking his head.

'Malin turns her back on you to boil the kettle. You did judo at university, so a chokehold is not difficult for you. And, as we know, you have used that grip before. You have a history of violence.'

'No, no, no, no, no, no.'

'You drag the body out of the kitchen into the living room and place it on the sofa. Mick is meant to find it in the morning. Sitting there, lifeless. Like a trophy. Then maybe you were disturbed. We know Halvar Mednick went in and found the body. Were you still in the apartment? Or hiding on the stairwell and watching him go in before slipping out of the building? Anyway, your ploy doesn't work out because Mick is not there when you arrive. But you think quickly. You go in and it gives you the chance to touch the body so that there will be an explanation for your fibres and prints when they are found, as they would inevitably be. That is why Mick attacked you. He must have had an instinct that you had killed her and exactly why you had done it.'

'Look, you've got this all wrong.'

Westermark saw Anita returning to her office. He wondered how best to get back at her. The stuck-up bitch. Her accent, her polished English, her attitude to him all drove him mad. Yet she was a challenge. Women did not turn him down, even if they wanted to. What made it worse with Anita was his desire for her. The need to conquer her. He fantasised about them fucking. And it was definitely fucking and not making love. She was all woman, and with a body that had matured to a peak. He was fed up with screwing all those young tarts that he picked up in clubs and bars. They were easy. Anita was special. The glasses, too, made her even sexier in his eyes. He would insist she kept them on when he got round to having his way.

But she had rejected him out of hand and she had to pay. He knew the best way. He had observed how Strachan looked at her. And Anita's unease confirmed that she might have feelings for him. He would ensure that the prick would go down for the murder, despite any efforts Anita might make to save him. He was guilty anyhow. That wasn't just down to his natural antagonism towards anyone whom Anita showed an interest in, but because he was convinced that Strachan had killed Malin Lovgren.

'Well, you didn't beat about the bush,' Moberg said approvingly when they met in his office afterwards. A sullen Westermark and a bright-eyed Olander were also there, and Moberg had given them the gist of what had happened. This cheered Westermark up.

'So it's obviously him.'

'According to Anita it is,' said Moberg as he flipped open the large pizza box that had been brought in for him.

Westermark shot Anita a surprised look.

'But do you think he did it?' said Moberg, who was sizing up his meal.

'Strachan certainly has given us the rope to hang him. He volunteered the information about the judo and he served up a motive on a plate. Would you do that if you're guilty? And he still doesn't want a lawyer. To tell you the truth, I just don't know.'

Moberg took a slice. 'The trouble is that we can't place him at the murder scene on the night.' He didn't bother to offer any pizza around.

'We need a confession,' Westermark hissed.

'Without one, we still haven't got enough to take to the prosecutor. Blom will go berserk when we tell her that Mednick's not guilty. She doesn't like being made a fool of in public. The commissioner's even worse. We'll all pay the price, so we'd better make sure any case we have is watertight.'

'I'm still not sure that the Debbie Usher story is complete,' said Anita. 'What happened to her could be the key to this case. Just now I was onto the Durham Constabulary, but they haven't many details of the case as it was years ago. Filed as a suicide. But I have the name of the detective who looked into it. He's retired now, but he still lives in the area.'

Moberg finished chewing his first piece of pizza. In a sudden burst of guilt, he pushed the pizza box into the middle of the desk. 'Help yourselves.' Westermark and Olander tentatively reached over and took a slice each.

'Right. If you can get hold of this ex-detective, get on a flight tomorrow and find out the full story. I don't even know where this Durham place is. Is it near London?'

'No. It's in north-east England. Not too far from Scotland.'

'There are flights over there, aren't there?' he asked doubtfully.

'Daily from Kastrup to Newcastle.'

Moberg picked up his second slice. 'OK, that covers that

angle. I'm still waiting to hear from Henrik up in Stockholm on the Andreas Tapper car crash. What else have we?'

'Bengt Valquist,' Anita suggested.

'The business partner. Is he a serious contender?'

Anita nodded to Olander. This was his chance to impress. 'He had opportunity. No alibi for the time of the murder. And he had a motive. Two, actually. One, Roslyn was playing around with his girlfriend. Secondly, and the strongest, was talk of Malin wanting to push him out of the company.'

'Right. Let's shake him up a bit. I think that's a job for you, Westermark. Olander, you can go along with him. It'll give you an insight into another kind of policing.' Anita knew what that would entail.

Ewan lay on his cell bed. His head was swimming. He was too frightened to succumb to a panic attack. How the hell was he going to get out of this?

CHAPTER 30

Anita turned the car onto the sliproad of the A1, which skirted round the south of Newcastle. This was Ewan territory. He should have been working here today but, instead, he was sitting in a cell in the polishus in Malmö. She couldn't make her mind up whether he should be locked up or not. He didn't look like a killer. Then again, killers rarely do, except in television dramas. She had found the interrogations hard. This was a man whom she was beginning to like. She had enjoyed his company. And she knew that he had probably been in love with her, or thought he was. The beseeching looks he had directed at her were enough to make her inwardly wince. She had wanted to say that she would do her best to give him the benefit of the doubt. He would get a fair hearing from her, even if not from the likes of Westermark, who had obviously made up his mind. When she had gone through her scenario of the night of the murder, Ewan had appeared dazed. Shattered. She couldn't help but feel a tinge of guilt. She knew she shouldn't because she was only doing her job. She crossed over the River Tyne and past the concrete mass of the Metrocentre. As the road swept up a gradual incline away from the Tyneside conurbation, she saw the Angel of the North; its powerful, rust-coloured, metallic aeroplane wings open wide in welcome to those arriving in the region. How many times had Ewan passed this spot? Anita wondered. And what was the point of her visit to ex-Inspector Gazzard anyway? Maybe he could throw some fresh light on the feud between Ewan and Mick Roslyn. Was Debbie Usher really the catalyst for Malin's murder? But would that help them convict Ewan? If nothing else, the trip would give her an excuse to visit Durham again. Inspector Gazzard lived on the edge of an old pit village about five miles west of the old cathedral city. If the case against Ewan was to be proved, then Gazzard might confirm the motive. Was part of her hoping that he wouldn't?

'He's not here.'

Westermark eyed fru Valquist up and down. Even in her youth, she wouldn't have been fanciable. Before he could say anything more she burst out with, 'Can't you people leave him alone?'

Westermark half-turned to the hovering Olander and gave him a knowing smirk. He was going to have to toughen him up after the police assistant had spent too much time fannying about with Anita Sundström.

'This is a murder case. If we want to talk to him, we'll fucking talk to him whenever we like.'

Fru Valquist's cheeks automatically sucked inwards in horror at the policeman's use of the 'f' word. 'There's no need for language like that, young man. If my husband was at home, he would take you to task.'

'I haven't got time. Where is he? We need to speak to him *now*!'

'He went back to Stockholm,' she replied defensively. 'On Saturday. He was very upset after speaking to that policewoman.'

'Shit!'

Fru Valquist aimed another withering look but said nothing.

'At his apartment?'

'I think so.'

'What do you mean, you think so?'

'I've tried to ring him a couple of times, but there's been no answer.'

'Is he with Tilda Tegner?'

'Don't talk to me about that trollop,' fru Valquist huffed. 'That's why Bengt is so upset. Her and Roslyn,' she shuddered. 'Awful, simply awful.'

'If your son rings, tell him to contact us right away.' Fru Valquist recoiled at the aggressive tone of his voice.

Anita drove into an early 1980s estate of uniform red-brick houses, built before the mining villages that peppered the countryside around the city of Durham had fallen into permanent decline. Murrayfield Drive was one of the many characterless cul-de-sacs. Anita confidently parked the car as she had now got the hang of the right-hand drive. By the twitching of the net curtains, she was expected.

Mrs Gazzard, a roly-poly lady, made a fuss of her. 'Come on in, pet. I'll get the tea. Just been to the Co-op and got these nice biscuits and some Battenburg cake.' It was lovely to hear the Durham accent again. The ex-inspector was waiting in the sitting room, reading his paper next to the coal-effect fire. A large flat-screen TV dominated the corner of the room. He rose from his chair and towered over Anita. He had thick grey hair, with a lick of grey moustache above lips that were clamped round a pipe. Anita wondered when she had last seen someone smoking one. A swathe of beer belly put a strain on the top of his trousers and showed that exercise hadn't been high on his agenda since retirement. He held out his hand and smiled broadly.

'By, they have better-looking coppers in Sweden than over here.'

She took that to be a compliment. 'Anita Sundström,' she said, taking his outstretched hand. 'Thank you for seeing me, Inspector Gazzard.'

'Forget the Inspector lark. Been retired ten years. Call me Billy.'

They exchanged small talk until Mrs Gazzard came in with a tray of tea, chocolate biscuits and slices of gaudily coloured cake. On a raised eyebrow from her husband, she retreated. 'I'll leave you to your business. But it's lovely to see you. All the way from Sweden. Imagine. They will be excited at church when I tell them.'

After she left, Gazzard apologised. 'Sorry about that. Brenda thinks anybody south of Yorkshire is exotic, so someone from Sweden...'

'No, she has been very kind.'

'To business.' He put his pipe back in his mouth, then immediately pulled it out. 'You don't mind?'

'Not at all.'

'You mentioned on the phone last night that you were after some information on the death of Debbie Usher.'

'Background really.'

'What does a death in Durham in the 1980s have to do with a Swedish investigation now if you don't mind me asking?'

'I don't know whether it has been reported over here but a well-known actress, Malin Lovgren, has been murdered in Malmö. Her husband was at Durham University – and so was the man who is helping us with our enquiries.'

'And do they happen to be Ewan Strachan and Michael Roslyn?'

Anita glanced at him quizzically. 'Yes.' She hadn't mentioned either of them on the phone. 'Roslyn was the husband. He is a famous film director in Sweden. The man we have in custody is Ewan Strachan.'

'So they've caught up with each other again.' He drew on his pipe reflectively. 'I know about Ewan Strachan. He used to write sports reports in one of the local papers, so I knew that he'd stayed in the area. But I'd no idea what

Michael Roslyn had got up to.'

'It doesn't seem to surprise you that they met up again.'

'Oh, it surprises me all right. However, what doesn't is that something unpleasant's happened. How did this actress die?'

'Strangled. Chokehold. Apparently they both did judo.'

'Aye, they'd been big mates, and then they fell out over Debbie Usher.'

'Can you tell me what happened?'

Anita took a biscuit and realised how hungry she was, not having eaten since a very early breakfast. Gazzard puffed on his pipe and let out a curling waft of aromatic smoke. It made her twitchy and she wanted to get out her snus, but he might find it odd, a woman stuffing tobacco into her mouth.

'Nice girl was Debbie, by all accounts. Nice-looking, too. From her photos, that is. She was a mess when she hit the ground after she went over the top of the tower. Do you know the cathedral?'

'I do, actually. I lived in Durham for a couple of years when I was younger.' The cathedral had been the first thing she had seen every morning when she opened her bedroom curtains.

'Well, you'll know that it's a helluva fall. It seemed pretty straightforward. A student jumping off the cathedral. They get depressed. Exams get them down. The Dean and Chapter used to lock the tower during exam times. Don't know whether they still do. Strange thing about Debbie was that it was just before Christmas. Virtually the end of term, when students are getting excited about going home for the holidays. It was about eleven o'clock at night. A couple of students, John Wilson and Alison French, were canoodling, or some such, close to the cathedral when this body descends from the heavens. Sickening experience for the poor youngsters. We were called in as a matter of course. Seemed like an ordinary suicide. Not that any suicide is ordinary, I suppose.'

'But you didn't think it was suicide?'

He pointed the stem of his pipe at Anita. 'No, I bloody didn't. Sorry, didn't mean to swear.' He glanced nervously towards the door. If he thought that was swearing, he should hear what she had to put up with from Moberg. She placated him with a wry grin.

'I went along with it at first. There appeared to be a tale of love and rejection behind her wanting to kill herself. And her friends did tell me that she'd been depressed after her break-up with Roslyn. Do you know about the involvement of Roslyn and Strachan?'

'Yes. Ewan Strachan was in love with her, and then Mick Roslyn stole her away, before leaving her.'

'That's right. I was able to establish all that. So, on the face of it, she might have had plenty of reasons to jump.'

'So what changed your mind?'

'First of all, there was no note. Now suicides don't always leave a note, as you know. But jumping off one of the country's most historic buildings is a grand gesture. She was rejected in love, and I'm sure she would have wanted to explain her actions. Her parents were heartbroken. By all accounts, she was very fond of them. She didn't seem the sort to have left no message.'

'Did you have any concrete evidence?'

'I wondered why she'd decided to wait until so late to jump. At that time of night, normally nobody is around except maybe the odd drunken student on the way back to one of the colleges. The cathedral's locked up well before then. Why wait up the tower for hours, then jump when no one can see you?'

'Working up the courage to do it?'

'I think if you wait that long, you'll have talked yourself out of it by then. There was something else. I went over John Wilson and Alison French's statements again. Something stood out. According to Wilson, he thought he heard a cry. This wasn't substantiated by French, but she was too distraught to remember much. And she had had too much to drink. But it made me think, like. If you're going to jump to your death, do you cry out? I think you just do it. On the other hand, if someone has shoved you over...'

Ewan knew that he had to act now before he went completely mad. He must talk to Anita. When he had been taken from his cell, he assumed that he was to be interviewed again and that that would be his chance. To his surprise, he was shown into a furnished room by the young officer Olander, who announced that someone was here to see him.

'I need to speak to Inspector Sundström. It's very important.'

'That is not possible. The inspector is away at the moment.'

'What do you mean "away"? Where?' Ewan demanded.

'I cannot say.'

This was disquieting news. 'When will she be back? I have got to speak to her.'

'Maybe tomorrow. Maybe Thursday. I am not sure. If you want to speak to Inspector Westermark or Chief Inspector Moberg, I will tell them.'

'No,' Ewan snapped. 'Forget it.'

'The British consul is outside. I will bring him in. I have to remain here while you speak to him.'

Olander went to another door, which he was about to open.

'Look, whatever your name is, can you make sure that as soon as Inspector Sundström returns that she comes and speaks to me. I have vital information that she needs to know.'

Moberg put down the phone. Westermark hovered by the window.

'Henrik says that he's getting nowhere with the Andreas Tapper crash. Talked to the Norrköping cops and Traffic. They're not stonewalling him, but they aren't being over-helpful either. They're a load of wankers up there. Anyhow, I've sent him round to Valquist's place in Södermalm and he'll have a talk with him. If necessary, he'll drag the bugger back here and we'll give him the works.'

Moberg got out of his seat and hoisted his sagging trousers up. 'Now I had better go and see the commissioner and tell him his prize catch has to be thrown back. It'll do fuck all for his credibility. He's not going to be pleased. Neither will that snooty bitch of a prosecutor.'

'The more I thought about it, the more I was convinced that Debbie Usher had been killed. There were only two possible suspects – Strachan and Roslyn. I was sure one of them managed to get her up the tower. I don't know what he did to persuade her – or maybe he abducted her – before hoisting her up and over the edge. Then he'd have had to wait until the next morning to slip out when the tower was opened up for the tourists.'

'Did you interview them?' Anita was now totally engrossed.

'Yes. Informally only. Me boss thought I was wasting me time. Neither had an alibi for that night. Both said they were working in their rooms. I couldn't find anyone to corroborate their stories, nor did I find anybody who sighted them near or in the cathedral that day. The last sighting anybody had of Debbie was in the Bailey, when a friend said she saw her walking past the Shakespeare Tavern, heading in the general direction of Palace Green and the cathedral. It was about five. She was by herself.'

'What was their reaction?'

Gazzard put down his pipe. 'Each one blamed the other. Not for killing her but for her death. Strachan said that she must have jumped because she had been rejected by Roslyn. Roslyn said that she jumped because Strachan refused to have her back. Both could be true, of course. Roslyn had caused all the mischief in the first place. But one of them was lying. I knew it. I know it still. I could never prove anything, so it got filed away as yet another sad suicide. I've never forgotten it.

Cases like that prey on your mind, don't you think? Unfinished business. Unsatisfactory. It still niggles. And now you come here and you're probably asking yourself the same questions.'

He leant down and picked up his cup of tea.

'And who do *you* think did it?' She braced herself. 'Mick Roslyn or Ewan Strachan?'

CHAPTER 31

As soon as Anita had left the housing estate, she parked the hire car at the side of the feeder road, just past the pub. She stared blankly out of the windscreen. She didn't take in the school bus that passed or the cars carrying the kids back to their homes. Tears were welling up in her eyes. Why was she feeling this way? Why did she care so much? Then the flood came. She jammed a handkerchief against her eyes in an attempt to stem the stream of moisture. Her shoulders heaved. All this churned-up emotion because ex-Inspector Gazzard had come out with the name that she now realised she hadn't wanted him to say. Ewan Strachan.

Moberg's meeting with Commissioner Dahlberg and Prosecutor Blom hadn't been one of his best. The commissioner had thrown the expected tantrum. 'What do you mean, it wasn't Mednick! I've gone on record on TV saying that we'd got the killer. It makes me look ludicrous.'

While the commissioner had blustered, Blom had roasted Moberg without having to raise her voice. Cutting and cruel, she had called into question his ability to run the case. She had a particular way of saying the word 'incompetence' that left no one in doubt as to its meaning. It took a Moberg eruption to bring the meeting back to a rational level: 'I thought we were all on the same fucking side! You can play your political games, but this is about catching a killer now. You can round up your scapegoats later.'

After that, Moberg had filled them in on Strachan and Valquist, and Nordlund's failed efforts to establish whether Andreas Trapper had died suspiciously or not. The only decision reached was to move Roslyn out of the safe house. They could no longer justify the expense.

Back in his cell, Ewan had time to reflect on his brief meeting with the British Consul. Martin Tripp was a British, Malmö-based businessman who had landed the consular roll by default and had never been called upon to do anything beyond the occasional official drinks party. A murder charge was way beyond what he thought was his remit or area of expertise. Exporting paper was more his thing.

'Dreadful business.' After he'd said it five times, Ewan's filthy look had shut him up.

Scanning the room, Tripp shook his head. 'This sort of thing doesn't do the British image much good over here.'

'It doesn't do my image any bloody good either!'

'Quite. I take your point.' He brushed an imaginary thread from his jacket lapel. 'Did you kill the actress?'

'No, I didn't.'

'Well, that's something. Thought I'd better ask. Are they treating you well?'

'They haven't started with the thumbscrews yet,' Ewan retorted sarcastically. 'Actually, they don't have to – their coffee is just as effective.'

Tripp looked askance. He didn't know what to make of this belligerent Scotsman. He just wanted to get out of the room as soon as possible so he could say he had discharged his duty.

'You know some awful northern rag has somehow got hold of the story? The embassy says the Foreign Office are worried it will be picked up by the nationals.'

'Bloody Brian!'

'Sorry?'

'It's nothing.' Ewan could see that Brian hadn't wasted any time making capital out of his appalling situation. And only one person was going to come out of this with a pay rise and promotion – and that was his idiot editor.

'They want to keep this business under wraps.'

'That's not what I want to hear.'

'Oh, yes, quite.' Tripp realised he had put his foot in it. 'I'm sure they'll do their best in the circumstances,' he said in an attempt to backtrack.

After establishing that Ewan didn't want a lawyer, he was able to escape. His sense of relief was as palpable as Ewan's frustration.

Ewan kicked his chair. He knew he might be able to get out of this if only he could speak to Anita. He should have mentioned it before. He conjured up her smiling image as he fought another bout of escalating panic. The distraction worked. But where was she?

The lights on the cathedral were magical. The awesome stone edifice on the rock above the loop in the River Wear rose majestically out of the darkness. The slender twin towers at the west end complemented the massive thrust of the one in the centre. Anita stood in Wharton Park above the railway station and stared across at the floodlit building and the neat Norman castle nestling in its mighty shadow.

Memories came rushing back. Durham had played a special part in her life. It was only now that she realised why it had meant so much to her. It had been the last time the Ullmans had been happy as a family. Her dad had loved it. An escape from Sweden, which hadn't become the socialist utopia he had hoped for as a young man in the 1960s. In his opinion, the country had been seduced by capitalism, whereas Britain was under a Labour government during their time in Durham. Retrospectively, Anita had been surprised at his stance, given that he worked for Electrolux, a symbol of successful Swedish free enterprise. But he had enjoyed the mateyness of those he worked and socialised with. As for her mother, this friendliness freaked her out. Where had the famous British reserve she had heard about – and had hoped for – disappeared to? But this was the North East, where strangers were affectionately called "pet" and people spoke to you on buses. Her mother's natural Swedish suspicion had been gradually worn down over their two-year stay, and she had begun to enjoy the chatty neighbours and shopkeepers and being asked next door for a cup of tea. And the more relaxed she became, the more the family seemed to bond. Anita realised that there must have been serious divisions in her parents' partnership before they came to Britain. Durham had papered over those cracks and even strengthened their relationship for a short time. It was the only period in her childhood when she felt really secure. If only they had stayed. Maybe all their lives would have turned out differently.

Anita had loved her school and had made lots of friends. Janet Trotter had been her best friend and the Trotters included her on a lot of their family outings. They had kept in touch for a few years, and they had always meant to meet up again. Of course they didn't, and the numerous letters turned into a solitary Christmas card. And that had stopped before Anita got married. Was Janet still living down there among the twinkling lights?

A train came zipping across the arcing Victorian viaduct at breakneck speed, heading north towards Edinburgh. It rushed noisily through the station below and brought Anita out of her reverie. She focused on the huge central tower of the cathedral.

Twenty-five years ago, Debbie Usher had either decided that life wasn't worth living any more, or someone had been strong enough to lift her over the edge and send her tumbling nearly 200 feet to her death. "In some ways her sin was worse". Ewan's words from his interrogation came back to her. They had struck her as strange at the time. Looking across at the cathedral, their spiritual implication was difficult to ignore. She didn't know if Ewan was religious. Was it a case of an eye for an eye? But if he had done Debbie in, why bother to murder Malin? Unless Debbie's death was to punish her sin, and Malin's death to punish Mick's. Debbie's betrayal seemed to have wounded Ewan more than Mick's selfish actions. Was it the chill air that made her shiver or the thought that Ewan Strachan could be a cold-blooded killer?

They were approaching Malmö and the traffic was thickening. Westermark had picked up Mick and was taking him to stay at his mother-in-law's, as Mick's apartment was still a crime scene. Mick's curiosity had been aroused by the detective who had come to tell him that his exile in the dreary farmhouse was over and that the police were sure there was no threat from ex-Säpo hitmen. He didn't know whether it was strictly true, but it was what Moberg had instructed Westermark to pass on. When Mick asked what was happening with Ewan, to his surprise Westermark hadn't held back. There had been none of the official caution he had experienced with Sundström. Mick was left in no doubt that Westermark thought that Ewan was guilty of the murder. What was more, he got the impression that the detective had taken a serious dislike to his old university friend.

'I don't know how the bastard could have done that to you. OK, so you screwed his woman. That happens. Inspector Sundström is over there at the moment. That place you were at university together.'

'Durham? She's over in Durham?' Mick was surprised that they had followed up his Debbie Usher suggestion so thoroughly.

'That's right.' To avoid ploughing through town, Westermark was now on the dual carriageway that skirted Malmö to the north.

'What does she expect to find in Durham?' Mick asked cautiously.

'Haven't a bloody clue. I think she fancies him. Probably trying to prove he's innocent. He certainly has the hots for her.' Westermark rammed his foot down and the car shot into the outside lane.

'Sundström's an attractive woman. Ewan was always a romantic idiot. And now he's killed ...' His voice trailed off. 'I can't really believe it. It hasn't sunk in. I thought his bitterness would have gone by now.'

They sat in silence as Westermark worked his way round the inner ring road onto the top end of Lundavägen. A few minutes later he parked the car outside Britta Lovgren's neat home.

'Safely delivered.' Westermark smiled. After spending the last hour with Mick, he thought of him as a kindred spirit. A man of the world who liked beautiful women. Just look at Malin Lovgren. He might also be a useful contact in the future. He liked the glamour of show business. It would be nice if some of it could rub off on him by association. That was where the most attractive women gravitated to. 'If I can be of any help, herr Roslyn, just ask.'

Mick nodded. 'Thanks. And it's Mick, by the way.'

That made Westermark feel good. 'I'm Karl.'

Mick leant over to the back seat and picked up his overnight bag. 'Look, erm...Karl. If you hear about any developments to do with Ewan Strachan, give me a call. Unofficially, of course. The police aren't very forthcoming, but I think I have a right to know what's going on. Could you do that for me?'

'Don't worry, Mick.' Westermark winked. 'I'll keep you in the loop.'

Nordlund had had a difficult day. And it wasn't getting easier. His frustrations over the Andreas Tapper car crash had been annoying. Finding Bengt Valquist was even more aggravating. When Erik Moberg had called, he was quite pleased to give his fruitless investigations a rest and get down to some proper police questioning. When he reached Valquist's apartment in Södermalm, the producer wasn't there. Or wasn't answering the door. So he went back into the centre of Stockholm to Roslyn's company's production office and managed to speak to a young woman called Agnes. She hadn't seen Bengt Valquist since the previous Friday afternoon. He had been expected in the office that day, but he hadn't turned up, which was unusual as he was normally very punctual and reliable. Why not try Tilda Tegner?

Nordlund had trailed back to Södermalm. Tegner's apartment was ten minutes' walk away from Valquist's. She was in. Not that she was being very communicative. She was in a state of mental disarray. She hadn't been able to contact Mick so had no idea what was happening with him. Why had he told the police about their affair? She hadn't dared to get in touch with Bengt, and he had made no effort to contact her. Was he still in Lund? After all this, would she ever get any acting work again?

'I haven't seen Bengt since last week,' she explained to the mature-looking policeman. He reminded her of her dad. 'Maybe he's still in Lund.'

'No, herr Valquist left Lund on Saturday, saying that he was returning to Stockholm. He didn't turn up for work this morning.'

'Maybe he's ill,' Tegner suggested, knowing full well he was probably hiding from the world because of the embarrassment she had caused him.

'He's not answering his door. I think we'd better go round and see if he's OK. I assume you have a key?'

The apartment was on the second floor. Nordlund rang the bell and received no answer. He turned to Tegner for the key. She handed it over and then hung back as he opened the door and let himself in. 'Herr Valquist?' The call was met by silence.

The apartment was very modern. No piece of furniture appeared more than a couple of years old. All the latest designs. Uncompromising and uncomfortable. On the walls there were lots of arty black-and-white photographs and two large, framed Roslyn film posters. Both featured close-ups of Malin. No knick-knacks or personal touches seemed to intrude –except one. Perched on a glass coffee table was a photograph of Tilda Tegner and Valquist holding hands on a beach somewhere. The kitchen and the bedroom showed no signs of life. Nordlund pointed at a closed door. 'What's in there?'

'Bengt's study.'

Nordlund opened the door. The telltale sign was the swinging feet. Nordlund would always remember how shiny the shoes were. Tegner's piercing wail was the other sign that Bengt Valquist had hanged himself.

CHAPTER 32

Moberg was in a foul mood. Valquist's death had thrown him. Nordlund had explained that he had found a neatly compiled suicide note near the body in which Valquist had written that he was taking his life because he couldn't live with the fact that Mick and Tilda had betrayed him. He had asked his parents to forgive him and said that he was leaving the Lund house and the Stockholm apartment to them. After calming down the hysterical Tegner, Nordlund had established that the handwriting was definitely Valquist's, so the death was unlikely to be suspicious, unless the pathologist or forensics came up with something unusual. The note didn't contain any confession about Lovgren, so he was unlikely to be the killer. Moberg had quashed his natural scepticism. He could never fathom how any self-respecting man could kill himself over a mere woman.

And they weren't getting anywhere here on the Strachan front either. Several people had been through his office already this morning and there wasn't a Strachan sighting to be had. CCTV footage had produced nothing. No one in the Värnhem area had seen him on the night. One young woman, living on the second floor of Lovgren's apartment block, did identify him from the following morning. He had gone in as she came out. Questioning the Hotel Comfort staff also drew a blank. The night receptionist confirmed that he had come in at about 9.30

on the Monday evening. He hadn't been seen again until the next morning.

When Ewan had awoken that morning, he was amazed at how long he had managed to sleep. The first night had been like living through a horror movie. Each time he woke up, he panicked, not knowing where he was. And each time, when he realised where he was, he panicked some more. This time he had stirred from his deep slumber with a clearer head. He lay on the hard bed and made a thorough review of his situation.

Was it as hopeless as he had first thought? The mention of Debbie had completely thrown him, and it gave them the motive they were so desperately searching for. But that was just conjecture. Would any judge and jury accept that someone would wait twenty-five years to get his revenge, especially as the murder couldn't have been premeditated? He doubted it. He was sure that they couldn't use forensic evidence against him. Of course, he had been in various rooms in the apartment. He should have told them about the phone call to Malin the night before. That was just plain stupid. It had raised their suspicions, and that was why he had ended up in the cell.

Ewan stood up. He did the silly little bending, stretching and head-twisting exercises his ancient osteopath had recommended to help the back pain that flared up occasionally. He had also suggested he sleep on a hard bed. He would have approved of the one provided by the Skåne County Police. By the time Ewan had finished, he had made a decision. If he couldn't speak to Anita by the end of the day, he would insist on a lawyer.

Moberg's temper hadn't been improved any more by the late afternoon meeting he called on Anita's return. His mood changed, however, once Anita had filled him in on her meeting with Inspector Gazzard and the ex-policeman's final conclusion. Westermark beamed with delight when she mentioned that

Gazzard was sure that Ewan Strachan had killed Debbie Usher.

'A double murderer,' he crowed. 'I knew he was shifty bastard.'

'And this old cop believes Strachan is responsible?' quizzed Moberg.

'Yes. He couldn't prove anything. What surprised him was that they had got together again after all the bad blood between them. What didn't surprise him was that there was trouble when they did meet up.'

'So we really are onto something. Well done, Karl.'

Westermark preened himself. Everything was going his way. Get this conviction, and he would move ahead of Anita in the criminal investigation squad's pecking order. This was the big one; the career-defining moment. His groundwork had triggered off this line of investigation, even if he had been carrying out Moberg's initial instructions. Anita's pathetic journalist would go down. She had lost. Then he would work on getting her into bed.

'Our other lines of enquiry have come to a dead end. Valquist is literally a dead end. The Palme thing may still be true, but I don't think it has anything to do with us. So, Strachan it is. The circumstantial evidence is enough to hold him but not enough to convict him. I still can't go to Blom without a sighting. We'll start again in the morning. But we'd better find something.'

Anita returned to her office. There were still lingering misgivings. Nothing she could put her finger on. She liked cases to be cut and dried. No room for doubts. But tonight she was too weary to think about them. She would go home and get an early night's sleep and get back into the office first thing in the morning. Then she would be able to concentrate. If Ewan had committed the murder, someone out there must have seen him. The fact that it had been on a bitter winter's night didn't help as not many people were abroad at that time. She was about to leave when Olander breezed in.

'How was England?'

'Useful.' She didn't really have the energy to go through her story again, but she felt it was only fair to update him. He was so keen. After she had finished, she picked up her overnight bag and made for the door.

'Oh, forgot to tell you. Strachan is desperate to see you.' Anita sighed heavily. She wasn't in the mood for it. 'Really insistent. Said he had some vital information for you. When I suggested he saw someone else, he didn't want to know. Only you.'

'Did he give you any idea what it was about?'

Olander just shrugged his shoulders. Anita stood there clutching her bag. She was undecided. A nice shower, a glass of Rioja and a good book – or going to the miserable cells? Did she owe Ewan at least that? He hadn't mentioned their drink in front of the others, so he deserved a visit.

'OK. You come with me. Westermark will think I'm plotting to ruin what he sees as his case if I go in by myself, so a witness might be useful.'

The duty officer opened up the cell, and Anita entered with Olander. Ewan, who had been glancing through a local newspaper, jumped up as soon as he saw her.

'Ani...' He noticed Olander. 'Inspector. Where have you been?'

'Durham. To see Inspector Gazzard.' Ewan wore a puzzled expression until it dawned on him who she was talking about. 'He remembers you.'

'Yes. He talked to me about Debbie. I'm surprised he's still working.'

'He retired ten years ago. Now, what do you want to tell me?' She had to admit that she was slightly apprehensive that he might come out with something personal. Something to do with them, their meetings. But she needed Olander there in case it was significant.

'Well,' Ewan looked furtively at Olander, 'I needed to tell you because I don't think your colleagues would want to listen.'

'I'm listening.'

Ewan gulped. His throat was dry. 'It's about Mick. Mick Roslyn. The night of the murder. Monday night. Mick wasn't in Stockholm.'

Anita stiffened. 'Where was he then?'

'Here. Here in Malmö.'

The tiredness vanished. Now Anita was totally alert. 'How do you know?'

'I saw him.'

'Where?'

'I don't know what it's called. Some street near Lilla Torg. I had gone for a wander when I first arrived. On my way back to the hotel, I saw him going into a building. At the time I thought I must be mistaken. Then, when all this blew up and Mick said he'd been in Stockholm, I assumed I must have been seeing things. It's only since I've been stuck in here that I've had time to really think about it. I know it was going dark, but I'm now positive it was him.'

'But he was on the Stockholm flight the next morning,' put in Olander.

'His name was on the flight list but I bet no one has actually checked whether he was on board,' countered Anita. Back to Ewan: 'Was he alone?'

'No. That young actress was with him.'

'Tilda Tegner?'

'Yeah. The one who was at the film festival in Edinburgh. It was actually her I noticed first.'

Anita's head was swimming with the implications. Her mind was flitting back over events, conversations and interviews that had taken place during the last week. A pattern was emerging.

'Would you be able to remember the building where you saw him?'

Ewan stroked his chin thoughtfully before shaking his head. 'I don't think so. Malmö was all strange and new then. I just know it was near Lilla Torg.' Then he clicked his fingers in a gesture of remembering. 'It was behind the Rica Hotel. I recall that. The building they went into was definitely modern. Opposite a car park, I think. Or an open space, anyhow.'

'Sounds like Mäster Johansgatan.'

'Will this help get me out of here?' Ewan pleaded.

Anita looked at him. He trapped her eyes with his. Maybe she had allowed herself to be pushed into thinking that he was their murderer. Maybe he still was, but they had some checking to do first.

'It might.' She turned towards the door. 'Come on, Mats. We've got work to do.'

'Inspector, I think I've been set up. I think I've been set up by Mick.'

Back in her office, Anita dumped her bag unceremoniously on the floor.

'Shut the door.'

Olander did as he was told.

'Do you believe him, Inspector?'

'I'm not sure, Mats. I'm not sure.' Did she want to believe him? 'There's only one way to find out.'

'Are you going to tell the chief inspector?'

'Not yet. We need to do a few things before we go in with this information. I want you to get onto the airline and the airport at Sturup and find out whether Roslyn *was* on the plane that morning. I also need you to check the taxi companies. Were there any fares that morning from Sturup direct to Östra Förstadsgatan?'

'OK, I'll get straight onto that.' Anita found Olander's

enthusiasm refreshing. 'What are you going to do?'

Anita was scrambling inside her bag in search of her snus. With a triumphant flourish, she produced it.

'I'm going to ring Henrik Nordlund. I need him to make sure Tilda Tegner doesn't contact Mick Roslyn.'

'Why?'

She had the tin unscrewed and a sachet popped into her mouth before replying. 'Because I think that herr Strachan may be right.'

Anita stood on the freezing platform. Olander brought her a coffee in a paper cup. Both were very tired. Anita had sent Olander off home at three and she had slipped into bed at five. The young police assistant had been a very useful sounding board as she had sifted through the facts and speculation to come up with a coherent case. But it would mean nothing without the discussion she needed to have in the next half hour, if the first train out of Stockholm was on time. It was 9.56am.

Among the wave of travellers sweeping in their direction was the familiar stooped figure of Nordlund with an anxious looking Tilda Tegner. She was dressed casually in black boots, jeans, a long turquoise coat and matching beret. Anita greeted them. 'Hi, Henrik.' He smiled wearily back. 'Thank you for coming down, fröken Tegner.' Tilda didn't reply.

'Are we taking fröken Tegner to the polishus?' asked Nordlund.

'We're here to do that. The chief inspector says you should go home and get sorted out before coming in.' Olander flashed her a surprised glance.

Nordlund didn't question her, though he shot her a doubtful look. He fished out of his coat pocket a brightly coloured mobile phone and handed it to Anita. 'Fröken Tegner's. Roslyn tried to ring her three times last night and left one text. He wanted her to ring him.'

'Can I have it back?'

'You can have it when we've finished talking.' Anita slipped the mobile into her bag and wondered whether she would ever be able to find it again.

On leaving the station, Anita didn't take Tegner towards the polishus but crossed the road to where the old Copenhagen ferry used to run from in the days before the Öresund Bridge was opened. The dock remained, though it served no function other than as a waterscape for the elongated glass expanse of the new Malmö University education department. Students trailed in and out of the university building opposite. The water rippled in the wind. Black clouds scudded overhead.

'Am I under arrest?' asked Tegner.

'No. You are helping police with their enquiries.'

'So why are we here?'

Olander was wondering that, too. He only hoped that Anita knew what she was doing because the chief inspector had no idea what was going on here. When Moberg did find out, he'd make sure he wasn't in the vicinity.

'A little chat.'

Tegner pulled out a packet of cigarettes and nervously lit up. The smoke she blew out mingled with her cold breath. The cigarette seemed to give her courage as she pointed it aggressively at Anita. 'It was your fault.'

'What was my fault?'

'Bengt. Bengt's death.' Anita had had a pang of guilt when she first heard about the suicide. 'It was you who told him.' This came out as an accusing shriek. A couple of passing students glanced over.

'You slept with Mick Roslyn. I didn't. You went behind your partner's back. I didn't. You betrayed Bengt. I didn't.'

Anita's words acted like a slap in the face. Tegner turned away, tears stinging her eyes. 'Tilda,' Anita's voice softened. 'I need to know about that Monday night.'

Tegner stared towards the water. 'You know about that night.'

'You said you were in Stockholm.'

'That's right, we were.'

'That's not what Mick told me. He said you were here in Malmö.'

Olander's mouth dropped open. Tegner spun round. 'Why should he tell you that? Why did he tell you about us in the first place?'

'He told me because it's true, isn't it?'

Tegner sucked hard on her cigarette. With the other hand, she wiped away a tear. Then she nodded.

'Where did you spend the night?'

'An apartment in Mäster Johansgatan. It belongs to one of Mick's friends. He borrowed it for the night.'

'Were you there all night?'

She shook her head. 'Mick got a flight down that afternoon. He came straight to the apartment and got there about five. I left about eleven.' Anita and Olander exchanged meaningful looks. 'I drove overnight to Stockholm.'

'I can't understand why you just didn't meet up in Stockholm.'

She gave a mirthless laugh. 'I think it gave Mick a thrill to do it with Malin and Bengt so close. It was also easier for me because Bengt was becoming very possessive. He might even have suspected us. He knew that Mick was supposed to have a meeting up there and was taking an early flight down here. And I was supposed to be driving north after leaving him in Lund, so, in theory, we wouldn't have had time to hitch up.'

Tegner's smoke was getting to Anita. She got out her snus tin. 'Do you know why Mick asked Strachan to come to Malmö instead of Stockholm?'

'He knew it would make life easier for Strachan. They have direct flights between Kastrup and Newcastle. Mick's used the service a number of times when he's gone back to visit his parents.'

Anita pondered this information as she took her snus. 'OK. We need you to come with us to make an official statement. Mats will see to that.'

Tegner flicked her cigarette into the dock and it hissed as it hit the water. Olander raised his eyebrows at Anita and smiled.

'Oh, this is yours, Tilda.' Anita handed over Tegner's mobile. 'Don't use it until you've left the polishus.'

CHAPTER 33

The cell door was opened. Every time it was unlocked, a little hope stirred, usually to be crushed as another meal was brought in. But this time it was Anita. She looked like death warmed up. Ewan was mightily pleased to see her as she was his only possible route out of this madness.

'Have you any news?'

She ignored his question and went straight into one of her own. 'What makes you think Mick set you up?'

Ewan sat down slowly. 'I've had plenty of time to think while enjoying your Swedish hospitality. At first, I just wondered about the timing of my arrival and Malin's murder. All very convenient. And then Mick turns up late at the flat, and it's me who's found with the body. Fortunately, you didn't immediately jump to the conclusion that I'd done it – not then anyway!'

Ewan waited as he concentrated on ordering his thoughts. He had to get this right. 'When you did get round to suspecting me, you couldn't find a motive. Then who conveniently supplies one? My old mate Mick, of course.' He paused thoughtfully. 'I tell you what keeps coming back to me.' Anita shrugged. 'His fucking film. That *Gässen* thing.'

'Why?'

'Seen it?' Anita shook her head. 'In the film, the husband murders his wife so that he can carry on with his mistress. The

268

wife, played by Malin Lovgren, is strangled by the husband. The "other woman" is acted by Tilda Tegner, who just happens to be Mick's mistress. Recognise the scenario?'

'It's only a film.'

'That's not it really. What strikes me about this whole business is that it's been stage-managed. From the moment I was invited over to Malmö. I think he's been after me from the beginning.'

'He supplied us with other lines of enquiry first.'

'If they had come to anything, would I be here?'

Anita had to admit that he had a point.

Suddenly Ewan banged his fist on the newspaper and made Anita jump. 'Mick's a film director, for Chrissake! He manipulates people, he manipulates their emotions, he manipulates situations. He *does* manipulation! And he does it brilliantly!'

Anita knew there would be trouble when she saw Nordlund sitting in Moberg's office. The distorted features on Moberg's angry face left nothing to the imagination. When Westermark came in behind her, she felt as though she had walked into a trap. She had hoped to catch Moberg alone.

'Henrik hasn't dropped you in it because he's not that sort of man.' Nordlund grimaced apologetically. 'But I was wondering why you asked him to come back down here with Tilda Tegner without me knowing. I was under the impression that I was running this fucking investigation!'

Anita kept calm. She held up a piece of paper. 'This is why.'

It stopped Moberg abruptly just as he was about to launch into another blast of invective. 'What's that?'

'A statement from Tilda Tegner. It shows that Ewan Strachan could have been set up by Mick Roslyn.'

Moberg turned enquiringly to Nordlund and then to Westermark.

'That's crap,' sneered Westermark. 'It's the fucking journalist.'

Anita smiled. 'Funnily enough, Karl, it was you who put me onto this.'

Westermark feigned puzzlement. This wasn't something he wanted credit for. He knew she was trying to get her *boyfriend* off. 'It's ridiculous.' This attitude was why Anita had wanted to speak to Moberg alone.

'It may be rubbish, but let Anita have her say. She's a lot of explaining to do as it is.' Moberg had reduced his level of anger to simple scowling.

Anita stared at the chief inspector. 'I'm sorry for going over your head, but I wasn't sure you would go along with it. I needed to sort out the facts, do some checking, and talk to Tilda Tegner.' She paused. Nordlund gave her an encouraging nod. Westermark just appeared petulant.

'Karl here told me that Roslyn hadn't been at the meeting he was meant to be attending in Stockholm on the Monday.'

'He was still in Stockholm,' Westermark said defensively.

Anita dropped the statement onto the desk in front of Moberg. 'But he wasn't. He was here in Malmö with Tilda.' All three men showed their surprise at the news. 'They were in an apartment belonging to one of Roslyn's friends.'

'So he was playing away. He's not the first.'

Anita gave Westermark a withering glance. 'I'm sure you're the expert.'

'Just let her get on without any fucking interruptions,' barked Moberg.

'Roslyn flew down on the Monday afternoon, not on the Tuesday morning as he claimed. We've checked with the airline. He was booked on the Tuesday flight but didn't actually board the plane. No taxi delivered a passenger from the airport straight to the apartment at Östra Förstadsgatan that morning. He met up with Tilda late Monday afternoon. Strangely,

Strachan saw them but thought he must be mistaken as he knew Roslyn was meant to be in Stockholm. Tilda left the apartment at eleven to drive overnight to Stockholm, where Bengt Valquist thought she had already gone.'

'OK, so he had opportunity.' Moberg was scratching his stomach again. 'How do you fit him in with the murder of his wife?'

'It goes back to Durham twenty-five years ago. Strachan and Roslyn fell out over Debbie Usher. Each blamed the other for her death. Roslyn may even have believed that Strachan had actually killed her. They don't see each other again until they meet at an Edinburgh film festival. It's there that Roslyn suddenly invites Strachan to come to interview him in Malmö. Even Strachan is surprised. Is Roslyn putting together his plan already?'

'What plan?'

'It's the old story of the middle-aged man who has found a younger model. Malin has done well for his career but she's not getting any younger. Was Malin holding back the ambitious Mick? She was a home-bird who shunned the limelight. Surely he must want bigger things. International films and fame? Hollywood maybe? Malin wouldn't have liked to be part of that. Now he's got a new muse, an actress who will fit in with his grander plans. But the beauty of his scheme is that he can get rid of his wife and get his revenge on Strachan as well by helping us pin the murder on him.'

'Hang on a minute.' This was Nordlund. 'Roslyn put us onto Mednick.'

'And the ex-Säpo angle,' put in Moberg.

'Yes. Let's take Mednick. We know he was fixated on Malin, but we only have Roslyn's word for it that he actually sent threatening letters, as opposed to lovesick notes. Conveniently, Malin supposedly got rid of them. As for the ex-Säpo hitmen. He put us on to them and asked for a safe house. Again deflecting attention from himself. And what did that turn out to be? Linas Tapper trying to tap Roslyn for money while peddling a story that may or may not be true. When those routes didn't work, Roslyn served us up a motive for Strachan. Clever; he's got his man and he's got away with murder.'

'So how do you think the events played out?' She could tell that Moberg was at least opening up his mind.

'Tilda has gone by eleven, but he's already got her to agree to an alibi if needed. That gives Roslyn time to go round to the apartment. Malin would be surprised to see him, but he probably said that he'd caught an earlier flight. It's late, so Malin starts to make him a cup of tea in his football mug. She turns away and he uses the judo skills he learned at university. According to Strachan, he was very good. Then he moves the body and sets it up on the sofa, and places the starfish pendant on her lap after it had come off in the struggle. We've assumed all along that the body was left for Roslyn to find. What if it was the other way round? Then Roslyn turns up half an hour late, giving Strachan time to go inside – the door was left conveniently unlocked – and be caught with the dead body. He's even got a photographer with him, giving himself a witness as to his time of arrival. Olander wondered why Roslyn was only wearing a leather jacket, having come from Stockholm on such a cold morning. Well, he'd only come from Mäster Johansgatan.'

Anita waited for the information to sink in. 'What we were beginning to think was a spur-of-the-moment murder was, in fact, meticulously planned.'

CHAPTER 34

No one spoke for a good couple of minutes. Moberg broke the silence. 'Now neither Roslyn nor Tilda Tegner has an alibi.'

Westermark shook his head. 'I don't buy it. With your version of events, Tilda Tegner could have done it.'

'She could have,' Moberg answered before Anita could speak. 'Or both of them in it together? That would make sense.'

'I don't think so.' They all turned to Nordlund. 'I've been with her since yesterday. She was very upset by Valquist's death. The grief seemed genuine to me. If she'd been involved in Malin Lovgren's murder, I don't think she'd have been so distressed by the death of her supposed boyfriend. Guilt seems to be the overriding emotion. If she was willing to get to the top by killing a rival or colluding in her death, then...' He opened his hands wide and shrugged. The point was made.

Now the focus of attention returned to Moberg. He was scratching his stomach again, which meant he was either having difficulty reaching a decision or he was hungry. He picked up a biro and started to flick the plastic top up and down with his thumb. The annoying, constant clicking only increased the tension. 'Henrik?'

'I think Anita's made a strong case. It's more watertight than the one against Strachan. Roslyn's lied. There's motive and opportunity.'

Moberg nodded. 'Anita?'

'We should bring Roslyn in for questioning. Strachan's up to you.'

Moberg looked at Westermark.

'I think that the only thing Roslyn's guilty of is screwing around and getting caught.' He glowered at Anita. 'The journalist did it. I know he did.'

Moberg's chair scraped back as he drew himself up. The office seemed to shrink as he did so. 'I'm afraid it's three to one. I'm going to see the commissioner and the prosecutor and organise an arrest warrant.'

'What about Tilda Tegner?' Anita asked.

'She'll keep.' Moberg trundled over to the door. As he opened it, he turned to Anita. 'You can go down and let your friend go.' He wagged an admonishing finger at her. 'But he's not to leave Malmö.'

After Moberg left the room, a seething Westermark eyeballed Anita, 'You've got this *so* wrong.' Then he stormed out.

Westermark walked straight out of the building, down the ramp, and headed directly for his car. He got in and sat in silence for some moments. Then he took out his mobile and toyed with it in his hands. He flicked through his contacts list until he came to the name he wanted and, after a momentary hesitation, he pressed "call". He didn't have to wait long for it to be answered.

'Hi, it's Karl. Karl Westermark. There's something you need to know.'

Anita gazed out of her office window over Rörsjöparken just across the road. It was a good place to go and clear the mind and soak up the sun or, if it was too hot, sit in the shade of the giant weeping willow tree, which in summer resembled a green-headed Rastafarian. The door opened behind her. The Ewan who entered was a pale version of the man she had first met. She could see that three days in the cells had been a shock to his system. She felt awkward. Even though she was responsible for his release, she didn't know what to say. Fortunately, Ewan spoke first.

'So you're letting me go.' She nodded. 'Are you to thank for this?'

'We're only doing our job. But you are not to leave Malmö yet. We will keep hold of your passport for the moment.'

Ewan suddenly grinned. 'Admit it; you're only doing this to keep me here so I'll buy you some more drinks.'

Anita was totally disconcerted. She had expected recriminations and accusations, anger and resentment. But he was laughing. 'Was I right about Mick?'

Anita was grateful that she could retreat into police-speak. 'I cannot say. But we are pursuing another line of enquiry.'

Ewan smiled again. 'So it's definitely Mick.' He held up his hand in acknowledgement that he wasn't going to get any more out of her. 'I'll bugger off, Inspector. The first thing I'm going to do on leaving this building is smoke two cigarettes. And the second is go to a spot where there are no walls to entrap me, where I can witness this beautiful earth as far as the eye can see. I want to go up your bloody Turning Torso.'

Half an hour later, Nordlund came into her office. 'Erik's got the arrest warrant. You, me and Westermark are to go with him to fru Lovgren's.'

'Isn't that rather heavy-handed?'

'He's not taking any chances after last time,' he said pointedly. Anita half-blushed at the thought of the fiasco of Mednick's arrest.

'OK.'

'And Anita, bring a pistol this time.'

CHAPTER 35

Once Ewan had gone past the university education department building and was headed directly towards the Turning Torso, the full blast of the icy wind hit him. It was an effort to walk upright. The cold was as raw and uncompromising as the surroundings of Stora Varvsgatan, which he was now walking down. The Turning Torso might represent the new Malmö, but there were still reminders that this had been the industrial heart of the city. To his left were the remains of the Kockums works, with its large spaces and box cranes, and to the right, a more modern office block. The solid Malmö Mässen exhibition centre and the squat Maxi ICA hypermarket beyond certainly weren't examples of Swedish space-age designer cool. But the towering Torso, just behind, definitely was.

He rounded the hypermarket and there, ahead of him, he saw it at close quarters thrusting into the gloomy sky. The nine white cubes, which were stacked one on top of the other at a jaunty angle, like a child's experimentation with building blocks, were each hijacked on one side by a cheeky triangular prism, making the whole a five-sided structure. On reaching the tower, Ewan found it was completely surrounded by a man-made water feature, with access to the entrance provided by a walkway into a glass portico. There was no denying that this was an audacious piece of design. Before its completion, many had thought it merely foolhardy. Ewan entered and walked past typically Scandinavian light wooden panelling, which surrounded the building's circular core on the ground floor. He approached the reception desk and asked for Daniel, Anita's contact.

The two cars parked opposite Beijers Park, a few houses beyond Britta Lovgren's house. Moberg and Anita got out of one and Nordlund and Westermark emerged from the other. They gathered round the protective bulk of the Chief Inspector.

'I don't expect him to put up a fight, but we have to be sure he doesn't try and bolt. Westermark, you go round the back.' Westermark nodded, though Anita couldn't help noticing how edgy he appeared.

As they approached the front door from the street, Westermark slipped round the side of the house. Moberg rang the door bell. He looked sharply at Anita. 'I'm handling this, so I'll do the talking.'

After a few moments, the door was answered by Britta Lovgren, who was taken aback to see three officers on her doorstep. She patted her immaculately groomed hair in a nervous gesture.

'Sorry to disturb you, fru Lovgren,' said Moberg. 'We need to speak to your son-in-law.'

'Mick? But he's not here.'

Moberg flinched. 'Do you know where he is?' There was more urgency in his voice.

'I don't know. He got a call on his mobile and left in a hurry. Why–'

Moberg didn't let her finish. 'How long ago?'

'Oh, less than an hour ago. He seemed very upset.'

'Do you know who the call was from?'

'I've no idea. He muttered something about having to get someone?'

'"Get someone"? To fetch someone?'

'What else could it mean?'

Just then Westermark appeared behind Britta Lovgren. She was startled by his sudden presence. Moberg didn't stop to explain as he turned away and stalked off to the gate, leaving the unnerved and bewildered woman. The other three followed.

'He's buggered off,' snapped Moberg, bringing Westermark up to speed. 'We don't want the bastard disappearing.'

'He might be coming back with someone,' suggested Nordlund.

Anita noticed Westermark shuffling his feet and looking distracted. The body language was evasive. 'Has he been tipped off?' she wondered aloud.

Westermark's head jolted up. Anita could see that her instincts were right. It was enough to alert Moberg, who fixed Westermark with one of his trademark glares. 'Well?'

Westermark gulped. 'I rang him.'

Moberg grabbed the lapels of his leather jacket and virtually hoisted him off the ground. 'You fucking imbecile,' he yelled in his face. 'What did you do that for?'

Westermark could hardly spit the words out. 'I thought he was innocent.'

Moberg threw him backwards and he ended up on his backside on the pavement. 'Now we've got to fucking find him! Christ, he could be anywhere.'

'I don't think so. When he said he was going to "get someone" he wasn't going to pick them up.' Anita spoke with a persuasive certainty. 'I think he's going to settle a score. Thanks to Karl's call, he knows it's all up. So he's going to get the guy he tried to set up for Malin's murder.'

'Strachan?'

She felt panic rising. 'Yeah. He's nothing to lose, and he wants to take his old rival with him. He would have had time to get to the polishus as Ewan was leaving the building.'

'Do you know where Strachan was going?'

'Yes. The Torso.'

Daniel had been very chatty. He had filled Ewan in on numerous facts and figures about the tower, none of which Ewan could remember, except that the Torso moved up to ten metres in the wind and some of the residents had complained of seasickness. The inside of the tower struck Ewan as part spacecraft, part lighthouse. Daniel had even taken him into one of the futuristic conference rooms on the fifty-third floor. Ewan wondered how anybody could concentrate with such staggering views out of the windows. Eventually, Daniel had shown Ewan how to reach the top of the tower, where normally nobody was allowed to go, other than maintenance staff and the man mad enough to go out and clean the building's 2,500 slanting windows. 'But as a friend of Anita's, then I make this the exception, no?' said the grinning Daniel with a confidential wink. He had been so effusive about Anita that Ewan wondered what the nature of their relationship was. Was he getting jealous again?

All was forgotten when he stepped through the white metal door and stood at the top of Scandinavia's tallest structure. He had emerged from the central core of the building, which up on the roof was circular, resembling a new, uncut Stilton cheese. Skirting the roof was a kind of elevated monorail track, which came up to his waist. Daniel explained that this was for the cleaning cradle, which was moved round until positioned above the windows that needed attention. As none of the sides of the building were straight, the workman guided his cradle carefully into the required position before getting out his squeegee. Ewan assumed that the only applicants for the job came from the local lunatic asylum.

The wind was quite strong up here, so Ewan didn't venture near the edge. Having escaped prison and a murder charge, he didn't want to spoil things by being blown off the top of the tallest building in Sweden. Despite the greyness all around, the view was still breathtaking. Malmö was laid out way below. He could make out the main landmarks like the castle and the larger churches. Despite all he had been through, it was a city that he was growing fond of. A city of parks and cyclists. A city of contrasts – a place that was growing more cosmopolitan, yet where Netto wasn't considered an embarrassing shopping experience. Over the expanse of water, he could see Copenhagen, which he promised himself he would visit next time. What really caught his eye was the perfect symmetry of the Öresund Bridge. Its incredible length made him appreciate what an engineering marvel it was. A large tanker was ploughing its way towards it. This was the gateway to the Baltic.

What was most exciting of all was that he was free, out of the cell that had trapped him for three days. Out here nothing could imprison him. He had fought endless battles to keep his sanity, and it was the recurring image of Anita that had saved him from totally losing control in that confined space. Up here, the fears that had taunted him, hour after hour, in that locked room were being blown away. And now the police thought it was Mick who had killed Malin. That really was a turn up for the old book. The bastard deserved to be locked up. It served him right for what he had destroyed all those years ago in Durham.

Ewan took out his packet of cigarettes. Despite his best efforts, he couldn't compete with the wind and he replaced the unsmoked cigarette. As he did so, he noticed the door open. From the flash of yellow maintenance jacket, he assumed it must be the window cleaner. Ewan turned his attention back to the view. From here he could appreciate all the green areas given over to the parks. Why couldn't they do that in Britain? Any public space was immediately built on by some avaricious developer with the connivance of weak and moribund local councils.

Ewan couldn't see the man who had come through the door

a few moments before. He must have gone round to the other side of the roof. It was now becoming really blustery, and he decided to go back down and then find himself a cosy bar.

'You fucking shit!'

Ewan spun round. Standing in front of him was a wild-eyed Mick.

Moberg pressed his huge hand on the horn on the steering wheel. The driver in front panicked and slammed on his brakes. Cursing, Moberg violently manoeuvred the car round the vehicle and jumped the red light, narrowly missing a taxi coming from the road on the right. Aggressive finger gestures were exchanged, but nothing was going to stop the chief inspector. In a country of careful drivers, this was like a scene from *Starsky and Hutch* bursting onto their streets. Westermark's car was hot on their heels as they raced past the station, then the central post office. Alarmed pedestrians rushed back off zebra crossings that they thought had been safe to negotiate.

Anita clung on to the door handle as she endured this white-knuckle ride. What her dominant fear was she couldn't decide – the lunatic driving of her boss or the worry that Roslyn had caught up with Ewan. She knew that she didn't want Ewan to be harmed. That bloody idiot Westermark! What had he thought he was playing at? He might have Ewan's death on his hands. Roslyn had already killed his wife. He could possibly have killed Debbie Usher twenty-five years ago, too. Moberg wrenched the car left onto Stora Varvsgatan and they had a clear run to the end by the ICA supermarket. Moberg rammed his foot down and the car very nearly became airborne.

They were circling each other like two cagey boxers, each waiting for the other to make the first move. Mick hadn't said a word after his first outburst, but his intention was clear. There was nothing left to be said. They knew why they were up there together. Ewan had opened his mouth to reason with Mick but promptly shut it. He knew it would be a waste of time. It was too late for that. Ewan weighed up his options. He could try and make a dart for the door, but that exit would be quickly cut off by Mick. When Mick pounced on him he knew that he would have the advantage of bulk, but that it would mean little as he was so out of condition. He could see that Mick worked out.

Despite the chill, sweat was running down his back. His mouth was dry. He was truly frightened. Mick was crazed. God, was it all going to end here? In sheer panic, he rushed at Mick and grabbed him round the waist and flung him to the ground. They crashed down together. Mick was temporarily winded as he was underneath. Ewan tried to get up before Mick recovered. Then he might make the door and the safety of the stairs. The tower was such a warren, he might be able to lose him. He staggered to his feet and tried to dash towards the door. He had nearly made it when Mick's arms whipped round his neck and shoulders, and he found himself being dragged backwards. He gagged as the crook of Mick's right arm pulled tight on his throat. He flayed with his elbows but he couldn't loosen the vice-like grip. He hadn't the strength or the stamina to stop Mick yanking him away from the doorway. The sky swirled in front of his eyes. He tried to scream. Could anybody hear him? Not in this wind. He was trying to make it as hard as possible for Mick, yet he knew that he was being hauled closer and closer to the edge.

They rushed into the building; Anita a metre or so in front of the panting Moberg. Daniel was in the reception area and smiled as he saw her, though his grin froze when he saw her running. 'Your English friend–'

'Where is he?' she shouted.

Startled, all he could do was point upwards. 'The roof.'

Without a word of explanation, Anita rushed to the

lift door and rammed her finger against the ascend button. A light flickered on to show the lift was coming down from the eighteenth floor. She swore. Moberg lumbered after her.

Daniel was about to ask what on earth was happening when he saw Anita pull out her police pistol. The question never materialised.

The lift arrived. The wooden door swished open smoothly and a young professional couple got the fright of their lives when they were met by a woman brandishing a gun. Anita unceremoniously yanked them out of the lift and she and Moberg got in. The terrified couple watched as the lift doors swished back and the woman with the weapon and the huge man with her disappeared. Before they could speak, another two men rushed into the building. The place had gone mad.

They stumbled back into the first piece of window cradle track. Mick had to loosen his grip and Ewan managed to prise away the arm around his windpipe. It was only a momentary respite as Mick then heaved him over the monorail, crushing Ewan's ribs in the process. Ewan summoned up all the strength he had left and managed to halt for a few seconds their inexorable progress towards the edge of the building by clinging onto the track top. He was even able to twist slightly so that he was side-on to Mick and couldn't be dragged. It was the wrong choice, as Mick's now free fist smashed into the side of his head. The pain was shattering. He stood reeling, desperately trying to hang onto some semblance of thought. It was hopeless. The second blow knocked him to his knees. He felt sick. He couldn't fight this any longer. His head was pounding so much that he couldn't reason. All he could think about was that he wanted it all to end.

The will to fight was seeping away. As if in a dream, Ewan was conscious that he was being pulled towards the second piece of track. He twisted again and Mick dropped him. He landed on the ground and lay there. For a second, it was a place of rest and blessed relief until he was violently hauled up again. Now Mick had got him to the track, which was next to the lip of the Torso. Malmö was swirling in front of him. It was so far below. Suddenly, he could hear his own voice, though it sounded as though it was coming from a distance. 'Please, Mick, please.'

Mick grabbed a clump of his hair in his hand. It hurt. 'Now you can join Debbie,' Mick shouted in his ear. Ewan's head was roughly thrust forward. Malmö seemed even closer now. He realised that he was half hanging over the edge. The tips of his toes were still on the ground, his stomach pressed against the top of the metal track and the upper half of his body was dangling over absolutely nothing. Bizarrely, despite all the pain and the terror, he noticed a yellow car driving down below.

Ewan made one last desperate effort to push himself away from the edge, but Mick's grip was too strong.

'Let go of him!' someone shouted. Ewan wasn't sure it was even in English. The yellow car had gone.

'Too late!' he heard Mick bellow just behind him. Ewan could feel Mick's muscles tense as he was about to give him the final push and send him spinning into oblivion.

And then everything slowed down. The explosion behind him was muffled; the wetness that splattered across the back of his head seemed to come in separately defined slaps of moisture, and the hands freed their grip on him ever so sluggishly. He nearly went over but must have caught something to stop his fall. It was so strange to see Mick passing him in slow motion, the top of his head bloodied and blown away, before he seemed to do an elegant somersault in mid-air and cartwheel all the way down and down. The last thing Ewan remembered was the faint sound of a splash.

CHAPTER 36

Anita squinted in the mirror and took her time to apply the lipstick. She didn't do it very often so wasn't practised at it. In fact, she wasn't that good at tarting herself up. It wasn't that she wasn't vain. She was at times. Normally, she couldn't be arsed. She never bothered for work and her desert of a social life meant that she hadn't been required to make an effort for some time. For years she had relied on her natural looks to carry her through, but that was changing. She couldn't stop age creeping up on her and playing cruel tricks on a face and body that had served her well for so long. She stood back and admired the effect. Not bad, Sundström, not bad.

She had to admit she was excited about this evening. It was Ewan's last in Sweden. She wanted to make it memorable for him. She still felt guilty about locking him up, though he had been seriously grateful to her for saving his life on the roof of the Turning Torso. That had been a week ago, and she still shook when she thought about it. If she had arrived a second or so later, Ewan would have been thrown off the top. She had followed procedure and had shouted a warning to Roslyn, but he wasn't going to stop. Fortunately, Moberg had reached the roof just in time to see what happened, so she had a witness to her actions. She had never shot anyone before and she prayed she would never have to do so again. It was a sickening thing to do. Was it duty or love that had made her pull the trigger? She didn't know. Moberg had commended her to Commissioner Dahlbeck for the promptness of her decision-making. Sweden had been shocked and fascinated in equal measure by the whole story, though there was collective relief that the Lovgren murder had not been carried out by one of their own but by a foreigner, even if he had become an adopted son. Everybody in officialdom was pleased that the case had been wrapped up relatively quickly and that they had avoided an expensive public trial into the bargain. The only person to come out of the investigation badly was Westermark. He had been suspended for his role in warning Roslyn, and an internal enquiry was to be set up.

And Ewan? He had spent the night in hospital before emerging relatively unscathed. The few bruises would heal quickly. The mental trauma of his experience might take a lot longer to come to terms with. She had only seen him on one occasion after he came into the polishus to give a brief statement as to the events on the rooftop. They had met for a coffee at the Malmö Konsthall gallery, not far from her apartment. It hadn't been as awkward as she feared it might be.

Now he was treating her to dinner at Elysée on Lilla Nygatan, close to the canal. She wanted to look good for him. Choosing the right clothes had been difficult – her choice was limited. Eventually, she had decided on the black and purple dress she had bought last year at Indiska and had never found an occasion to wear. It was as short as she dared wear these days and had a shapely neckline, but without the worry of her boobs falling out. She knew what would go well with it – her Lotta Lind starfish pendant. As she put it on – it was turquoise rather than Malin Lovgren's deep blue – she reflected that she had got that all wrong. She had thought its discovery would be the key to the case. She smiled ruefully at the mirror. That was just one of a number of mistakes she had made.

Now she was ready for Ewan. She was pretty sure that she would invite him back to the apartment afterwards. She had rushed around tidying up and even did some much-needed dusting and cleaning. More tellingly, she had changed the sheets on the bed. Well, you never knew what might happen. Whatever did, she had a feeling that this could become a more meaningful relationship than she had had with anyone since Björn. She wondered how Lasse would take the news that she had found someone new. Maybe now that he had Rebecka, he would be fine with it.

Sudden last-minute thought. Should she wear her glasses or not? Vanity said no. Practicality said yes. She wanted to be able to read the menu. Practicality won. She reached for her coat. If the opportunity arose, she still had one question that she needed to ask Ewan. He might not know the answer, but she could no longer ask Roslyn whether he had murdered Debbie Usher. She wanted to be able to put Inspector Gazzard's mind at rest.

Ewan waited nervously inside the restaurant. Anita had chosen well. Elysée was both cosy and sophisticated. Classical striped wallpaper, old pictures and portraits and glass mirrors achieved the French effect he assumed it was striving for. The padded leather chairs shimmered in the glow of the inevitable tealights on the tables. The music was eclectic, ranging from Roy Orbison to Vivaldi, via Miles Davis. As he perused the menu, he kept glancing towards the entrance. Was she being fashionably late? It was a big night for him. It could be the cherry on his rapidly expanding cake. The last few days, which he had spent at David's flat, had been eventful. His extraordinary Swedish experience had turned out very nicely, thank you. Ewan couldn't help smiling to himself. He had been at the epicentre of what had turned out to be a huge story in Sweden, where his face had been plastered all over the media. And in Britain, too, thanks to the articles he had written and Brian's desperate bullishness. He had even done interviews from a Malmö TV studio with both ITN and BBC's *Newsnight*. Things would change when he got home. *Novo News* would be history. A high-profile job within the group awaited. Maybe even a national paper would come sniffing. A book? Now that was a thought. As long as he didn't have to work for Brian again, he would be happy. And, best of all, he had fallen in love with an amazing woman. Even more astonishing, Anita seemed to be keen on him. For the first time since Debbie, he felt that he had met the love of his life.

Anita arrived fifteen minutes late, full of apologies. On leaving her apartment, she remembered his passport, which she was returning to him officially. The meal went well. Ewan had avoided piling too much on his plate from the complimentary self-service salad bar, despite the mouth-watering choice. Then he had a fancy mushroom dish before settling for a beautifully tender, thin steak. He had ordered a Rioja, which Anita seemed to love. Conversation had come easily. Nothing was stilted or forced. They just seemed to get on naturally. And he had cracked it at last – he could imagine Anita totally naked. The thought gave him an illicit thrill.

Anita had a large wine glass in her hand and took a gentle sip. Over its rim, she fixed Ewan with a mock stare. 'You still haven't told me about that Scottish lord who ended up in Malmöhus.'

'Ah, yes. James Hepburn, Earl of Bothwell. I discovered why he was imprisoned here.' He put down his knife and fork. The plate was embarrassingly clean. 'Before his time with Mary, Queen of Scots, he came over to Copenhagen and fell for Anna Tronds, a Norwegian noblewoman, whose father was a famous admiral serving as Danish Royal Consul. This was a time when Norway was under Danish rule. Bothwell got engaged to Anna and left for Flanders. Haven't discovered why they went there. Then the wicked Bothwell announced he had no money and persuaded Anna to sell all her possessions and to ask her family for money too. He then failed to marry her and disappeared with the dowry.

'Then he gets caught up with Mary, Queen of Scots, kills her English husband, Lord Darnley, and then marries her. However, it didn't last long as they were defeated in battle and he escaped to Scandinavia to raise an army to put Mary back on the throne. But his luck ran out. He was picked up off the coast of Norway without proper papers and taken to Bergen, which just happened to be Anna's home town. While under arrest there, she made an official complaint against him. Even then his charm seemed to have worked and he persuaded Anna to take his ship in compensation. She agreed, but the King of Denmark heard about the English wanting him for the murder of Lord Darnley and he was brought here to Malmö and thrown in your local prison. And I know what that's like,' he added with a smirk.

Anita flushed. She didn't want reminding. 'Did he ever get out?'

Ewan nodded his head. 'Out of Malmöhus? Yes, after five or six years. But then he was sent to the dungeons of Dragsholm Castle in Denmark. They say you can still see the pillar he was chained to. After ten years of captivity, he went mad and died.' Ewan shivered. 'I'm not bloody surprised. Three days inside your place and I was going insane. Enclosed spaces freak me out.'

Anita reached across the table and placed her hand on his. 'I'm sorry. It should never have happened.'

He manoeuvred his hand round so he could squeeze hers.

'It's OK. I could always forgive you anything.'

Their eyes met.

'Anita, you look fantastic.' She beamed. Her pleasure at his remark was evident. He knew he was hopelessly in love.

'That pendant really shows off your neck. It's lovely.

I've seen one like that somewhere before.'

Anita removed her hand and it automatically went to the pendant. She absent-mindedly fingered it gently. 'It's from my home town of Simrishamn. It's by Lotta Lind. Just like the one that Malin Lovgren wore on the night of...'

Ewan saw her face change slowly from one of proud reflection to puzzlement and then on to appalled horror. '*Herregud!*' She shook her head in disbelief. 'Mick was trying to kill you because he *knew* you had murdered his wife. Thanks to me, you were about to get away with a perfect murder.'

'I don't know what you're talking about.'

'The pendant. We never released that information. You could only have seen it on Malin that night!' She couldn't shake the incredulity from her voice. 'It *was* you, wasn't it?'

Ewan stared at Anita. This was the face of a woman who had captured his heart. He never thought he would fall in love again, but it had happened. He couldn't lie to her, not any longer. He nodded. 'Almost exactly as you described at the police station.'

Anita struggled to get the words out. 'And Debbie?' she whispered.

What the hell!

'Yep.'

Other titles in the series

Murder in Malmö is the second in the series of the best-selling crime mysteries featuring Inspector Anita Sundström. *Meet me in Malmö* and *Missing in Malmö* are the first and third titles.

A gunman is loose in Malmö and he's targeting immigrants. The charismatic head of an advertising agency is found dead in his shower. Inspector Anita Sundström wants to be involved in the murder investigations, but she is being sidelined by her antagonistic boss. She is assigned to find a stolen painting by a once-fashionable artist, as well as being lumbered with a new trainee assistant. She also has had to restore her professional reputation after a deadly mix-up in a previous high-profile case. Then another prominent Malmö businessman is found murdered and Sundström finds herself back in the action and facing new dangers in the second Anita Sundström Malmö mystery.

Other titles in the series

Missing in Malmö is the third in the series of the best-selling crime mysteries featuring Inspector Anita Sundström. *Meet me in Malmö* and *Murder in Malmö* are the first and second titles.

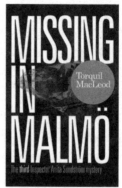

When a British heir hunter fails to return home after a trip to Malmö, Inspector Anita Sundström doesn't want to get entangled in a simple missing person's case. She shows a similar reluctance when her ex-husband begs her to find his girlfriend, who seems to have disappeared. But when the mysteries take a sinister turn, Sundström finds herself inextricably involved in both baffling affairs, one of which seems to be connected to a robbery that took place twenty years earlier. As the cases begin to unravel, tragedy awaits the investigating team in the third Anita Sundström Malmö mystery.

Meanwhile, enjoying the hot summer away from Malmö, Anita Sundström is on her annual leave and is showing Kevin Ash the sights of Skåne. Their holiday is interrupted by the apparent suicide of a respected, retired diplomat. After a further death, Anita finds herself unofficially investigating a case that has its roots in the 1917 chance meeting of a Malmö waiter with the world's most famous revolutionary. All she knows is that the answers lie in Berlin.

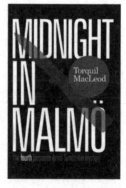

Two investigations that begin and end at *Midnight in Malmö* – the fourth Inspector Anita Sundström mystery.